Debatable Land

By Candia McWilliam

Nan A. Talese

DOUBLEDAY

New York

London

Toronto

Sydney

Auckland

Debatable Land

Candia McWilliam

PUBLISHED BY NAN A. TALESE
an imprint of Doubleday
a division of Bantam Doubleday Dell Publishing Group, Inc.
1540 Broadway, New York, New York 10036

DOUBLEDAY is a trademark of Doubleday, a division of
Bantam Doubleday Dell Publishing Group, Inc.

All of the characters in this book are fictitious,
and any resemblance to actual persons, living or
dead, is purely coincidental.

Book Design by Gretchen Achilles

Library of Congress Cataloging-in-Publication Data

McWilliam, Candia.
   Debatable land / Candia McWilliam. — 1st ed. in the U.S.A.
      p.   cm.
   1. Scots—Travel—South Pacific Ocean—Fiction.   2. Sailing—
South Pacific Ocean—Fiction.   I. Title.
PR6063.C85D43   1994
823'.914—dc20   94-26104
                                                              CIP

First published in the United Kingdom by
Bloomsbury, London

ISBN 0-385-26310-4

All Rights Reserved
Printed in the United States of America
March 1995
First Edition in the United States of America

1   3   5   7   9   10   8   6   4   2

COLIN McWILLIAM
1928 · 1989 · FIRMITAS
UTILITAS · VENUSTAS

The tropics vanish, and meseems that I,
From Halkerside, from topmost Allermuir,
Or steep Caerketton, dreaming gaze again.
Far set in fields and woods, the town I see
Spring gallant from the shallows of her smoke,
Cragged, spired, and turreted, her virgin fort
Beflagged. About, on seaward-drooping hills,
New folds of city glitter. Last, the Forth
Wheels ample waters set with sacred isles,
And populous Fife smokes with a score of towns.
There, on the sunny frontage of a hill,
Hard by the house of kings, repose the dead,
My dead, the ready and the strong of word.
Their works, the salt-encrusted, still survive . . .

—From *Songs of Travel*,
ROBERT LOUIS STEVENSON

Debatable Land

One

The washing that went on in Alec's house when he was a child was carried out with a fervour that had something in it of atonement. There was no washing out, though, what lay deep in the flesh of his mother and father, the distant coastal whiff of fish.

Today, a man of almost forty, he looked from the window of his hotel out to the southern sea to whose care he was preparing to commit himself. He had packed for the voyage and now had only his thoughts to collect. Over the boulevard from the hotel was one edge of the Pacific, docile and oily at this margin against the sea wall, imponderable further out under its blue reception of the wide sky. His own North Sea never brought itself to so melting a blue. The hot air here did not move but hung and sank on its own weight. He thought of the argumentative air of Scotland. The thought punched aside his homesickness somewhat.

He had come so far from home in order to see it clearly. As a painter he lived by light, and he feared that the light in his head was going. Having taken the decision to live on water with strangers, he had to keep his own respect by sticking to it. He could sail, he would be fed, even paid a little. He had found a boat. It remained only to cast off.

An uncertain passage in the *Odyssey* has Tiresias speaking of a land without salt. Odysseus mentions this place to Penelope even before they first sleep together after their long parting. Is Odysseus preparing the ground for another great journey, this time to the saltless land? Is Homer ensuring that his epic has the ragged edge that adventure has in life? Or is he describing, perhaps even unwittingly, that saltless state of being that makes people take to the sea or to another sure source of fear when they have no need to, when they have come to feel the savour gone from their daily life and a deathly blandness consume their works and days? If a land all salt will not support life and a sea greatly salt is called dead, it is also the case that deprived of salt we long for it and will lick stones to get it.

It was in such a saltless state that Alexander Dundas was collected from his hotel on the seafront at Papeete by Elspeth Urquhart and brought to *Ardent Spirit*.

No one now on the yacht needed to be at sea. Her owner-skipper was happiest there but also had more than one anchorage on land. Logan Urquhart was a Scots American of fortune who doubted his own courage and was timid though successful with women. Each time he wrestled physical fear he needed to do it again a little sooner; metaphysical fears assailed him but receded after each trial of the body and will. In common with many rich men, he confused enlightening introspection with womanish indecision, and in so doing he lost the feline self-knowing power of the transcendent tycoon. Moreover, Logan Urquhart was young, only forty, and had morals, for which he respected himself.

Elspeth was his wife, and was grateful for it. She loved the boat and had suggested the name *Ardent Spirit* for reasons of her own, when asked by Logan to think of something to call the material beauty that was slowly forming in a cold concrete barn on the East Coast of Scotland. For all the miles she had sailed, Elspeth did not yet consider herself, as she did her husband, a sea creature. *Ardent Spirit* she had named for the old name of the liquid that has shaped Scotland as ornamentally and destructively as seawater. Its own place in her life lay deep and only tidally admissible. It was not she who was the drinker, but often enough she wished she were. She feared she had not the allure of firewater, that her own spirit was not ardent.

Because of the presence of others, Elspeth was able to conceal her maritime insufficiencies with forms of overcompensation that she felt made her monstrous but could not hold herself back from. She undertook the housework on the boat with a masochistic vigour that newcomers noticed, speculated about, and then took for granted, imagining it to be to do with being spoilt on land, or perhaps childless. The four-hour watch system was the only reason for broken nights known to Elspeth, a soft-looking woman with an untidy body that she kept hidden. Logan

3

had the blond hair of a man with brown hair who spends half his life at sea, and arms hard with muscles from winching up sails the size of castle walls.

Ardent Spirit's wardrobe of sail was kept in a bin just astern of her main mast, each heavy-sided billowing sail folded down to tameness and at last silence and kept in its own bag, labelled in black stencilled letters on the whispering Terylene: Genoa, Big Boy, No 1 Spinnaker, No 2 Spinnaker, Storm Jib. The rarer sails were kept in the fo'c'sle, under whose floor lay the sewing machine for mending sails shot through by the wind or in a bad gybe punched in by the spars.

In the fo'c'sle were to sleep two men, Alec Dundas and Nick Pedersen. Alec had found the job advertised between old suits of sail and exhausted moorings on the thinning English coast, in the back of a sailing magazine he picked up waiting at the hospital for Lorna, the nurse with whom he lived, to stop working and come home with him. The magazine seemed in that hospital to be the leavings of lives unimaginably emancipated, lived between sea and sky, not bandages and botched periods of perforated sleep. He read the advertisement:

Strong man with some experience of sail required for last leg of Pacific voyage. Keep and fair wage. Apply box THA7A55A.

The simplicity was enough. He flew to it from the life he had organised around himself, to which he had become averse. He had sailed a little around the river's mouth at Cramond, and knew many words out of books of the sea. His contained manner

4

and the enthusiasm that unfolded from him had recommended him to Logan Urquhart; those, and his being a Scot. Alec wrote a letter and they spoke twice by telephone; Logan sent an air ticket, explaining that it was more usual to hire in port, but that he had taken to something about Alec. From this Alec realised that he was about to enter a world with freedoms and restrictions he had not contemplated ever before. He felt as though he were joining up. A lightened sense of duty and a beautiful unnatural surrender came over him.

Alec's mother Mairi said that her hands had been cured to salt hams by a working life gutting and filleting the fish brought in to the processing works. She'd hold up her hard-rinded hand, and take a shivering thin knife up to it, to show where she'd carve off the salt slices, snick along the side.

To keep a grip on the fish, to hold them from squirting out of the grasp, his mother and the other fish girls would salt both hands regularly, pressing them into deep vats of rough salt. Each girl had her own knife, black steel with her name burned with hot wire into the wooden handle. These knives were left behind at night. Like a pen, each knife in time became modified to suit its user. Some knives had come down from mother to daughter. The rate was forty fish a minute for small fish, say herring.

His mother said she could feel down her knife, with a faint near-magnetic charge trembling through the blade, if there was roe in a fish, if she'd not already been able to tell from a jowly look to its belly. She could sense the grain of a fish along the knife, the way its flesh pulled in arrows of muscle away from the backbone, and the freshness of a fish was for her not crudely a matter of smell. When the flesh began to sicken, she saw it and knew that the fish had been kept waiting by the weather.

The floor in the processing works struck a cold up your legs bitter as ice. It was slippery with the snarls of guts that had been thrown to the bin and missed it. The guts of these small fish had the look of dropped yarn and the cats that haunted the place played with them, making cats' cradles. Swim bladders beaded the floor like bits of mercury, tough as seaweed to tread on even through a rubber boot. The floor was hosed down twice a day with a disinfectant that stank of tom-cats and someone in a city's idea of fir trees. The floor was faintly canted, its lowest end at the dockside, so the water and guts could run out through small drains that ran down to roans over the harbour water where gulls waited.

She told him that these gulls took kittens from time to time, blind and newborn or just emerging into seeing, with milky marble eyes. The gulls took out the eyes at a swoop without even the mercy to devour the rest of the creature. His mother had dropped a stone on one such kitten, though it pained her to do so. The wee cat was mewing at the gulls. Their own kitten cries out of their hard screaming beaks mocked it. The kitten had been so surgically murdered that in every way it appeared new and hopeful but for its absent eyes.

The cats sometimes had their kits among the salt sacks behind the sheds. The babies could not keep out the salt, being born bare and blind. So there were preserved litters, pink and rigid, among the straining jute sacks. If you pulled the salted kittens away from the fat woven sacks, they were printed with the coarse weave and flaked in their folds with crystal salt. You could see everything that was to make this small thing a cat hardly begun but present, flaps of ear, tricorne nose, distinct pads like white raspberries. It was all there but the late flattering luxury of fur and whiskers.

There was one persistent orange tom who would walk away from work with Alec's mother, sometimes as far as her bus stop on Leith Walk. He would rise up on his back legs and biff her hands as though he were heading a feather. His balls stuck out behind like an apricot under his tail. Alec's mother thought the smell of the fish had sunk to her bone. She could imagine the cats digging her up to chew on her, so she told him, to suck on her fingerbones.

Jim, Alec's father, said he could not smell it, but that was no surprise. He was a fishmonger. Certainly she smelt it on him, for all he was so clean and had a different white coat each day. Her own nose detected each distinction; she suffered, like Alec, from perfect nasal pitch. She caught the lot: the oily smell of herring; the salt-blood tang of mackerel; the gloom of cod; the washcloth vapour of cooked roes; the pipe-smoke and zoo smell of smokies; they were all there, in his hair, on his hands, folded in his body.

His blue van, shared with his partner Fordyce Macrae, had shelves of slatted wood in the back, and stalls to hold the buckets firm as he drove on his deliveries over the hills of the city. Anything over he would sell to housewives before he went to work at the shop. He parked the van down by the clock at Canonmills, by the Water of Leith. The women stood in a woolly queue, their net bags ready for the morning's catch. Every one of them wore a hat on her head, or a headscarf. Hair is a modern accessory. Alec's father made a parcel of even the smallest purchase, two skate-knobs for a minister's housekeeper, a single roll of coley for an old man without teeth. Taking the fish in his left hand he placed it dead centre atop the pile of grey-blue paper, and folded it with envelope ends to stop any leaks, pulling out his left hand at the last moment to give a squaring-off slap to the parcel. He made out receipts with care from the pad headed "Dundas and Macrae". Each action came to him easily. He was in his element. The silver streets of Edinburgh in the fresh morning might have been rivers to him.

Mairi was not so aswim. She feared the sea, that had reached her grandfather down from a foredeck at night and pocketed him deep in a net heavy with starfish. The ominous weight of starfish in a net has fishermen miserable before they find a man in it, a drowned comrade become a mass of hungry muscular stars.

Alec she had named Alexander for her grandfather and it was upon him that her hopes of rescue rested, optimistic and transparent as a message in a bottle.

It was not that she disliked fish. She merely wished it in its place. At night when she smelt his father's and her own mixed sleep it cannot have been that of warm-blooded animals resting between dry sheets and under wool in a house on dry land, but that of seals among weed and wrack. Then perhaps she felt the deck slip and her own grip loosen and the sea open.

Maybe it was on mornings after such nights that she cleaned with even more zeal than usual, abrading and scouring and sluicing until she left the house with a clarity of air and freedom from dust whose unwitting effect was solely marine.

———

Nick Pedersen had one pair of shorts and a pair of spectacles that were held around his neck on a string black with sweat, salt and oil. He lived at sea and was at home on it wherever there were winds. His calmness and slowness to speech gave him the apparent dullness that was his great advantage in foxing people. He had begun his life on the hot metal presses, in Essex. At these presses, his father had tweezed and dropped letters, spaced them with beautiful tense spaces held open by discretion and metal, and locked them into their formes. When he saw that the work he had pined for was disappearing, Nick told his father of his plan to get out on to the sea and his father had told him to do it while there was still room on the water. He spoke of the sea as though it were a page growing ever more crowded with poorly spaced letters.

Nick was admired in many ports for his patience. He could fix all engines, even the sulkiest, even the engines of fridges. He did not see the need for patience since it was interest that lured him as he dismantled the questions set before him and reassembled them as answers. He had a swot's face and pirate teeth and the newt-like body often thought of as intellectual. His reputation arrived before him in harbour. Logan had put out the word in ports across the Pacific that there was a place for him if he wanted it on the last leg of *Ardent Spirit*'s voyage from the Panama Canal to New Zealand. Over oceans the gossip travels in bounteous sneezes, chatter reaching islands at dawn, multiplying with the lifting sun and moving off to infect and settle the next atoll before the abrupt darkness. Nick was curious about the boat and joined her in the Marquesas.

Sandro Hughes was a New Zealander. If the Scots are the

most emigrated people on earth, the New Zealanders must have most nationals afloat, outside of a navy. The boats of New Zealand outnumber the people on water as do the sheep on land. Sandro's mother came from North Italy. In Auckland she ran an Italian restaurant called the Check Tablecloth, where she made Italian food with a New Zealand flavour. Lawyers came every night for her oyster cocktail in a sundae glass. One or other handsome son waited at table, combining the mother's punctilio with the father's aversion to what he saw as fawning.

Sandro and his brother Luca alternated their periods of absence from the flat on top of the restaurant, to spare their mother the loneliness of life with a man who had decided to resent the native land of a wife he had once chosen for her eyes, her cooking, her forgiving unwillingness to close up against what she did not know. Sandro, at twenty-four, had made it twice to the Panama Canal but the first time his papers were lifted in Colon City and the second time he got drunk with a man who said he was a mercenary though he had no detail of where. In the morning Sandro saw the boat that would have taken him through to the next sea, held in its place in the deep canal by straining ropes and heckled by dirty pilot boats that seemed to threaten its sudden departing smallness among the great precipitous ships of purpose, trade, tourism, national power. He was left behind by these things and did not much care. At last he found *Ardent Spirit*, after reading a postcard on a board in a bar. After five different men had checked him out over two afternoons, he met Logan, who took him on.

Sandro had, instead of the patriotism he might have, had not his mother divided and his father made repulsive such an idea, a high romantic regard for sailing boats. He loved them and learnt quickly the mood of each boat he lived and worked on. *Ardent Spirit*, for instance, had a list to port before certain winds and under certain combinations of canvas. At her best, she sailed more perfectly, more nearly silently, than any boat he had been on. Her ornamental interior he noticed and did not mind, while Nick saw it and was irritated somewhat at details that he felt were pointless enough on land. Sandro forgave the vessel's fine innards and her well-made solidity, even the sofa cover patterned with stylised marine knots, the shelves battened to measure for books, the tantalus socketed in its cupboard, the rotating captain's chair plugged with buttons, before a chart table big enough, really, to eat off, to sleep on.

And it was so that above, on deck, such detail lost the note of frivolity although it was incidentally elegant, being entirely bent on purpose and maintained at a level that might be called groomed. Each rope, for fear of catching and holding and thus, at such great weights of sail, tearing off a hand or foot, was coiled invariably, discreetly, concentrically, paid down inside itself—even if it had to be so in exactly the same manner again two minutes later. Winch handles were stowed as though they were sharp knives. The deck was smooth and white and close-set with only the regular golden freckle of brass screws to hold it. Towards the bow the hardly visible curve of the deck took the eye like the wing of a hovering bird as its two sides approached one another precisely, minutely, the tessellation of the pale wood meeting without demarcation.

Sandro shared his cabin with Gabriel Shepherd, whom Logan had taken on as cook. She was tactful about being female. So far the only disturbance she had caused him was by her occasional mutterings into a small tape recorder. She was describing the journey to her mother, to whom she regularly sent these tapes. Sandro listened from the lower bunk (he had offered Gabriel the choice of whether to sleep above or below; embarrassment must not even commence in so confined a space or it spreads more treacherously than a silent fart) as she spoke rather shyly into her machine, whose absence of response in the silence sometimes seemed a bit rude. Often, he was struck by how different was Gabriel's account of things from any he might have given, was giving, he supposed, in a more cryptic way, in what he told Gabriel was his diary but what was in fact the long letter to his mother that he stopped writing only to post and then at once resumed.

Gabriel was an English girl, come to try out the world, Sandro supposed, before going home to an English man. She spoke in the old-fashioned way and wore a nightgown, under which she undressed, even when the watch system meant her sleeping times came during the day. Nonetheless, although she was slight, Gabriel was tough; she could crack walnuts in her palms and go up in the bosun's chair's spinning and creaking harness, where she'd hang at the top of the mast doing chores sixty feet up at a tilt as though she was taking cobwebs off the moon with a feather duster for fun. Sandro listened, not knowing that he did so, for any mention of himself in Gabriel's tapes. He knew the backs of her legs and her feet's soles well from lying exhausted in his bunk below hers. Both of them knew the other's unthinking habits since they had seen one another in states of extreme exhaustion usually shared only by pairs of people who are coupled, and are able only to brush tired shorthand kisses on to one another at the beginning or end of shifts with work or sleepless infant.

It was Gabriel's Englishness, in a way, that had brought out the ill temper of everyone eating breakfast. The relief at leaving hot, expensive Papeete was considerable, like at last having a drink of water or a shower, two things paradoxically rationed at sea.

The berth at Papeete was no more than a busy road, noisy at night and heavy with the fumes of traffic, beer, fast food, so that living on the boat felt more cramped than it did out at sea, where their accommodation was not exposed to the curiosity of all strangers. At night in their urban berth, a glaring lamp was set up in *Ardent Spirit*'s shrouds, to discourage drunks from coming aboard to sleep in her sail bin. The hatches had to be shut, or pranksters would creep over the deck to drop cigarettes or worse in on sleepers, so it was suffocatingly hot below. The harbour water had a skin of oil that made the water move slowly and left black smears of dead rainbow on the white hulls of the boats lolling, tied stern-to up to the pavement along which roamed tourists in various stages of disillusion with the place, a paradise handled.

Only when approached as any other colonial town did Papeete begin to reveal such charm as it had. The decontraction associated with earthly delights withers when it is a question of affording the water or the apple, but not both. The dissension in the saloon of *Ardent Spirit*, that first morning for all six together at sea, concerned cheese.

The cheese was from Paris, the city that administered Tahiti.

Plastic Port Salut, flown to New Caledonia and brought on a cargo ship to Tahiti from Noumea, with such tropical essentials as heated rollers, fake tan, artificial flowers, pineapple juice and the hair accoutrements known as rats.

"Ten pounds for a piece of cheese that has travelled the world by three different forms of transport, signed all the relevant forms, hung about in at least two warehouses and remains absolutely unchanged by its experiences. It is a narrow-minded cheese," said Gabriel, "for narrow-minded French consumers."

Unpleasant emotions about the French are unleashed by French colonies in some sorts of Briton. In Papeete, it was not hard for the most Francophile to see things reflecting badly on the administrators of the island. Among sights more glancingly combining the best of the cultures here melted together, the stately transvestites walking abreast punctuated in their reined-in strides by a little black poodle, the green pharmacy cross nicely medicinal in a street of *boulangeries* selling sorbets like frozen inks, in the sheer shade of mountains ribboned with silver waterfalls, there was to be seen a Frenchness that was less seductive and that did not include the people colonised except as they were of use.

Logan Urquhart was not wholly for spirited opinions in women unless voiced with concision and consonant with his own feelings on the matter. In this case he agreed to the extent that he found the French greedy and pusillanimous while admiring some superficial aspects of their culture. He was wary of going too far this early in a voyage when he had to live so closely with his wife, a Scot who keenly felt the Auld Alliance of blood and philosophical speculation with the French. Elspeth often expressed feelings about the English similar to those Logan held about the French. He wondered sometimes if her talk about the French was not worn like costume jewellery to make herself interesting at little expense. Since, anyhow, he imagined he could predict what Elspeth might say, he prepared himself for a period in the conversation during which he anticipated she might speak; so he began to think of other things, a uxorious habit even more practical on a boat than on dry land.

It is odd, thought Alec, that this boring conversation is no less boring because we are tipped up in the Pacific Ocean by a miracle of wind and water, moving through their agency to another place we shall fail to understand, discuss clumsily, forget, and then, as time builds lies into beauty recollected, recall transformed. Why did I come here? Why did I think I could change things in my life without changing myself?

As the tropical day began with its misleading purity to steal into and refresh them all, so they each saw ahead in this early heat of ill-temper the real danger of anger in a confined space and each, without knowing he or she did so, made a delicate concession and turned words through the uncomfortable degrees of angry argument to the pleasant pastime of exchanging differing opinions. The two women, Elspeth and Gabriel, led in this, conceding repeatedly and denying their own seriousness, until each danger was past and every person on board was returned to the position most conducive to peace, forward movement, and the maintenance of the status quo.

Having come to this extreme place to assess his own life among strangers, Alec felt his misgivings weigh him down. Had he not simply recreated, in farcically condensed form, the diffi-

15

culties he wished to sort out? Was the extremity of the situation, shut up in a pretty husk with five other souls between planets and sea monsters, not just a newer nightmare, more vulgar because so rich in psychological archetypes?

Suppose he were casting the play of his own life. Logan, the wooden but powerful rich man, would have to be his father, the fishmonger. Elspeth, who seemed to Alec alternately garrulous and blank, and with something insincere lying in her, was unlike his mother in every way he could think of. It was not possible to think of her saving milk-bottle tops in a heavy silver ball or taking the washing to the steamie in a pram. Neither the stern rectitude of saving, nor its dignified rewards, he thought, could ever have struck so pampered a character as Elspeth.

Nonetheless she was a diligent housekeeper, if that was what you called a woman who cleaned a boat inside as though the polish and rubbing would cause the thing to grow roots off its keel, flip upright, sprout a chimney and turn into a house. Could Elspeth have undiagnosed hydrophobia? He would try her, perhaps, later.

Alec's mother rose at four-thirty to clean the house and his own and her selves. The water she heated up in grey pans you could boil a sheep in, on the old Raeburn fed with coke from a metal scuttle. The noise she made pouring the coke was the noise of steeply dragged shingle under surf. She riddled it with a rod that glowed like a tiger's tail. Soda crystals fizzed as they went into the water, down the lavatory pan, down the bends of the double sink. He heard her flushing out the house's dirty secrets, before she came to get started on his own.

Alec being a landlubber and a bohemian prude took Sandro

and Gabriel to be lovers. He was that bit older than they were so that he suspected all young people of falling on one another when he was not looking. He thought that they, having so much he feared to have lost, must have everything he had not. He could not see that they were fleeing, often, from the trivial shape of their own thoughts and might wonder what he might have to tell them. Their handsome appearance and physical ease with the ropes and the wheel made Alec feel weighty and exposed if new sails were hoisted when the wind changed. At home he had sailed in small boats; the scale of this one made him afraid of accidents. He was the last to join this company and already he was wondering behind what false exterior to shelter. He had not yet properly left the land.

For the present, he thought it best to hang like a mackerel does in the water, not visible from below because its silver belly is only a floating mote against the paleness of the sky, not visible from above because its black-mapped blue back is incorporated with the contoured surface of the blue-black sea.

He continued to cast the central characters in his life from the people he was confined with on *Ardent Spirit*. If he had met almost no one, he thought, as spoilt as Logan and Elspeth Urquhart, he had met almost no one as unspoilt as Nick Pedersen. For a man as secretive as Alec to share any room with another person might have been unbearable. Like many secretive people, he was inquisitive, and had been through Nick's belongings one afternoon when Nick was sorting out the inert gas system on the second refrigerator, in the saloon. The other was in the galley and held large items such as joints of meat.

It was not possible to think of his mother, whose life had

17

after all been damaged and sustained in different ways by the sea, understanding the point of this sumptuously wasteful toy that was for a time his home.

Their house in Edinburgh was the grey of spurned beaches, made of concrete harled with small pebbles that appeared to have been picked from the noses of hills. It was a house built on quicksand promises, assembled from components, as notionally fit for humans as is a hutch for rabbits. The front door and three windows equalled those on the house's other half, so you might have folded it together for the doors to kiss and the windows to look into one another's eyes.

Alec had a usefully forbidding presence, though he was not tall. His black hair, red cheeks and white skin gave him the crisp appearance of a knave on a playing card. The condensedness of bearing that belongs to dark Celts was coupled in him with a capacity to become invisible, so that not many people saw how much he was taking in at his pale-blue eyes. No one could have guessed how much he took in or how he saved it. His greatest greed was behind his eyes.

The cleansing of Alec as a child began daily at the basin. His mother checked him over as though she might return him to the shopkeeper if she found a mark. She pushed his poll up the wrong way lest vermin might be resting in the shade of a hair. She soaped behind his big ears and under his small arms, in the cleft of his neck and down the knobs of his spine as though she was cleaning through to the bones.

One morning, unrewarded by the view down the plug, he strained his eyes up under his smarting lids as his mother skinned him with a flannel seemingly made of thistle-silk—and saw a delightfully shattered world, a dazzling reorganised frost-garden.

The lower pane of the bathroom window had been installed with modesty not revelation in view. Its thick glass was moulded in a million asterisks, a frozen field of dandelion clocks. If you looked through it at impossibly close range everything—the leaning iron washing-pole, the shed, the other cockle-brown houses—exploded into smithereens. The weatherproofed green shed where Jim's budgerigars lived became a fountain of bottle-glass, a green fanfare to a newly splintered world.

This pane of glass was not as limited as its immobility at first led Alec to fear, since within its frame it recorded changing weather and seasons, the times of day, domestic rhythms. In itself nothing but a new way of seeing things, it made of a mo-notony that had seemed unshakeable something incomprehensi-bly new that was also comprehensibly familiar. It was as though a ravishing abstraction had grown out of a flowerpot.

Even long grudging Edinburgh days of sea mist offered themselves to fracture and reinterpretation through that frosted bathroom window. Each child hunts for a solution to the bore-dom of being no one but itself. Alec's first answer was a sheet of modesty glass.

The mania of his mother for cleanliness also played into his hands, or eyes, since the washing line was constantly changing its wardrobe, from dancing white-and-blue teacloths to his father's white work-coats with their wind-filled arms untypically gesticu-lating. Once when it was snowing his mother took out the rugs to beat them with her cane carpet-beater, for the fresh snow to suck out the ingrained dirt. The fractured red and yellow of the carpets, the persistent seething flakes, the privacy of what he enjoyed as he pressed his cold face to the starry window, gave him a sense of being real that did not otherwise outlast his dreams.

That his first self-discovered pleasure took place in a bathroom was much to his mother's innocent satisfaction. If it was otherwise for his father he gave no word. Strangely, it was part of Alec's gratification to lock himself in in order to look through the—he thought of it as his—window. He did not speak of the window to either parent, each of whom he now as an adult supposed naturally came to a separate conclusion from the other about their eight-year-old son.

They thought he lied, but it was just the way he saw things. Alec sensed that he was pale in the bright colours of the modern street, not up-to-the-minute, not developed, his nature not fixed. He was not modern, nor old-fashioned in a way readily understood by modern people.

He was folding and settling his thoughts, as though ready to stow them for the life to come at sea. What I carry, he thought, is the memory of a time that should not have burned away so fast. What is called progress has consumed the fabric of our towns like fire, where war has not acted the mad dentist. Or does every man feel this as he ages? Our lives have been stretched beyond enduring by history and the result is that people welcome inanition, which is available in more forms than ever before. How I fear the young, although I am not old.

Alec ascertained that Nick Pedersen possessed a knife with a marlinspike on a lanyard as dirty as the string on his specs, an old green Everyman of *The King of the Golden River* that smelt of cinnamon and cat, and a Chinagraph pencil tied by, for Nick, rather extravagant nylon twine to a small, plastic-coated book showing commonly seen fish of the Pacific.

Perhaps Nick was more like Alec's mother, with his frugality and patience? But his want of possessions was an emancipation not a discipline against gross pleasures, and his patience did not seem to have enclosed and snuffed out the fire of his nature. No, for the moment it must be Elspeth, since she was the consort of the ruling male.

Alec picked up from the end of his bunk the newspaper he had bought two days ago. He had found it in a supermarket next to a pile of *Club International* on whose recurrent cover was a pink blonde dressed as a parcel. Browsing among the exhausted *saucissons* and Normandy butter costing its weight in gold were women more lovely, more exotic and more naked than the pink parcel, who seemed to represent an idea of sex uniquely Anglo-American, at once clean and creepy, more useful in confirming than gratifying masculinity. This look, the pink parcel and all Alec associated with it, he thought deserved the bulbous generic name "porno". He had picked up his newspaper and a small box of violet-scented indigestion cachous; he imagined caches of sweets would be found on a boat, but he would need something to suck if things became miserable. All his life Alec had taken small stolen sweets to bed at the end of wretched days. Sometimes he awoke with a cheek full of syrup, a reservoir of melted comfort.

The headline on the page of the paper to which he now turned read: "*Won Chiu Lee s'est pendue dans une boucherie après une dépression de 64 ans.*" It was wonderful to think of the relief death must have brought to her, the peace, the deliverance from blood and meat and the routine of the butcher's shop. Remembering the early mornings his father had to work, going to the docks when the sky was brown and the gulls screaming around the boats, Alec tried to translate this memory into its equivalent in a French Polynesian butcher's shop run by Chinese. All he could think of was the horrible obligation to use every part of the animal but its squeal, which was used up entirely at the time of slaughter, presumably. Supposing each pig to have thirty yards of gut, how many miles of pig's intestine alone must Won Chiu Lee have washed? Enough to rig a schooner with sails made out of sewn sow's ears.

"I am writing this," Alec's first sweetheart had written, "in my pyjamas." In fact she had been dressed, she later told him, in stout boots and a flowered dress that had reached its autumn. That first love was an *allumeuse*, indiscriminate, involuntary, dejected when her flirtatiousness was pointed out to her, not on account of having been found out, but on account of the lowness of her habit and her addiction to it. It was as though she chewed gum without being aware of it, not merely sappy, minty chewing gum, but the juicy, pink, softer bubble gum that you couldn't stop yourself winding around your tongue or concentrating into a wad at the tips of your teeth before inflating it into a bubble of precarious rosiness that might burst in your face, and sometimes did.

The relief from my mother's clarity offered by such a girl set my life's habit, he thought. Have I always to take the longer

22

road? My parents worked to give me everything that made me strange to them. I hanker now for the simplicity you can no more work for than faith, which it seems to me they had.

Light was changing its weight and pulling the sky out down towards the edge of the sea at the end of that first day out of Tahiti. At the bow of the boat the anchor chain girned with a faint but surprisingly serious sound, as though the stone knight on a tomb were waking and beginning heavily to stir in his burdensome carapace, the stone conjunctions of his armour beginning painfully to grate into articulation. In the fo'c'sle it was less easy to forget the boat's vulnerability. Although he felt he would settle into the sleep-fracturing watch system after only a few days of it, Alec was still constantly nervous aboard, with two forms of unease. Among people still strange to him he felt a protracted and almost physical unease that was the tense social pain of a term begun, or a long stay in another family. The greater unease was a fear of falling short of some still-unpresented ordeal. In trying to keep himself ready at all times to respond to some practical mishap that might smite the boat, Alec chafed at and wore down the distance he kept habitually between himself and others. He wondered if the utter unfamiliarity he had forced upon himself would not merely force himself more into his own company.

An excited, thin-skinned hypochondriacal trance, like the sensation that precedes flu, enclosed Alec during his first days at sea among the Society Islands. That there was a right way to do things in this ordered, constrained community was clear, but he watched so closely and so much that the other men did not feel easy with him, and he was overcome by the self-distaste of the intelligent mimic. He had hoped that intelligence and practical ability would tell him what to do, but many of the words were new. Nothing could release him from his fearful sense of impersonating a man on a boat at sea. He felt a gap in himself where instinct should have been, a gap intelligence took time to fill.

He awoke to a roaring that seemed to pull downwards, and a looser crunching grinding, accompanied by the hard sudden noise of a big rebellious engine thrown into reverse. His open-mouthed dreams had been full of talk and tinkling and the booming of men; he realised these sounds came with the peaceful down-hauling of sail.

What was afoot now though was not peaceful. In the bow the anchor had thundered down, but there was a twitching in the boat. Her anchor was dragging, poiseless and lame. The engine was holding the boat off rocks or coral. So much he had picked up from listening to the talk.

Had they left him to sleep because he was no use? No one could have remained asleep, and Alec could not pretend to have. He went above, emerging from the companionway with a face full of feigned alertness. Between the shrouds of the tall mast he saw, perfectly set and disorderedly edgy like an uncut gem, doubled in the milky sea, the raked sides and cleaving shadows of the island of Moorea.

"It's holding," said Logan. In these moments of expert flurry, his American accent came through, manly, assertive. Solid behind the wheel he spun to perfection even with his left hand, he set his white beauty of a boat to rest in the skirts of the high island.

Elspeth looked from time to time at her husband with a peculiar air of rehearsal and artificiality. It was not possible to imagine that this boat was in any way hers. Gabriel seemed more adult although she was by perhaps eighteen years the younger, as she sauntered yet executed the right moves under Logan's and Elspeth's eyes, that watched her without either watcher engaging the other's regard.

The sun was yellow and oval, dropping visibly as the sky turned thinly green. Towards the sun moved wide lavender shadows on the smooth sea, stepping towards a rim between the sea and the sky. The sides of the island shivered with rich, defined vegetation of a green now almost devoid of yellow. Three hundred yards from them, the island's shore seemed to pull the darkness in towards the land, reining veils of shadow in from off the sea.

The sun was sucked down to the sea in the last degrees of its declining, just falling as the air tipped and formed into drifts of breeze.

The green flash will come now, Alec thought to himself, and I will know I am in the south. The sun should fall down through the sea and show a momentary stripe of light behind the ocean, as though you could cut down through the sea with a knife of light. He hoped to see an orderly cross-section of teeming ocean, laid bare and rational like past history set down to be understood.

What he saw was the sun, yellow in its moment of joining the briefly ultramarine horizon. The sun fell into the sea, shooting through from behind it a deep beaming triangle of burning green, a green flash through the long water it had fallen far within. Though cool, the green was blinding and it lingered in yellow lashes of light behind the eyes. A red sunset would have soothed; there was no setting to this sun, just a hot falling and then whole darkness, momentarily black and full of the aftermath light that had gone, without, yet, new light.

The sky returned to purple and the island become a profile only. Venus came up, red Mars behind it. Dim Jupiter began the night.

Inside the reef, *Ardent Spirit* hung in the water bright like a star in the sky, but held in her place, at last unmoving.

Nick began to put down hooks for night lines to get fish, as they would every night they anchored, to keep up food supplies without using storage space. He put a heavy hook down you could have hung an ox's carcass from, baiting it with a phosphorescent rubber squid.

"Outside the reef there are sharks. In Nuku Hiva there are more fishermen with one leg than with two. Some of the kids there are stitched all over, cobbled really, you'd say." Sandro's New Zealand voice kept his remarks light. The continual interrogative in his tone made the words buoyant.

"I've seen a leg took down to the bone by those rows of teeth," said Logan, "and I never wish to again. It's the way the shark's skin snags and draws blood that gets me, every bit of the shark made to draw blood. I've seen a man . . ."

"Let me get you a drink," said Gabriel, something nurselike in her tone. The plain words in the star-enfolded place seemed to make briefly a family of the individuals at sea.

"Tonight, and as long as we stay here, we sleep all night in preparation for the open ocean. After that, once we're making long passages, it's on to the watch system, in pairs, four hours on, eight off, unless the weather comes and we need all hands," said Logan, pouring out naval rum. Its high alcoholic tang and sugar-and-tar smell filled the night, overlaying salt even.

Later, when Alec got up in the night, he did not know the hour, but he pulled himself up on his hands through the fo'c'sle hatch. Just six feet from him in the bow leaned Logan looking up at the stars like a man making a vow.

Or he could have been counting, Alec decided, back in his own cramped berth in the fo'c'sle. He did not know why he had this gentle but piercing impulse to trim Logan's heroism, his romantic scale. It was the satirical deflation of a son towards a father, the snobbish non-combatant squeamishness he felt to-wards soldiers, heroes and other romantics. How else, though, to face the sea?

When Alec was eight he went through into a dark room, the dark room, the Camera Obscura. It was on a shepherded school trip to the heart of Edinburgh, the cooler city of the seven hills. Their destination was up by the Castle which sits aslant its de-funct volcano, set across a small valley, containing the railway, from the main eighteenth-century thoroughfare, Princes Street. Small shoals of schoolchildren in coloured blazers moved con-stantly through the "sights" of the city. A city so rich in itself could be said to be all sights.

They were learning their history, the history Scots learn with different heroes and different victories from the English. They were taught to expect perfidy and misprision from an English-man, should they meet one. Alec knew how they talked, from off the wireless and from imitating them. They spoke as though their chins were noses, like horses.

Alec was in a group of clean small boys in shorts, their socks held up by strong elastic, their temperaments pugnacious, impressionable and not yet priggish. As an identifiably bookish child he had more enemies than committed friends but he was not soft. Already he had learnt the self-reliance of the only child and the banked arrogance of the single-minded one. Boys are more loyal in childhood than girls, something to do with girls' rehearsing for change and adaptation and boys' preference for consistency in practical matters, so Alec had at that point the friend he had known all his life, who lived next door. In the street the boys were not so close, for Hector's physical dash outstripped Alec's own, but at school Alec solved Heck's work since he found it uncomfortable to concentrate.

Hector was an adept at childhood, I realise now, thought Alec, and I had not the knack. He was a sprite, with thick red hair that stood up like a crown of leaves. Will that hair be white now, or fallen? Red hair burns out so young. Alec poured more water into a toothmug. It tasted of mint and cigarettes, not salt.

The many steps up to the dark room were themselves dark and the boys bumped up them bouncing their satchels, more interested in being out of school than in being where they were. Alec had no idea of what they had been brought to see. Heck had a metal musical instrument, called a kazoo, which he had been told would be confiscated if it appeared again. It was a flat, squared-off tube about five inches long, with a circular mesh hole an inch from the top, out of which, if you equipped it with a disc of hard lavatory paper and hummed, an amplified version of the humming came. Heck would give kazoo performances on the street, writhing and dipping and leaning back from the waist, darting forward suddenly like a striking snake when he needed applause. The only pleasant sensation whatsoever produced by the kazoo was a faint buzz against the lips of the hummer, a kind of first-kiss ache, it now seemed to Alec as he recalled it, the thin skin prickling with too much minute sensation.

Heck had the kazoo in his blazer. Alec knew it was there and that his friend relished offending where he most especially should not. Alec's lifelong reluctance to disobey rules was already itching at him, so he was edgy as the group settled in the cramped upper room, the Camera Obscura.

In the dark they stood around a low white bowl, about a yard wide, while a tubby man, dressed in the civvy uniform of a commissionaire, tried to get the measure of them, like someone shaking a bag of sugar for lumps.

"Here in this room you will see your own home town, brought by a periscope and mirrors down into this white dish. I shall indicate the places I mention with the baton I hold here in my hand." He tapped the white stick thrice in the bowl, into which light at once fell from a tight point above it so that the children stood about an inverted cone of light. The light was not electric or warm. It was the light of day. It seemed refreshing in that room that smelt of serge and boys.

"Very well. The mirrors, Ian, please." A cranking sound came from a corner. A small man in the brown overall ironmongers wore at that time looked up with the furtively busy movement of a rodent. He was turning a handle whose noise described its effect, the circular motion pressing up into, disengaging and raising metal bars attached to plates that moved with a squeaking sigh and a more precarious, delicate sound, like teeth in one's own head.

"Thank you, Ian. That'll be the mirrors marrying now. Tighten up there, Ian, till I see it clear. There we are. The city of Edinburgh, boys, laid out in a bowl."

Not the whole city at once, but parts of it in turn spilt down by the mirrors into the bowl, a tour the boys could not have accomplished on their inattentive feet. The colours were the same as when the boys had left the world outside of the Camera Obscura. The quality of high brightness they had was on account of the darkness from which the eye looked. There was no impression of the idealised colour of film, its incipient sunsetty glow. The colours were true to the tabby, pewter, lilac and soot of the slate and smoke of the city.

"One mile in length runs Princes Street whose stores are used by the highest in the land. Over here the North British Hotel, whose clock you will observe is a punctual five minutes fast. Passengers at Waverley Station therefore," he waved the baton, "are less likely to miss their trains. The two great galleries of Scotland are here at the foot of the Mound, sorely in need of a clean as you will observe from the state of the Queen." The baton flicked a youthful coal-black Queen Victoria seated on the roof of a low-columned building on whose black steps a man scraped at a fiddle. No noise, of course, came.

"The Scott Monument further down Princes Street is a memorial to a great son of Scotland the Laird of Abbotsford. You will see him at his books inside this," he took a breath as though about to use a phrase from the French, "highly ornamented example of the neo-Gothic."

30

Ian turned his crank again and the sound came as a shock. It was peculiar to see the town alive but not to hear its life. As though taken over by the invasive silence to be found in involuntary church going, the children redoubled their silence, if you can double nothing.

Alec began to ache, not with boredom so much as concentration. The spin of the greasy iron sounded like the chain of a playground swing, slowed only just bearably. Alec was nervous in the comfortable way a beloved child of regular habits feels hunger. He was about to know how to allay what ailed him.

The man in his uniform began again. The decorations on his chest were slim bits of colour like a girl's dress caught in a door hinge each time he bent forward into the cone of light.

"Here of course we have Princes Street Gardens, open to all for recreation. The world-famous floral clock may be seen just here, giving the correct time in many colourful blooms, kept fresh by careful replanting. Only in the depth of winter does it rest. Are there any questions now?"

Since a couple were embracing next to the congested planting of the floral clock, one of the boys had to speak, to release the tension.

Heck asked, "Is it the flowers keep the clock going or the other way about?" At that moment the door of a small house on a stick set behind the floral clock burst open and a stiff wooden bird was ejected. It bobbed three times. The sound it made, inaudible to the boys, apparently shocked the couple whose deep embrace they had been following in detail. The man had his hand behind the woman's head as though he was injecting her with his face. When the bird sprang out, they leapt apart as if they had just found out they had been making a mistake.

It was a surprise to Alec to see that neither of these people was distinguishable as a person who had recently been kissing. He thought it must show somehow.

"The gardeners keep the clock going. And here we have the Mound itself, aye, Ian, right you are, heated underground in winter, boys, as you may know, by a warm blanket lying just beneath the surface, recently installed at no small cost." A maroon City of Edinburgh bus was straining like a beetle up the steep hill towards the Old Town, leaving the Castle off to its right. It was a cold mistless day with a hidden glare of sun that from time to time flashed off glass or metal as they made their cooped tour of an airy city into which they had never roamed so far, whose sea they saw at the one reach of their Olympian view, whose lion-shaped presiding hill, Arthur's Seat (Why is Holyrood? Because it looks up Arthur's Seat. Alec thought the riddle before he meant to, out of habit laid too long to wipe out), and dark crags at the other.

At some point during that afternoon a ladybird blundered on to the dish where the city displayed itself tantalisingly bowlful by bowlful. Alec realised that he had been walking about the streets with the same unaware confusion as the insect now showed, marching through and over people, houses, churches, gardens, schools, law courts, graveyards, libraries, as though only it was real and they were just light thrown by a mirror. It stood unaware among the thorny arms of the crown on top of the High Kirk of St Giles. It meandered down the wide, granite-laid streets of the New Town, before falling over the edge and out of his sight into the daytime darkness.

Most peculiar of all was the silence from these streets, whose surface was of setts, blocks of stone laid brickwise, a surface that, outside of the Camera Obscura, gave richness to the sound of vehicles and a stony literal accompaniment to the progress of people or horses.

Here was their city, voiceless, displayed. The silence kept Alec's attention and enclosed him. When Hector took out his kazoo and began to polish it on his backside, Alec was for a moment in terror of the noise he knew must come, as though he had made a decision for life to choose sight above hearing.

Under the boat the water divided and remet itself around her keel. The two lappings of the water on each side of the boat were separately audible, and beneath them the deeper licking the sea made at the island's hidden reaches ushered a lower and graver sound over the sea's surface, under the talk and human movement on the boat.

By the time there came tugs on the night lines set for a night catch, everyone slept, Logan in the sail bin among his floating beauty's robes and veilings, and his wife in their cabin with a book, open, over her wet, shut face.

Alec's withheld, inland demeanour began young. Not long after his visit to the dark upper room, the Camera Obscura, he started to take an interest (as a man might take a drink) in places. The habit was not one he was brought up to, and at first he did not know how to look or what to look at, but shortly he realised that Edinburgh was full of secret places.

These places were the first rival of his mother. In them it is possible that she felt the first move of her son away from herself and her own controlled despairs. His interest in houses and things she could not separate from what she feared to be an interest in the complex, subtle, fierce life of property and those who had it. She feared the lullaby the handsomeness of property might croon to his conscience.

"Will I not come with you?" Mairi asked her son sometimes, though she did not want to look all day at grey buildings that glinted in the same dead way as mountains of fish. Going up to town suited her for an ice or an outing, but not for tramping up hills and staring down them and asking sour old women to get a look at their ceilings.

Alec walked the city to get a sense of it like a policeman with a beat. Some of the streets were so steep it seemed you would fall out of them into the sea, that lay there always at the mouth of the town, fuming up into mist or sparkling up into the city so the minute particles of mica in its stone flashed back like salt thrown up by the wind off the water. Alec pined to take the red iron rail bridge over to Fife, into the country that occurred as visible echoes in places within the town, elbows of green, spurs of black rock among the heaped tall buildings of the Old Town and lying under the leggy bridges of the New Town.

"What difference will it be? How are the houses not the same there as here with us where we stay? In our part of the town?" The word she was not using was morbid, though she might have had she known of his frequent visits to churches.

The almost fetishistic belief in action that Mairi had was the heart of her energy, her stamina; she could not gather what her son was accumulating by his wandering habits. Moreover she began to fear that he was not (no boy could) spending all this time in *looking* only.

"Tell me where you go."

"All over up town."

"What do you do?"

"Look. See."

"Who do you see?"

"Mostly no one."

"*Mostly*. Someone?"

Now he would have to invent suitable friends. What could be better than an old lady?

"Oh, I see an old lady."

"I see. How old. My age?" Alec was too young to hear the wife in his mother. And now he would have to find an old lady.

"What is her name?"

"I don't know." He did not, indeed.

His mother, unwilling to accept that her son was spending hours away from home on account of motionless compilations of materials, could more readily understand it if he were up to emotional mischief, practising for his departure from her careful love. He concealed his innocence, and thus began the unravelling between his mother and himself. He was ten.

The next day was between summer and autumn. The leaves were not yet fallen. On the branches they appeared resigned and would in a day be wistful, then gone. Their yellow was too milky to be quite dry yet.

Alec must today find an old woman to befriend him at speed. It was a Tuesday. His mother had a half-day and she was to come to tea with his friend, whose address he had failed to write down, although he rightly knew the way there. It hurt his dignity, this pretending not to know where a place was, but he had to in the circumstances, not yet knowing *if* it was. He would accompany his mother to tea.

Old women went to wash clothes, they went to kirk, and

they went shopping. He might find one at the steamie, any of the many churches (could he risk an old woman not from the Church of Scotland?), and at the shops.

What type of old woman it must be had not exercised him until he came to choose, perceiving that there was considerably more difference than you would have thought. In appearance, they were similar in essentials, of course. Hat, coat, terrific hefty handbag, painful shoes (he was after an old woman his mother would deem respectable). He'd give the steamie a miss. It was so noisy, how could he explain he needed to borrow an old woman?

Alec walked up Drummond Place to the playground called the Wreck. So it was. The iron toys creaked in their cindery bed. Purple flowers with long pods like needles grew and sank overnight. The dogs came here to lay black dirt in the nettles and squirt hot green sideways pee at the gulping shaky stanchions of the swings. There was broken glass on the ground and a hole in the fence at waist height that had no meaning that was good. The talk among the children here was of men who offered sweeties and of the parky threatening a good beating. The one bench was misleadingly curvaceous as to its iron, but without a back. In its green paint were messages of love. The words "Fuck the Pope" were written as casually as "Gordie for Sheila". More personal messages described the skills of girls hereabouts in geographical terms: "Donna goes Russian", "Donalda can French".

Alec sat down. The brindle dog with a stiff tail and white eyes came over to him, the blind Commander pulled along behind.

"I can tell you like dogs. Yes, he's a particularly fine bull mastiff." The old man spoke to the presence he felt, heated, ruffled, bothered. The dog snuffled at Alec's grey shorts, leaving its dribble, like hot cobweb jam.

"It's his coat I chose him for," said the blind Commander, whose back was scattered with soft, perforated flakes of skin and several lost strands of white, whose face was growing hairs at the points most exposed to wind, where a gargoyle will first wear. "These markings are exceptionally fine. It's the black on the brown I greatly admire, an effect like that of," he seemed to wander and he stroked the air with his right hand that held the loop of lead and his left a bird's breadth from it, "of, I don't know if you recall, but on a hen pheasant." He did not have a hat on, but the Commander seemed to adjust what was not there.

It was a day whose sunshine was being withdrawn, though when Alec lolled back on the bench's springy rusting bracket, it was faintly warm, and the iron swings sent out their heavy tang. He wondered what the Commander thought he was, how he saw him in the eyes that saw the brindle dog.

"You are a boy of perhaps ten." For a time Alec was alarmed, but the Commander did not move except to pat his dog's hard flat head and dejected muscular shoulders. The interestingness of old people, so different from their charm, revealed itself to Alec as it hardly ever does to children who are not themselves apparently peculiar.

"How do you know that?"

"You smell, I mean no offence, like a puppy."

"I need an old lady," said Alec. He explained, finding it not difficult because of the swift understanding the blind Commander showed of what it was privately to want to escape and to see.

"I know where we can get one, but we may have to hurry, and you must help myself and Dunvegan on to the bus."

The bus ride was not unpleasant, though Alec was worried about the time and had no watch. The blind Commander had a watch that was embarrassing, because it lived in his pocket and chimed and was held to him with a necklace. It was eleven-fifteen by the time the three of them reached Jenners.

The solemnity of department stores, like that of liners and the obscurer Victorian Gothic churches, veers close to farce. If one person laughs at the absurdity of the elaboration, at the redundant ceremonial, the splendiferous equipoise of the over-weight enterprise is threatened, the displays shimmer, the grandeur is revealed as mummers' tricks. When the discrepancy between the general tone of manners and the high formality of the great department store was less, to visit such a place was a small act of celebration. It had not yet become camp. The satirical bent of the lowland Scot kept Jenners, modest before it was grand, afloat on Princes Street.

"Haberdashery would be the spot," said the Commander. "We'll leave Dunvegan with the commissionaire. We're able to take him in, but old women are terrible for not looking where they are going."

Alec had admired the crusted edifice he was now entering, but he never would have gone into the place. Inside, there were layers of banisters up a great hall, all with women taking time so slowly that there was a luxury about their browsing. He saw a child, barely recognisable in clothes like those of a man doll. He was sitting on a stuffed dog the size of a table and getting his hair cut by a bendy man in striped trousers.

"Violet on the hair, Archibald, today, or Bay Rum?" asked the hair cutter, using the silver scissors to conduct his question.

"No such silliness. Water alone has no shame to it," came a voice, and Alec noticed, sitting unyieldingly on a polar bear, a woman all bone whose rigid clothes were navy blue throughout. She rose. Such thinness might have been illness.

"They will pay," said the fine but obscurely client old lady.

"Thank you, Nannie," said the hair cutter.

And in a new voice, now the child was standing, a small male of the governing class, no longer a wee man on a stuffed dog.

"Goodbye then, sir."

That there were so many towns in the one had only begun to glow in Alec's mind. Now he was learning, as though he were lifting clothes from a trunk, about other ways of life.

Haberdashery was small things you would not remember to buy until you needed them, such as pins, scissors and ribbons. A short rotating stand dispensed cumbersome shaped pads with straightforward illustrations of how to insert them into a frock to collect sweat or make your front stick out more.

Certainly Commander Bruce was correct. The supply of old women here was considerable.

"Try tartans, Alexander."

Alec led the blind man to an alcove where some blindness might have soothed. Wiry women in black manhandled wide bolts of cloth from the shelves and chucked them down on to a long wooden counter, marked in inches, feet and yards along its far edge. In the ease and custom of the women Alec recognised something of his mother. The tartans were splendid, too bright, jarring, over-square. A softness was missing that he knew by instinct was part of the secret of the look of Scotland, its fractions, hints and modesties of beauty.

"Do you see any old woman you like the look of?" asked Commander Bruce.

It was not a question to answer with the truth. No answer was needed, however. An old woman was approaching, downy-faced and in a hat and hard shoes, with some humour in her face, though.

"Is it that time yet?" she asked the Commander. "Or are you the early one?"

"Alexander, my sister, Miss Bruce. Muriel, this is Alexander whom I met at the Wreck."

"Is that the right name for it?" Alec asked. He thought it was just what the kids called it.

"Short for recreation," said Muriel Bruce, not bored or teacher-like. "Will you take lunch with us? We generally have our bite at lunchtime on a shopping day."

"He'd rather take tea with us, Muriel. His mother wants to meet you. For tea. That is the plan."

"In that case I must purchase some fancies with Dunvegan's damaged biscuits. Have you our address, Alexander?" Only a woman of poise or habitual perfect forgetfulness could display such calm.

"It's Nelson Street. Seven. The top flat. Dunvegan's bowl is outside the front door. When do you generally arrive for tea engagements? I suggest three-thirty. We shall not be formal." All the while he spoke, the Commander's hand was throbbing like a pecking chick against the spruce-and-burgundy tartan roll at the top of the gamut of stiff plaids. No one could reach the tartans,

Alec realised, but they all held back from budging the blind old man with his softly beating, trembly hand.

"We might just set you on the road for your bus, Alexander, before we make our own way."

"I know the town. I get about without help."

"For the company then?" enquired Miss Bruce, since she was curious, and kind. The complicated slowness of life with the old, different again from the irritating but protective slowness of life with a parent, fully came to Alexander when, later, he found himself explaining to his mother over a cold fried egg piece, the reason for the lateness he hoped always in future to pin upon the Bruces.

"So there is an old man also?" said his mother.

"Blind," said Alexander.

Mairi wondered whether this was better or worse.

"For eyes he has a brindle dog name of Dunvegan," replied Alec, trying out some ways of talking he had heard that morning.

His mother prepared herself, as she watched her son, pink and white and black like a fruit tree in spring before hardening into leaf, take the last meal of his simpler life. Gently, she untied the first string between them.

In Nelson Street (it was "in", not "at", for the flat was his first great house, apprehended as somewhere not home and, more than that, a site where things were possessed for a reason) Mairi sat on the sofa with her feet on a zebra skin. When the afternoon seemed to be about to upset her balance, she looked down at the stripes, bringing first the black stripes, then the white, forward into her eyes, moving focus precisely in alternation as a person will do to reorientate herself after a swoon.

The room was dark, but Commander Bruce got about without harming the tottering arrangements of objects.

"It has been here since we were children, almost all of it in this room, though we have added to the other rooms some things we have found." The oldness of the things ceased to be their only trait. Much of the stuff was so old it had returned to childhood. A cavorting ostensible ugliness led the taste of the Bruces towards the purchase of large, heavy things that had they been animals would have been buffalo, okapi, iguana, beasts disproportionate, ungainly and on further contemplation affectingly expressive of a human past without self-consciousness.

The sugar came in an ostrich egg, halved and set on a foot of blackened silver. The room hardly shone, though it did glint, with slipping velvet, tormented horn, snapped ormolu, and colours made to be flattered by dust, to shine through grease—coral, amber, the slick internal pink of shells.

On the top shelf of a red-and-gold set of shelves cornered like a pagoda with bells was a giraffe-coloured shell the size of a bugle. Its point was jauntily to one side, the pearly throat the conclusion of a series of angled spirals abstract as a puzzle.

The Commander said, "We bought it for the story it told." Alec saw a speech bubble come from the mouth of the shell, a cartoon thing anyhow for its size and markings.

"South seas, all that. Here he lies, you know, where he longed to be. Home is the sailor, home from the sea. Or home from Edinburgh." The Commander tweaked at both his trouser knees and smoothed them, making as much noise as he could with his quiet tweeds in the company that was not getting his drift. He regretted that he had lost his visitors with his words.

Dunvegan crossed and recrossed his front paws in his sleep,

as though anxious to change the subject. His black claws tapped on the floorboards. He shook his ears with a wet sound.

"Robert Louis Stevenson, a fine man, a writer, was he not, Mrs Dundas, I believe you are right, was a child not far from here. The junk shops around are surprisingly full of items that he might have used as an inkwell. Or might not."

Neither Alec nor his mother knowing whether to agree, to laugh or to give up as one does when looking for something that does not really matter, kept quiet.

"You would like to see the instructional tortoise, perhaps?" Miss Bruce said to Alec. "And we ladies must leave the men. I have a question to ask your mother, in the sewing room. It concerns something most important to do with trimmings." Tact, irony, speech taking no account of a child, combined to confuse Mairi while she was allowing herself to be charmed, that is, manoeuvred, albeit in this case for her own good.

The instructional tortoise was disgusting, frightening, not that clean, and never forgotten by Alec. The small purposeful animal sat, varnished in the laborious throes of taking a step, on its cretonne grass, held down by wire loops over a middle nail on each foot. From one side, though too smartly finished, like a shoe never worn, the tortoise was as you would expect, whorled shell, leathery weak pits at the entry of limbs between the domed shell and the plastron (the Commander passed on the words he had heard as a boy; they were part of the instructional tortoise). When you turned around the tight glass-and-wood case, the other side of the tortoise was its self within. The taxidermist, observing the evening-dress mimicry of nature on the first side, had exactly halved the shell and divided the comforting outer parts, leaving only the right-hand side of the tortoise clothed in shell and skin. The left-hand side was clean bone. Dry as lace-bobbins, the small bones were set in a lively, halted, recreation of a step that could not arrive. The skeletal side of the tortoise, being at least apparently frank, was more lively, when you were used to it, than the overdressed seeming right-hand side. The most painful part was the harsh division down the centre, from which fixed line the tortoise could hide nothing of its secret, witty, vulnerable and complicated most internal workings. It seemed rational, like a watch that might be set going, but of course it might not; the life had been explained out of it. The instructional tortoise was a curiosity, a confident attempt to reveal and to teach, more usually displayed in illustration on paper where liberties are more easily taken without pain.

"It has a glass eye on the right-hand side," said the Commander, "about the size of a young pea. Remarkable. I saw it when I could see. I was younger than you are. A man came to our parents' home to rejuvenate the stuffed animals. He was a vet, with a sideline. He supplied pelts all over the east coast and was known for his lifelike mounting. The motor car, when it came in, was at first apparently of some use to him, but it is not a clean killer."

Alec was in surroundings wholly unfamiliar, surrounded by incomprehensible plenty, addressed in a confusingly courtly manner by an old man who spoke in a way he had not heard before. The things to be seen in the flat were not such things as he connected with something like money; would you buy old things?

The cold dark communal stair, a feature of the city's palatial streets, built behind swooping façades as flats from the beginning of the New Town two hundred years before, had been a reassurance to him. There must be countless such different ways of life going on all over the town, unknown to him, unknown to one another, behind doors leading off unheated stone stairs, flight after flight.

"There are many gardens, all about the town," said his mother, returning to the room, with Miss Bruce. Later, when he thought of his mother, trying to collect all he remembered of her before it blurred, he remembered sharply she had sung these words, in a high voice full of assurance and contentment. Beside Miss Bruce she seemed a girl.

That was before he had his other mother, who came next.

In Moorea, the morning sun melted the last mist, closer to the last resting place of Stevenson than to his birthplace, but heaped high in stone like it. Only a purple cloud stayed as though caught by the island's teeth. Alec awoke from dreams of high heaped buildings, the dream he associated with Edinburgh, and heard two things.

Gabriel was talking into her tape recorder, though he could not hear the words. Nick was leaning down through the fo'c'sle hatch with a pronged piece of white metal like a short crowbar, an inch thick. There remained only a faint bend in the fish hook that had once bent like the elbow of an arm wrestler. Something had been powerful enough almost to pull it straight while they slept.

Not knowing he knew the words till he said them, Alec said, "God knows the breaking strain we had on that line."

The people on the boat had become "we" in the face of the sea.

Two

On the boat, Elspeth was thinking out loud. "So they introduced a snail to Moorea and the idea was that it would gobble up the huge edible snails that had been introduced artificially themselves, twenty years ago, for food. The giant snail ate everything, not just what it was supposed to. The second wave of foreign snails was even worse, and carnivorous. Species of plant and insect grew scarce as they were eaten up. Now the first, indigenous, island snail is endangered and people come from America and all over to try to track it down and beef it up and train it to fight back in the name of biodiversity. People are wishing they had the old wee nuisance back."

"What a lot you do know," said Logan. He did not like the way she, having perfectly good information, made it implausible in the way she set it out. He did not look women in the face unless he was explaining things to them or setting out to seduce them. Otherwise, in a beautiful voice, he gave orders. He did not need to pitch them high. He was a man for whom people did things, for their own reasons.

"The ecology of islands is fragile that way," Nick said, but it was not annoying. They even hoped he would continue. He did not have the polymath's trick of talking in brightly formed sentence-long paragraphs. He went on eating Weetabix, feeding himself from the front of the spoon. It was a large spoon, no different from a small spoon to him in the matter of eating; had it been an engine part he could have gauged dimension precisely. "In small enclosed places with highly organised finite interdependencies you can't afford to unbalance a single thing."

Elspeth and Gabriel were coming by now, the fourth full day in Moorea, to seek one another out. The forgettable conversations that distinguish the domestic female day could not take place at sea, where there were no shopkeepers, no bus drivers, no familiar strangers. Gabriel, being younger than Elspeth, did not need and had not established so many of these links, but Elspeth realised each time she went to sea how she missed such small advances into disinterested warmth.

The escape provided by these secessions from life on dry land was more partial for the women. The sense of being away and free can shade with a change of wind into the sense of being caught and trapped, painted in to a picture one did not choose to be part of.

The chopped time of watchkeeping, twenty-four hours divided into six stretches of four, quickly establishes itself. The body adapts by cutting off the dawdling sleep that is rich in enquiry and reconciliation with the day just gone. Even in the deepest sleep, too, the body is attuned to the boat. All through the sleep on a boat, by day or by night, you listen for some clue from the air as to what it intends to do. On a sailing boat this speculation is the medium of all preoccupation. The wind breathes into everything. If it is not there, its absence is felt like a distant but fresh bereavement.

The company on board were between the land and the sea in their sleeping habits as well as their anchorage; they had not yet begun to work fully on the watch system, although Nick and Sandro tended to split the night between them to listen for dragging on the anchor chain. Nick hoped to see the fish that stripped the hooks each night. All they had caught was a shark pup that was more interesting to gut than to eat. It had fed with such uninvolved gusto that its belly spilled out fifty-seven unmarked silver wrasse, shiny like foil birdscarers. *Ardent Spirit* was anchored a few hundred yards out from the island; as the day began, the sound of mobilette engines could be heard from the land, and sometimes a papery chopping, palms being cut by machete blades. The flat sea took the noise straight over itself from the high island. There was no modifying shore. Beyond the boat, over the reef, the water crisped and broke, caught from beneath continually, combed to shreds and flung again.

Gabriel, wound up in a pareo of flowered cotton, seemed nonetheless unexotic, her bare shoulders fine, not private or suggestive. The cloth wound round her was not introspective and alluring like a sari, but to the point, as an Englishwoman will have her clothes, modest, practical and apt as an apron. Her hair was tied up and fixed with a jawed clip. The freckles glowing below brown skin would soon join up to make her the colour of a hazelnut. Elspeth was untidy even in one single piece of cloth; her pareo seemed ill cut. There was an incoherence to the various colours of her skin, tan back, red shoulders, white legs and undersides, that was pitiful, infantile. The high bones of her face were overdramatic for her apologetic demeanour and insistent self-effacement. As two feminine types, the certain and the unsure, they seemed, if only physically, exemplary. The subtle expression of character and habit in feature had begun in Elspeth, being older; Gabriel's character was apparently of a piece with her wholesome body and face.

Nick was holding the tender to the side of *Ardent Spirit*. At the back of the solid rubber boat a powerful outboard engine was clamped to the wooden transom, and resecured by ropes. Disaster beyond the small accident was foreseen on the tender as on the big boat. The extreme provident caution that must accompany adventure is cousin to the theoretical pessimism parents deploy.

"Who's coming?" Nick called up to the deck.

"We need oranges and needles." Elspeth hung over the wire rail. She was hovering and would not commit herself until she saw what each other person was doing.

"I'll stay and put up the awning and housekeep the sails. I'll swim in later, could be, and catch a beer," called Sandro who had been to Moorea before and knew it as well as he liked to know a place.

Logan came up. A silence lay over the others. They waited under his decision.

"I'll take in the hills one more time," he said.

"I'll do the shopping." Gabriel spoke crisply.

"Could we take the Zodiac?" Alec was not yet familiar enough to state what he wanted without asking what was done in such a place. "And find a beach maybe and look at fish?"

Logan looked at him as though assessing a difference between face and market value. Then his own face loosened, and he smiled.

"Sandro, get the diving gear, and pass it to us."

Alec had dived before, in grey sea off Kintyre; he had hated it. The complete severance from others, which he had not thought to fear, shocked him. He was surrounded by a greatness to which he was nothing, but not as one is nothing under the stars; under the sea it had been for him like an unmourned death. Down there, he longed to hear words again, to use them, as he had never longed before. Below the upper surface he realised how his inland taste for solitariness was reliant upon the presence of absent others.

"He might prefer a snorkel." Elspeth was looking in a deep compartment aft of the life rafts. In it were oxygen canisters, wetsuits, spears, flippers. The snorkel she pulled out, and the little mask, seemed like bath toys. "The fish will be pretty right at the top. You can almost just stand and stare at them."

She passed the snorkel and mask down to Nick. Her slow soft body met the wire and marked at once, once at the shin and once on the right forearm. In her skin, shine was replacing glow.

"Astonishing how you can pass up what's really challenging," said Logan, "but it's different for women."

He was pleased with some timidity in his wife, not having intuited, as she had, Alec's misgivings about diving.

"The horrendous thing when a person gets the bends," he resumed, responding to something in the air he did not know he felt, "is the angles they get into in their pain. A guy could snap his arm out of its socket and not feel it. The pain is that bad. They can dislocate a limb." All the time he had a rapt look on his face. He looked like a child telling an important lie. His tone was one of grave reiteration, a tone of amen.

Everyone who was by the rail listened to hear if he had more to say. When his statements had ebbed, Gabriel, in an exhilarated voice, said, "Have we the waterproof fish book? Have we the rug? Have we got money? Petrol can? Antidotes? Just thinking aloud, sorry," she said to Elspeth, who had indeed forgotten the hornet-venom antidote syringe her husband required but forgot at all times.

Elspeth went below.

Nick, Alec, Gabriel and Logan waited for her in the Zodiac. A flat supply boat came around the tip of the island, leaving a low pinkish welt of smoke. It was heading back for Tahiti. The fan of its wash passed under, through and past *Ardent Spirit*, and slapped hard on the Zodiac. Nick lowered the flukes of the outboard into the water and settled himself to its port side, with the tiller against his side.

Logan was checking the dials on the gas tanks of the diving gear. Gabriel had her basket on her knee, and her shoes. Her feet were bare on the floor planks of the Zodiac. In that large air it came to Alec that she had scent in her hair. In her ears she had put pink studs of coral. These did not distract from her air of appropriateness.

"Logan, your antidote, you forgot it," called Elspeth. It had not been where she kept it. So often did he lose things he might have hidden them to pass her heavy time.

"Thank you, dear," he said, though she heard the harder words within what he said, and began to consider ways of pleasing him in his absence.

"Give me that," said Gabriel, putting out her hand for the syringe, "I'll keep it safe. I can administer it too."

She was a useful girl.

Logan unlooped the Zodiac's stern line. Elspeth threw down her painter, less tidily than she wished. It was one of the things she was trusted to do around the boat. The seamanship required was about sufficient.

The grey rubber boat turned and set its prow to land, leaving three "V"s, two within the frilled widest, behind it. Sandro, cross-legged on white sheets of sail on *Ardent Spirit*'s foredeck, looked up and waved, smiling with the sail needle curving in his teeth, adding to his smile.

Elspeth divided by two the time she had anticipated having to herself; in half of it she must make good the rift that had begun to make itself felt between herself and Logan.

"Drop me, I'll shop, and then you can collect me and take me to any nice beach you find." Gabriel spoke firmly. Her back was straight, her hands locked behind her back on to the Zodiac's port rowlock. There was a chain around her neck, Alec now saw, small as grains of sand, falling into the shadows between her silky bones. As they approached land, she seemed to adapt herself for it, by a transformation effected not with effort but with tact. He tested his interest in her like a man testing a foothold. He sensed that interest taken in her might be what she was used to; women who take tithes will receive them too, well beyond youth, and Gabriel was young.

"I like shopping," said Logan. Alec realised that his own interest in the girl might well be a natural response to the more urgent interest of another man. The triteness of the animal life in humans struck him even while he saw from the streaming boat the black and green heights of the island ahead, the grey-green field of serried pineapples, and the jetty from which children jumped, knees up around their ears, smacking into the water and swinging out of it again in glee, never learning the pain of the water's smack among the shouting and companionship that went with it. I am coming to life, maybe, thought Alec, and must not hold it off.

Alec resented the way Edinburgh was being trained into new shapes around its residents. Cranes seemed apt and birdlike at the docks, wading among the ships. Stalked into the city, they stood in craters not made by bombs only. The sadistic dentist was getting to work on the too-regular Georgian smile of the New Town. The even-tempered crescents and elucidating squares were an affront to the disjunct spirit of the times. As for the medieval wynds and tenements of the Old Town, they must be rinsed and swilled away to make space for what was to come. Rinse and swill and spit, to make way for colossal bridgework, up-to-date false teeth.

It is hard for humans, thought Alec in Moorea, to reside within an artificial smile without recourse to something stronger than marital sex or the word of God.

On the streets at home there are people living like snails

without shells, slowly, featurelessly, uncleanly. A house, many of them have learnt, is a fragile thing, a shell, easily crushed. Its removal will remove part of yourself from you.

Another change had taken place, among the staggering drunks. Loquacious, angry, grandiloquent, falling over, these people had for as long as he could remember congregated near the railway stations and at the warm mouths of tearooms, hair-dressers' shops and matronly hotels. At the docks and in the Old Town they would group, hellishly festive, and allow themselves in the year's cold seasons to be impounded by such organisations as the Salvation Army and the Mission to Seamen. Many were old soldiers and sailors; some mutilated, though the limbless more often took to music—a mouth organ, a tatty set of pipes and a thrown-down bonnet on the pavement—than to alcohol. The hard drinkers were great talkers and boasters, gesticulating like generals talking strategy. When Alec was a child they were the wounded of a war. The pallid and silent heaps he saw now had been harmed at peace. The heat of carousal the old drunks used to give off had been replaced by a chill where the publicly intoxicated congregated. A drunk on the street would now very likely be middle-class, his desperation floated closer to the sur-face than in the days of the saving of faces. There are wet trou-sers where the trousers have been made for the wearer with silver pins and tailor's chalk.

Up Gabriel's neck grew soft pale hairs in a pattern that ended in two arrows that went deep into the stronger hair.

"I'll shop, too," Alec said, seeing these.

Nick, though he did not discuss what he wanted until it had

been established Logan did not need him, was going to look for the conquering snails and some trace, maybe, of their victims.

"Tell you what, Alec, then, you shop and we'll collect you. It's an unbeatable experience in these coves," said Logan. Gabriel gave Alec the shopping list.

The Zodiac nosed the jetty. Logan stepped on to the land and tied the boat up. The sureness of his movements was almost balletic, the graceful product of instinct and practice.

"There's the shop," he said to Alec. "We'll walk you up there. I'm tempted to see if we can get a goat slaughtered by the time we set sail. Can you butcher or is it like diving?"

So he had noticed, not by words but by some bullying intuition.

"I can butcher," said Nick.

The shop smelt of coconut, orangeade, sweat, petrol, beer, and quiet, perpetual frying. It was dark and hot with a concrete floor and muttering deep freezers, one full of parcels of hard meat in paper, the other of frozen vegetable macedoine and fanciful ice-cream desserts with names like minor works of soft music, *Fantaisie en Rose, Aubade en Robe de Chocolat*. In the low freezer were also kept beauty preparations. The shelves were deep in the attempts of French manufacturers to recreate American food and American food giants to conjure some sophistication. Drums of soda crystals and aggressively named washing powders had been shaped into impromptu chairs on which men sat with soft drinks in cans. A whole wall was dedicated to food for between meals, Cheez Wizz, Cheez Balls, Tandoor Chow Mein Pizza Bites, and sweet drinks. Pineapple and strawberry Nesquik stood next to Eucryl smoker's tooth powder.

On a door that must lead in to the back of the shop was the poster of a controlled nuclear explosion at Mururoa atoll—a tall gaseous spire of bruise-coloured uncontrol with an orange heart and a sheer glare of white in its core, reflected in a quiet blue sea and sustained by the outraged blue sky. This poster was sold wherever anything was sold in these islands. It had become a good photograph, a labelled image in place of rage, a picture marketed before the word "controlled" had lost any of its shocking cynicism and still marketed by people almost familiar with this habitual outrage done by the French on land and sea and air and water.

Insecure wooden crates of Sprite and Lilt were stacked up in the back, with baskets of the rolled-up posters among them. A collection of feather dusters stuck soft and lush from one roll of posters, a polythene petrol-syphoning tube slumbered among others. Through the blue corrugated plastic roof in which tinselly fibres flickered, came the striped light of day. The rich aromas of drains, roasting fish and beer came from the garage at the side of the shop.

Alec found six hard green oranges in a net and bought some mandarin segments in syrup and a pot of Dundee marmalade to enhance them. By the counter he was amazed to find jars of sweeties he'd not seen for years, among the Chiclets and taffy and Lifesavers; there were nougat prawns, jelly penknives and drunk men's eyeballs, even Berwick cockles, though here they were labelled Killer Snails in the English and *Super Escargots* in the French, in deference from one colonising power to another.

As a small boy, Alec took to visiting the poorer parts of the New Town where people better off and less respectable than his own family lived. They were maybe university people or young doctor couples renting. A fair number of them went without hats. In their rooms at the front you might see a violin or an easel. Cars were infrequent, cats innumerable. A lot of the women in this part of town had their hair down and wore trousers.

He enjoyed his visits to these parts because they were so different from his own district, because the visits were secret, and, he saw now, because he was attracted by the way of life. Then he just wanted to carry on in his own way without too much attention and these people in their voluntary oddness seemed unlikely to observe him. Alec was averse to confrontation to a degree that kept him continually mildly compromised; he disliked telling the whole truth in case its edge should, no matter how paperily, cut someone. Least of all did he wish to harm—or tell the truth to—his mother.

Her legs by now had eely varicose veins up behind her knees. Her black hair had a wing of white. The shadows round her eyes had always been dark but they were no longer matched by her high colour. She had much disliked a year spent cleaning clams on the gutting floor, the clattering shells and pluggy, featureless creatures.

"At least fish have an expression. A clam has no features. There is nothing to get to know," she said to Alec, a remark he only now, as he thought of her under this shady heated afternoon's remembering mood, recognised as either dangerous or sad. She would have been horrified had he suggested to her that she was implying a wish to gut only creatures familiar to her.

It was rather that she was casting about for something to meet her eye. She was lonely in a way that is part of the sort of marriage she and his father made. Alec was no companion for her. In her idea of him, her ambition for his future, she had, with considerable sacrifice, resigned herself to his life's betterment, as she saw it, at the expense of their closeness. She wanted him to become the sort of young man who did not know women like herself, although she also wished him to retain in himself her backbone and steely standards.

She was not, either, a demonstrative woman. Tears she retained by working in her house until their time had passed over.

Alec took pennies from his father and mother, from small stores hidden in places unknown to the other but known to him. He could smell out pennies anywhere with their copper and verdigris tang.

Mairi collected pennies from the time of the young Queen Victoria, whose profile appeared on them with a wispy ribboned bun at the nape of her slender neck. The name for these pennies was "bun pennies". They were smoother, naturally, than more recently minted coins. Their smoothness gave them a silky warmth.

He stole these treasured pennies from his mother for their face value, to buy sweets and squibs. The money he took from his father Alec took from his one coat's hem. He regularly made a hole in his father's left-hand pocket that his mother regularly mended. He took pennies from him at the shop, too, muffling the ping of the till with a hastily dropped pint of mussels or, which must be worse, he thought, a song.

Mairi had a chipped front tooth, the left rabbit-tooth as you looked at her. The enamel was gone in a grazed dip that did not reflect light. She chipped this tooth on the stone of a peach. Jim bought her this peach when she was expecting Alec. He got it from out of the box where they put the bruised fruit at Rankins the superior greengrocer. Fordyce Macrae, his partner, had heard that fresh peaches cured the morning sickness. With just the few fresh peaches to go by in her pregnancy, Mairi could never be sure, she said, if they'd held down the sickness, but she did enjoy the flavour, around the bruises.

"So I bit right in to the first peach in my life and inside I meet this chunk of wood that takes a piece off of my tooth. White they are, so they're soft with it, my teeth, made of sugar."

She was fond of sweets though she had chosen not to work at the chocolate factory that had been the other place to work near enough to home when she was a girl. She'd a cousin who had worked there as long as she herself had with the fish-gutting. The cousin reported that you went off sweets early on. She took to drinking vinegar water to whisk the sugar-spinnings out of her tubes. Satin cushions were a favourite with Mairi, snips of sheeny boiling in shades of shot pastel, plump and cornered like film-stars' pillows. She more often was able to afford an ounce of cherry lips or a McCowan's chew, a rubbery ingot of toffee sold three for tuppence, in a twist of greased green-and-red tartan paper.

The continuity in the names of sweeties eaten by Scots children is considerable to this day, Alec thought as he stubbed and blotted the flakes of stale croissant from his teeth in the shop-shed in Moorea. The most doted-upon sweets, the penny treats babies start on to bring out their sweet teeth, are named not for their industrialist overlord or by committee, according to market forces; they are named with deference to the addiction that is as strong as the addiction to sugar among the Scots—a nostalgia for the nation's happy childhood.

Happy childhoods return to haunt self-deceivers mostly. Those who have had them seem to sink into an adulthood that is a state of depletion, or to advance without consciousness of their luck into a happy adulthood. In childhood, the moments of consciousness that we later recall occur precisely when we are not happy, but those high moments transform themselves by a miracle into a memory of happiness, as though stones had hatched. What makes them sweet to us is that they took place during a time we have forgotten but which is part of ourselves. Memories yielded by that time are as from a golden age, although their gilding has almost certainly been subsequent.

He thought of Mairi, and her fondness for old-fashioned sweets: soor plooms she relished, sugar greengages like the eyeballs of ginger cats, and Berwick cockles, red-and-white pellets tasting of face powder and mint, puffing to dust against the gums, leaving toothpastey mastic between the teeth. Old English was the unlikely name of a sweet she favoured, a dense pack of Spangles with several peculiar tarry and spicy tastes like cargoes, wrapped in pyjama-striped papers. Their smell lasted as long as tobacco's.

She accumulated small scars, at home and at work. The cuts were all on her left hand, the burn marks on her right. Her inner right arm had a four-inch burn scar from the iron. The burn-blister puckered and swelled with water like syrup in a balloon, till it burst. Alec had enjoyed kissing that scar, which, untypically, she would allow. Perhaps she thought all that education was making a healer of him. It was like kissing a flattened mouth, puckered and thin-skinned.

Her cleaning habits led to fingers fraught with hangnails and a right index-finger bent over in a curve from rubbing and rubbing the washing up and down the drubbing board, the polish cloth over the stairs and down in under the banisters. The cleaning she gave to it was more dignified than the house itself, the gardens of crystals diluted and sluiced down the tremulous plumbing and over the thinning linoleum, the creamy cakes of beeswax smoothed over and fed into the few limping chairs.

Furnished in the fifties, the house contained a random sample of the design tics of those dingy-fancy years. Geometric but disunited, cocktail-hour shapes, nothing to do with his parents' way of life, lay in chips on floor-coverings, floated on the fabric of curtains, encountered one another in indifferent swarms on the paper coating the walls. Whatever the materials might have been, his mother did not question. She cleaned. For her the essence of things was what counted. The appearance was of little consequence. By cleaning she made the house good. She fed the household gods with Chemico and Parazone and spirit vinegar.

The oblivious are blessed, being in a state of nature. Alec lost this grace and emerged into the open-eyed struggle at the age of five.

They were in the fish van, all three, the family. Alec was comfortable in the back, sitting wedged between the slatted shelves with his arms around his knees. It was early evening, rainy, the street lights burrs in a mist that was an atomised dampness berried by the fat warm raindrops. The ceaseless windscreen wipers making gulls' wings on the screen, the van's heater, the road sign that told him it was five miles till they were back in the city, all held him in a rich suspension. He rocked with the movement of his father's decorous but over-careful corner-braking. He looked out through the back windows of the van, two squares of night decorated with a few distant lights making ribbons. They had been at the sea, which exhausts small children and rocks them down to sleep.

Alec must have looked as though he were asleep. His mother turned to look at him and for once allowed her face to pour love. Her profile was rueful, as though she had put someone dear out to sea on a bad night in an open boat. He tried to introduce a holy look to his, he knew, already appealing features. I may have let a tear swell between my lashes, he thought, tasting his behaviour as the dusty flake of stale croissant.

He enjoyed her access of love that was worship, almost. He had not yet come to mind being claimed. He liked being no-where, enclosed, unheld but cared for, being driven from some-where to somewhere in the warm, distantly fishy back of the van repeatedly but irregularly rocked without risk as the gears and brakes engaged and bit. From within his own piece of darkness he liked seeing without being seen, knew that he liked it, knew that for the present he should hide how much. He stood outside himself as though he had unzipped and stepped out of it. The sense of separation from part of himself was satisfactory. He felt like the golden entire yolk that has been scooped free of the clinging indefinite albumen.

Elspeth had finished beating the matting over the side of *Ardent Spirit*. She chose the side off which the wind was blowing so that no dust blew on to the hull. She swept the boat below, having first dusted, though it seemed to her that salt was the dust of the sea more than dust itself, and set the matting down again. Being a woman who preferred large cooking implements and a kitchen through which she could walk, leaving sheaves of flowers and bowls of eggs about on its tables, she did not much like the seven-eighths proportions of the galley, nor its satisfying, expedient, but somehow smug dovetailings. At sea it was useful. At ease it was an impersonation of a thoroughly workmanlike kind of something she would prefer to be rather less practical and more forgiving. She was a mistake maker, also a mistake rectifier, but the sea does not allow for mistakes.

"Tea, Sandro?"

"Thanks." Which was yes, not no.

"Will you come?"

"I'm bad for time," he said. She was unsure whether she should distract him. She set the weighted mug down on the deck behind the gathered field of sail.

"Ahoy," called a voice, ridiculously.

She replied in the same way, not to offend.

A hand rose up from the starboard gunwhale, holding from the base like a bunch of flowers an ornate, dappled, shiny-throated seashell twenty inches long. Within something slow-stirring seethed and a few bubbles came. She looked into it, expecting at least a face.

"Take it, or don't you want it?" said the voice. "In exchange let me aboard. I've got the family."

"You'd better come round to the steps," she said. If she put the shell down would it walk? Was it a snail, and if so did sea snails make marks? How would she explain silver paths over the decking to Logan?

"Talk is you have a fridge aboard and the kids haven't seen

one of them since Home," said the whippy man before her. "This is my better half. Doesn't say much for me."

"Home" had been spoken importantly and she took the lead.

"Where's Home?" she asked.

"The old country. Same as yourselves."

On her stern *Ardent Spirit* bore her name and her port of registration, Aberdeen.

"Scotland, then?" asked Elspeth, although she did not think it likely. The man had a southern voice overlaid by the bark of the sea.

"No. England." He had been abroad a long time, Elspeth thought, if he could make that foreigner's error, thinking Scotland part of something calling itself England.

Two children with red hair whose curls met like bubbles in a bowl looked wretchedly at Elspeth. On their boat, moored, she now observed, perhaps fifty yards away, a dog was howling and jumping up. The guard-rail was netted. The red dog kept leaping and muttering, wagging its tail all the time. The arm holding the shell was getting tired and Elspeth held the mollusc out to the children.

"No fear. We want to see the fridge," said the children. Miraculously, although they had come from another boat, they seemed to have shoes as grubby as children who have come in from a garden. How foolish of her not to have waited before doing the cleaning, so that her gesture made for Logan might also be received by him.

"I'm Elspeth," she said to the wife, whose clothes were much more respectable than her own dusty pareo and laddered swimsuit. This woman was decked out for a refreshing meeting of the Women's League of Health and Beauty; she had repressed hair and ankle socks. Her eyes were brown, unhappy, but even then not beautiful. She had a sweet smile.

"I'm his wife," she said. So there was to be no trade of names.

"Got any drinks from a tin?" asked the larger child, a boy.

Elspeth had to do something with the shelled creature. She was aware of the living movements inside its hard whorl, as if someone had handed her a newborn in a cone.

"I'll deal with he," said the dominant visitor in his facetious voice, as distinct from his formal voice, or the voice he used for his wife, "and you help Elspeth with the makings," he instructed his wife.

Had it been a kitchen on land, Elspeth would have invited the woman to sit down while she made her a cup of tea. As it was, the woman stood just outside the galley and watched Elspeth. She emerged at last with relief only to find the two children having left the fridge door wide open and several sampled cans of sticky drinks left around the saloon, even on the chart table. An open fridge is a dying engine, she thought. He has often told me that on his patrols of the house for spilt electricity or overblown light. She shut the door of the small inset cabinet fridge, allowing herself one deep draught of its delicious artificial cool. She would have to dispose of the cans later and alone or the waste would be discovered.

When it was not lonely, the sea could provide an imprisoning gregariousness of heightened bourgeois anxiety, Elspeth knew, except for those free spirits who either had nothing or held things as nothing. The tiring appetite to collect and possess, that

should be swilled away at sea as it is in the desert, could sometimes become a terrible itch, especially among wives who were
losing heart for the life and children who had not asked for it.

"She's gorgeous. Just gorgeous." Elspeth smiled at the
mother of the two children in thanks. Perhaps if it was a long
time since they had been in England the children would like
biscuits too. The serious-mindedness of British biscuits is not
accurately reproduced by any other nation. She brought from
the lead-lined dry-goods store some digestive wheatmeals and a
roll of ginger snaps.

"These two here were just one and two when we left, you
see," said the husband. Elspeth could not see the shell, but did
not like to ask. She put down the tea tray in the shade of the
awning. Now she saw that the mother had red curls too, but
something had caused them to lose spirit.

"We teach the kids at sea, away from bad influences. Milk
and two sugars. When in Romania, I always say."

"And they learn a lot from places we visit," said the wife.
"Plus there's a school on the air."

Elspeth pictured a shoal of flying fish in the sky.

"The radio is truly excellent in that respect. All over the two
great oceans are little children at their lessons. Magnificent ser-
vice. On the same lines as the system in the outback. Of Austra-
lia."

"Only wetter," she said.

The wife looked at Elspeth. It was a look between admira-
tion and fear. Elspeth knew how that look felt on her own face.

For some time the husband discussed radio frequencies. At
the end of periods of talk, receiving no response from either his

hostess or his wife, he set springs for himself. "You will say that I am dogmatic perhaps in saying that . . ." "Contrary to what is generally thought to be held to be the case . . ."

Elspeth made two more pots of tea. The two children had joined Sandro up in the bow where they did what they were told among the swathes of folded sail. She could hear Sandro instructing them to fold the sails, and saw the soft geometric dance sixty feet from herself and the excruciating tea party she was holding in spite of herself as something ideal and free, an abstract epitome of what was mysterious, childlike and full about life under sail as against the life of occasion and adult ceremonial.

"You may not agree here . . ."

Elspeth did not like to be rude, was not normally so, but she thought she heard the Zodiac and she knew that she feared more to irk her own husband than this one. She interrupted.

"That beautiful shell. Where is it?"

"I've set it up for you, never worry, just off the stern."

"Set it up?"

"You'll be wanting it for a trophy. It's not after all the stuff of which pets are made." It was the facetious voice. His wife laughed. Elspeth didn't. She was short of time.

"I got the bugger to stick its head out and I hooked and weighted it. Sooner or later it'll part company with its shell, you can flush the thing out with a strongish scouring substance. I often as not use soda crystals. And there you are, a conch to call your own."

Off the stern rail, sure enough, Elspeth saw a line hanging, from which must be dragging the shell and its ever more taut body, losing suction with every minute.

68

He sensed not her disgust but some misgiving.

"Of course it does smell a bit. It's the length of time taken, cardinally."

"How long?" asked Elspeth.

The Zodiac sound had gone. Smoke was going up at points among the green crevasses of the island, soft blue amid the blackening green. The sun was starting to fold the pale sky away in preparation for the stars. The others must have found a good beach. Perhaps that would keep Logan banked and protected against the pain his ill-temper inflicted upon him.

"A week or so. But no worries, you can continue the operation under sail."

The creature she had hardly seen within its squint-mottled spire had been mottled too, in an orderly, glamorous way, as only animals or the rarest primitive textiles can be. Two soft probes about the size of a small child's fingers, but extensible, had emerged—the horns, she assumed, such as a snail has. Did she not recall that these were eyes? The sheer pearly mouth of the shell must be being battered by the silent boneless creature as it was dragged out of its one lodging, that was part of itself.

As bores will, the visiting husband became suddenly bored. It was always a matter of regret to him how ungrateful people could be. This was a classic case, now. This woman didn't know when she was lucky. He looked at the pointlessness of *Ardent Spirit*, and allowed himself to congratulate himself, just for once, on the tight ship he ran for his family.

The biscuits were finished.

"It'll be torn loose from its muscle plug by now at any rate, so it's only a matter of time before it's a goner," he said. He could not resist it. Only a woman with nothing much up top would get precious about a big snail with spots. He could see that was it. Never had a moment's pain in her life, he supposed. Which reminded him.

He gave his wife the angle of his face and back that expressed his want of entire gratification. She stood, and smoothed her lap. Crumbs fell to the deck. In places were the footmarks of the children.

"It's been pleasant. I hope also for you."

The red dog began to howl now. There was a breeze that ruffled the water. Spars of sunlight tightened about the sky. It was like being within a shrinking parasol the translucence and colour of rice paper. The green of the island was black now, the blue smoke white. Even the red curls of the children had lost colour.

At the steps down the side of *Ardent Spirit*, Elspeth said goodbye to this family, hoping to convey to the mother that she wished her well in her lonely enterprise, to the children that escape would be easier for them one day than it ever might be for their mother, and to the father that he would run out of victims one day.

She was ashamed because she did not know whether to unloose the tormented sea creature or whether Logan, reflecting that it was already harmed beyond help (he was good to animals and things that did not speak), would wish to keep the shell for its undoubted handsomeness.

In order to put off her thought, she repeated her cleaning operations of the morning. In his cabin, Sandro was playing the harmonica, old, melancholy, predictable ballads of the sort that had convinced her, when she and Logan met first, that at last she knew love as other people understood it, a great thing binding them not to one only but to many others, all swayed by eight notes and about fifteen words. She had not, before she met Logan, heard popular music.

"Cherry, Cherry, baby," wailed and hummed together the buzzing windy sound of the mouth organ, while Elspeth set to doing what she had already done.

By noon and after two Hinano beers Nick knew a bay that had never known a shark attack and was not private. Keeping fairly tight to the shore, he steered the Zodiac and the passengers, more slowly now, so that the shopping was not soaked by the bow wave, along the coast of Moorea until he came to the sixth inlet on. It was hardly a beach, more an ingress. Leggy mangroves stood over it on webbed legs sunk hard into the beige sand.

Logan, Alec and Nick jumped into the surf and pulled Gabriel in with the rubber boat until it was two thirds up on the sand, then handed her out and pulled the Zodiac clean up, making her fast to a mangrove that held up its hands in a histrionic soothsaying gesture, pulling down the air.

Among the mangroves, along the fiery sand and even into the shade, white crabs the height of cats tiptoed and suddenly sank. Their swift incomprehensible movements made the noise of many pencils used by keen but apprentice writers on paper shot with slub. Several of these crabs lay dead and emptied of flesh, blowing light as paper bags among the rooted mangroves. From time to time a coconut fell.

"They split your brain if they land on you. Never sleep under a coconut palm," said Logan.

"Hard not to." Nick looked up. High before the sky it was all palms unless you were almost in the water.

"Split your brain, I mean it. The remains would be two poached eggs in a bucket of blood, should one of these," Logan picked up a coconut still in its case of copra, and palmed it as if affectionately like the head of a mastiff, "one of these happen to light upon you."

"Not light," said Gabriel. Logan and Alec laughed immoderately. Nick seemed to know they were playing a game in which he had been dealt no cards. He sat on a palm tree that grew parallel to the ground and two feet or so above it, and wrote in his small spiralbound notebook, the size of a book of stamps, with a thin pencil of chestnut brown. Sometimes he made longer lines and paused; he was drawing the deserted armour of a sand crab.

"Have some disgusting picnic," said Logan. "Pitch in."

Beer, rum, limes and the ropelike shadows of the mangrove limbs made a crazed mirror of the hot hours they were there on the beach. Nick had gone, no one was clear when. They relied on him to return at a sensible time because he could tell where and when he was from looking at the sky, understood the imperatives of tides and never kept anyone waiting. Logan could do these things but preferred to have them done; he saved himself for extremity.

Alec slept, his head wrapped in a towel through which he continued to hear the scratching sound of the crabs as they pencilled incessantly and suddenly sank beneath the sand. Through the towel he heard sighings, rattlings, whistlings and moans he took to come from vegetation. There was a sweet caving in and a regular hard thocking as though a man unseen but close were cutting down a resistant, fibre-clothed, slim tree. He could not hear Logan and Gabriel in any familiar way.

Although he had seen it in others, his own death was still theoretical to him. Even in his sleep he knew he slept and enjoyed the knowledge. When he imagined death, he did so in terms of life, of what would be gone then and how brightly in the shadow of death these things shone. Not graveyards nor funerals could put him in mind of death: the yards were too full of personalities and irreverent energy, and the constant threat of being moved, by the entablature over a mother, the small sarcophagus of a child, the garrulous encomium of a mason aslop with words even in stone.

Funerals were too close to parties and to family life, with their social constraints and embarrassments, to aspire to touching on the abstraction at their heart, the missing person. What he had felt at every funeral he had attended was a kind of common human love, almost a reaffirming inclusion, that had reassured him that he like other men had a heart. He had felt this sense equally with those greatly loved lying in the bare box and those cared for in a mild way. He had not tried the funeral of a stranger, which might be a form of theft.

If any places struck him with the transmitted sense of death, museums and libraries did. So richly did they seem to throb with what he loved that he felt them imperilled by what is deathly. He feared the death of imagination as a devastation. To him the end of the imagination would pour salt into any meadows that remained fertile on the earth, and plough it in so that there would be an end to things for all time. The annihilation of his own imagination he knew would come; that of some men somewhere on the abandoned earth he had to believe would somehow continue to burn. That was his faith and he had never confided it to another; for that reason he held a form of conversation with the principle he had to believe was not his only, coming closer than he recognised to prayer.

It irked Alec that the sorting through of his thoughts was akin to prayer, but always so conscious, as though he were reciting. He had hoped that the relinquishing of land for sea would bring prayer or some closer than before approximation out from himself, like music.

His thoughts choked him with their words.

If each man—thanks to the aching cauliflower we carry in our skulls—is walking along a tightrope in his life, I am the man who cannot move when most he would. The reason is my eyes; they paralyse me with all they tell. My eyes show me the glistening narrow wire I must walk, but they show me other such slung paths, stretched above me or below, and they reveal to me also the declivity below, and the distracting faces of those who watch and hold their breath.

About me I see the confident forward movement of those who look straight ahead, travelling along their apportioned slim wire in company with wives and children. Where is their courage from? What visor have they come to wear that holds their fixed gaze ahead?

Far beyond where my own gaze tires are the ropes that at heart I wish to walk. They are not lit. They are invisible, taking their colour from that which surrounds them. Occasionally perhaps someone who has found and trodden one of them has left a trace, an emblem you might call it, of himself. These paths are scattered with faint, tactful, discouraging, and beautiful symbols of holiness or art. I do not want quite to be holy, too uncorporeal for a painter, a Scot at that. But I do want to be good. Not good at what I do, which I judge almost impossible beyond a certain disheartening competence, but the still harder thing, good.

The difficulty with goodness is that it is severely practical as far as I can see. It's a case of practice making perfect. The daily, hourly, minutely demands that the practice of goodness must make sit athwart certain aspects of my nature and my habit. The only way for goodness to be carried out is with the unconsciousness of habit. But I cannot put my consciousness to bed like a bird under a cloth. So I stand at the commencement of the wire in a bright spotlight that is half conscience and half vanity and I hold my breath, and freeze.

I should be halfway at least across the wire by now but I stand looking, frozen, uncommitted, not warmed even by fear. I am not afraid, I am conscious. If I could set one foot before me, the stillness and chill might be stirred, my life take its first breath, my virtue awaken. As it is, my habits of control and distance hold it cold, unborn. My eyes inform me, freeze me.

It is so that they also feed me.

A painter must live by his eyes and the messages they impart. I do not feel, however, that I fully inhabit my life and days. I am within and yet without myself. The painting seems to be a superficial matter, a trick I can perform that will delude a number of people but not myself. I seem not to be capable of much more than looking and recording; what I wish for my work is that it should bespeak an achieved moral ease I cannot pretend to possess. If those who watch and comment upon me do not see the safety net, I know it is there and I know too that I must rip it away or at any rate test it.

Each of us has his own safety net. It is often as not self-deception, yoking itself companionably to false need. In the North (by which I mean Scotland) it can be sentiment and it can be wrath and it can be a God who combines the two. My own (and I will be deceiving myself here very likely since we all have more than one of these nets) is an ironical non-involvement interwoven with that solution of all cowards, a long perspective.

I also—but for how long?—have the constitutional tendency to hope that characterises fairly young men on the hunt for a mate.

Should I jump, it will be worse for me than death. I will be caught for the rest of my life in the safety net, condemned to a life of disengagement.

Minds meet in meaning, and I have met no one as close as the person I have harmed and who is not yet dead, so I can't think of her at peace.

For an exile, there are no continuities, merely succession. I am at the middle point and I must move. I burn, but the only light I see by is the light of that burning. I fear in the night sometimes that I have no soul. Should I wait for love or bring it about? Stevenson, who played as a child on the same brown river as I did, said that to marry was to domesticate the Recording Angel, that after marriage, there is nothing left for you, not even suicide, but to be good.

Eighty feet above Alec, the palm leaves rattled. Along his body the sand conveyed a minutely concessive crystalline heat. The crabs scribbled from left to right over the continually rubbed-over sand, their writings erased by winds that could not be felt by skin.

Once he heard a dog whimper. It seemed to be out at sea. Later in his reverie, it may have howled, almost like a woman, although that seemed to be on land, even close by. The water threw its voice.

At the funeral of his mother, there had been a trick: never to look at the box itself, and always to comfort others before they might broach you. She died without ease, sweating herself into a pool of salt and bone in the bed where his father continued to want to sleep. After his mother died, she was very clean, there was no more swabbing and filthy linen to be taken out. They burnt the last sheets, his father and he, ashamed of what she would have said about the waste, but unable to bear the truth that might come to them if they once more washed these sheets: that she was not alive to make them once more dirty.

All through her sudden dying, the vengeance her body took on her lifelong cleanliness was brutal. Gore came from her when all she wanted was to rid herself of waste. Her ears and nose marked pillows overnight as though she leaked bitter secrets. Her throat was black with deposits as though she had used filthy words all her life.

So for the first twenty hours after she died it was a honeymoon. Alec and his father, gently and with no sense of who was bridegroom, washed her and calmed her face into forgetting the hard last breath that had come from its mouth like a saw. They washed her hair with a little bowl of suds and dried it in muslin, folding and pressing the hair till it was dry between the layers of cloth. The nightdress was white, long, cotton, maidenly. Inside it they had settled her for peace and dignity, padded against the loosening of all the body's last shames, that had tormented her late days. From the garden they brought two bunches, one of lavender, one of rosemary, and that was the end of each bush for these hot herbs decline in the wet of the North.

Alec assumed, and it was so, that his father would want to stay that night with his mother. When he took tea to them in the morning, he forgot and put two cups on the tray. When he remembered, outside the door of his parents', now his father's, room, he stopped and wondered if he should take off his mother's cup.

He did not do so. When he went into the room the air was not perfectly sweet. His father was talking to his mother, nagging her about her neglect of herself. He seemed to be bossing her about the journey she was to take.

"It is not far. You will not feel it. I will be here. The boy is good. Will you listen to me at last."

The cryptic link between these two hard workers, his dead mother, his living father, seemed to grow flowers from its hard wood before his eyes. But he cast them down for fear of being seen to listen with his eyes to secrets he had not been invited to hear.

He had not seen it because they were old and ordinary and his parents. His mother looked on the bed in her nightdress no age at all, and his father turned to him like a young man. The

78

two of them had been still far off old age. His mother late in her forties, she would not tell him how late and he would make certain not to learn at the funeral, for that would hurt her feelings, his father fifty-two and all muscle and pep and opinion.

They took her off on a stretcher. It was the first time her face had been covered and he feared her shape, shrouded, also the steepness of the turn around the landing on the stairs, when the stretcher had to be jolted and turned at angles only feasible for the dead.

When the undertakers had gone, his father said, "I'll be sure to die down the stair."

Outside there were gulls in the air, large-footed, greedy, white as snow. Alec and his father, who ordinarily ignored the birds at the docks when they came to crop carrion and nab good fish, went indoors and fetched every scrap there was and threw it on the lawn for the birds. The party of the gulls was loud and abrupt. Their clamour and their careless appetite eased the silence that had filled the house. The white birds with their yellow feet and rapacious bills seemed literal and firm against the wraiths Alec did not wish to allow into his life, the insubstantialities of a life with his mother gone. He did not cry. He tried to by saying the words, "My mother is dead," in various forms to himself. All it did was make him realise that he would never make an actor.

His father wept abundantly and these tears took him soon to the bosom of Alec's second mother, his mother's sister, the arrangement practically a formal dedication of her pain and his father's. The habits of his new mother, Jean, were not precisely those of his first mother, but the sisterhood gave a consoling slant of resurrection—or haunting—to the sway of his aunt's marriage to his father. He did not use the word stepmother because they all agreed it was a hard word and one that his first mother would not have liked to be used of her sister.

The gap of time was nine months. Had the woman been unfamiliar to him this might have pained Alec. As it was, he saw his father sheltered by his aunt, and in his turn sheltering her. At twenty-six, Alec was too old to feel the unmerciful, whole-hearted, puritanism of youth. At first he was unsure of his own reaction. Was it right that he did not mind? Was he deficient in love to his father, secretly relieved to pass him once more to the care of a thrifty, provident, sober, woman?

He could not answer his own suspicions. He was glad only to see his father calm.

When he began to wait to watch his stepmother lift the washing tin or to stretch up to pin damp clothes to the line, to check whether her clothes rode up as his mother's had, over flesh creased like petals by the elastic and buttons of ma-tronhood, he saw nothing to it but a sort of zoological enquiry.

He began to seek a new place to live when he surprised himself by spending an afternoon off work going through her clothes and smelling them. Some of the clothes Jean wore were her sister's, kept. The anger set about Alec with unclean heat.

He was rapacious. An unnatural murderous lust assailed him not with his second mother's differences from his mother, not her particularity, but her resemblance to his mother. The ac-knowledgment was sickening. He was isolated and conforming to the myth he least recognised.

Still he did not cry. If he might slam his second mother into his arms, beat her into his father's tidy bed, then he would cry, perhaps. He would not let it happen, must protect them both, his father, his second mother. By failing to weep for his mother, his controlling mind forced his body to seek another kind of outburst with her near-effigy, her sister.

"She is a second mother to Alec," said his father, of his wife and sister-in-law who was in her sister's kitchen chopping vegetables with a little knife she'd herself gifted Jim and Mairi even before they were engaged. "A second mother, the very same."

Jean wore overalls in flowered cotton. Her body did not smell as his mother's had, of fish and the emetic scouring toxic stink of cleansers. She smelled of gum and human hair and acetone, the materials of wig-making. He smelled it in her clothes when he pulled them from the washing basket pretending he had lost a sock of his own, then fell into a handful of his aunt's strait cottons like a dog on meat.

The other people working at the museum were relieved that Alec, by his abstracted air, was clearly up to something with a lass; it was the best way after a death. Bed is the only answer to a grave.

Alec longed to be free of his aunt. To this end he began to read and look at words and pictures he hoped might divert him into preoccupations more natural. The artifice and dated domestic insistence in even the lewdest set pieces (rolling pins, a Kenwood mixer more luxurious than anything his mother or aunt ever might have had, rollers, bedroom slippers, even a slippery looking eiderdown with a brushed-nylon underside such as he had seen in an Embassy Coupons catalogue) tended, as all symptoms will, to confirm his fever. He looked for his aunt among these girls and women and because she had been a girl and was now a woman, he found her there. He could place her, knowing all he did of her modest nature, in these scenes, and believe it. He could mask her, strip her, harm her.

He worked hard, ineffectively. This was put down to bereavement. When he found the flat, it was in the centre of town, not far from the Bruces, now in their eighties, a high flat with the one big room and a view over the city that fell down to the sea, over to Fife, and included many gardens.

When he left home, he explained that he had stayed too long anyhow and then stayed on because of his mother's illness, and now that his father was settled it was time to set up on his own.

Jean said, "You'll visit, then?"

Was she after all in the same mind as he was?

He calmed himself. "Often enough. You two newlyweds need time to get to know one another." It was a dreadful thing to say, the remark of a dirty old man who did not know either of the people he addressed.

She kissed him goodbye and where the overall brushed his coat he felt a scorching come through to him. His father hugged him, also, during which operation his conscience throbbed like a cut corn.

The city provided him with a distraction from his paining heart during the first year his mother passed in the earth. He watched the crowstepped tall closes clamp about the night and heard the tenements settle like trees full of children. The castellated schools, turreted also for good measure, like as not, became castles by night, with maybe the one window lighted. Across the city the gas lamps were succumbing to a less hesitant form of lamp, and the renovators were setting to the buildings with chemicals to clean off the Industrial Revolution. He lamented the occlusion of glittering grime by explicit lighting and shadowless sandstone. He watched the amelioration of Edinburgh from his window by day and was relieved when darkness returned the city to its secretive, undeclaring self. Cranes were up over the town, three of them, high on hills. Often he cycled behind lorries labelled, "Forward-Looking Demolition Our Speciality".

Through the Frenchified haircomb of wrought iron worn by the civic building two streets beyond his own, he watched a window, idly but repeatedly. It was lit at about seven these winter nights and the shutters were never set in place until the resident, a woman, had looked out up to the stars and over across the jagged city.

"Not a bad fit," said Logan, some feet from Alec who was surprised the first voice he heard was that of a man, so deep was he in a maze of preoccupation with the women who had indirectly led him to this beach.

Gabriel, turned black and shaped like a rubber doll, looked down at him.

"We're diving, d'you want to snorkel?" The impression was of playtime, with different games. Alec enjoyed the cheap exclusivity of feeling left out.

After Logan and Gabriel had taken the Zodiac out to the blue, he watched them fall back off its edge into the water and briefly envied them their belief in other elements than thought and feeling.

Once snorkelling, he was again a child, and happy. The gaiety of the bright world so close below was unstopping, a continual dazzling display as though flowers could gossip. Drifts of pompous-faced black fish with eyes like pugdogs pouted at each other, followed by haughty blue fish long as an arm with inbred noses and blots on their shield-shaped gills. Some shoals moved like the light on waves in a painting and were gone, others were electric bars the size of a textbook underlining. The silent bustle and fierce colour held him happy as he forgot everything and listened with his eyes.

Inland, but aware of the time, Nick carefully drew the pursed mouths of the three, various, gastropods he had tracked down.

In the deeper water, Logan stroked the blue lips of a velvety black clam the size of a chair and moved away each time they closed their helpless distended frill. Close to his face, stretched open into an expression of ecstasy by the mask over her eyes and nose, was Gabriel's. Her eyes obeyed his own as she watched him pull away from the passive, clenching, clam.

Three

The graffiti on the huts and cafés off the road that made a circuit between the mountains of Moorea were in the rounded, looped writing that is taught in French schools. Occasionally romantic, the words were more often resentful of the distant administration that had formed the very way they were set down. "À bas la France!" was written on one maroon stuccoed wall that yellow and pink plumes of hibiscus brushed in the evening wind; the letters were as assuredly French as the script in the first Babar books.

Nick hired a bicycle from a man with strong hair like a wig and a frangipane blossom behind his ear with a Biro. When he was a mile or so away from the beach where he had left the others, he smelt garlic and pork and the gluey richness of *haricots*. The café door was held and fixed open by a springy growth of vetch that had grown around it so that it could not move. Hens came and went through the plastic ribbons that covered the doorway. Black coffee had burnt near by that day.

"Can I get some water?" he asked, his thirst woken by the sound of falling water splashing down the mountainside behind.

A woman brought him bottled water. He paid the comparatively large bill in the way you had to in these islands, without translation into any other currency. Nick as a rule bought little and appreciated much that came free, so he understood a certain fairness as he took in the shining moss wet as a bath sponge, the ticking undergrowth that tipped towards flat black rocks, the fungi white like cheese stacked at the side of the café's window at which quivered gingham curtains.

Leaving the bike with the woman, Nick pushed in his green metal chair. It twanged as it hit the table. The island was full of reverberations. The inanimate seemed to react as though it lived.

If he found any snails he would be pleased but what he sought most of all was the heart of the island.

He held on to fibrous palm trunks as he made his way up to the water he heard. Soon his sweat was mixing with the mist of water that a deep waterfall dispels as it falls down. From up here the cove where he had left the others was not dark but the green of water over white sand, the colour that is most associated with the Pacific, the colour of lull within a reef; beyond the reef he saw the blue ocean, almost violet against this inner sequestered blue that was not blue either, or not the celestial, European blue. This was a colour not of contemplation but of sensation. It did not calm the eyes so much as stretch and drench them.

He was now deafened by the falling water above him, though he could see no pool. The rock seemed to repossess the water as it struck. The plants all about were colonised by other plants. Petals seemed so fat with water you might snap them off and suck them. The growth of green all around was so full of itself it ripened, rotted and germinated in the one season.

In fact, seasons, offering the appropriate system for natural life and death, were too orderly for this profusion.

Ardent Spirit looked flat and small and white from here among the green and noise and wet. Her two empty masts were all that made her more than a white gap on the water. If he took off his misted specs and screwed up his eyes so that his lashes caught prisms among themselves, Nick could hallucinate that he saw Elspeth on the boat and what looked like children.

He began to move about on his hands and knees among the ferns and mosses, lifting them carefully as you lift tissue from a botanical illustration. When he had collected the various snails into his Dijon-mustard glass, taken from the boat's rubbish, he looked up at the fractioned sun through the palms and set off down towards his bicycle. He had just finished making a lid for the glass with a handkerchief when he heard the hungry yelp of a dog.

It would soon be dark. They could not leave the reef by night or they might misjudge the narrow channel that had been dynamited through it for the passage of boats. Warm abrupt rain came. When he looked up at the crown of the waterfall it was surrounded by a vehement double rainbow. The impression was of a shrine for a shakily authenticated miracle.

The bike spurted sparkling water from its wheels as he

freewheeled through new puddles on his way down to the beach where the others lay. Gabriel was on her back with her forearms flexed behind her to take her weight. Twice Logan reached and seemed to remove things as small as insects from her, with the dissatisfied absorption of a sharp-eyed bird. Alec lay some way from the other two.

"Nick, you are a timepiece in yourself," said Logan. "Will you give us a hand, now you're here, with this thing?"

They stowed the shopping, pulled on sweatshirts, and plucked out the crabs that had made it into the Zodiac. Some crabs had died and been eaten by small scavengers during the afternoon.

Gabriel sat up in the bow while the men launched, held and climbed into the rubber boat. Nick lowered the engine and started it, steering towards *Ardent Spirit*.

She grew as they approached her. By the time they touched her side she was their home again, their burden and their way of escape.

"You are the mollusc man, Nick," said Logan later. "Perhaps you can tell us what to do with the splendid creature currently parking its custard off the stern."

Nick thought of the three land snails he had found after his hunting under fizzing ferns. He had released them. They were all specimens of the dominant carnivorous snail, at different stages in its lifecycle. The idea that a raptor might in its youth impersonate its victim seemed intelligent and horrible to Nick. He had found two large edible snails mating in a mess of froth, and one half eaten, the size of a cow's tongue, loose but muscular.

The lights on the mainmast and spars gave enough light to show the markings of the shell and its resident, when they hauled it up. Large and primitive—what a hopeless combination for a mild-mannered marine creature. Nick stroked its mottled probes and received a polite response. But the poor thing was lolling loose in its shell. Besides, it too had been half eaten, by something that appeared to have had pincers. Even within, the flesh of the big shell was skewbald.

"Soak it in bleach or cleaning soda, I should, Nick. The shell, that is, after you've pulled out the beast. We shan't eat it. Use the flesh for bait when you lay the lines tonight." Logan was at the charts with his dividers, plotting their course at the chart table. "What can we expect to eat, Gabriel?"

"Dorado ceviche and noodles." Gabriel was enjoying the galley still, and, since this afternoon, working for Logan had become something full of promise to her. She turned the flesh of the fish in its souse of lime juice and chilli. Having stripped the skin off half a dozen tomatoes she had frisked through boiling water, she chopped them and laid them around the shrinking, whitening dorado slivers. The smallness of the galley and the adaptations of technique and habit it demanded of her conventional repertoire exerted a challenge over her that she felt, now while the ship was at rest, to be laid out clear as a trajectory set in stars. She dared the sea to show her up. Yet she was also relieved that the galley was a place where Logan did not often come. The element of fear that went with her being drawn to him needed some cessation. It is wearying to serve at all times, even when it is sweet most of the time to do so.

Charts have the unimprovable truth of discovery in their words. They admit that little is yet known though much said, and most of it fearful. Not much advance has been made, when you look at the charts, since the time when plumb lines were all the sonar there was. No satellite steering but a sextant, Logan thought, as his mind and body had been cleared to do, of the sea and its conquest by men.

"The only real advance is in the killing of pain," Logan would say, when he spoke to men who did not go to sea. "Where you might have had to knock a man out with your fist if he got hurt, now you can carry morphine and just shoot him up."

The morphine was kept with the guns, in a safe hidden behind the tantalus. It was the boat builder's joke, though it did not bear repetition. Logan and Elspeth knew about it; no one else.

"Huahine tomorrow?" asked Sandro. These islands were like suburbs to him, different from one another in small ways but not so different from home, and full of people who did not mix with one another except in the most intimate ways, for love or work.

"Six o'clock start. We'll shoot clear of the reef like a bullet from a gun. Say hello to your mother from us all, Gabriel, if you're going to do the words for home now." She had actually been coming into the saloon, but she apprehended that he did not at present want her visible, and she found a way of making the thought a romantic one. Perhaps he was thinking of how best to tell his wife.

Gabriel's suntan deepened pinkly. That was all a blush could now do to her. Not even Sandro had mentioned her talking into the tape recorder. She smiled at Logan from along her eyes, as though to put him down. Elspeth watched him for irritation but he just grinned and went back to making pencilled lists of figures.

"Anyone mind if I put the generator on for a while?" asked Nick.

"Fire ahead," replied Logan. Nick looked around, but permission had been given and no one questioned it.

He checked the generator, made a solution of soda crystals in a polythene bucket and wedged the bucket in the lazarette. When he had, he hoped, pierced the big sea snail mortally, he felt for its anchorage of muscle and severed it. The snail that fell overboard was dappled like a new fawn and as long, two feet of stretched dead muscle gone slowly slack in pain. He put the shell in the crystal solution. It was a hot night now.

To drown out the sound of the generator that gave them the benefits of artificial heat, light and cold, Logan put a tape into the machine. The solemn glorious pomp of Purcell's "Dead March for Queen Mary" rolled over the water.

To its accompaniment Logan and Alec each began to plan his own funeral. Elspeth lay on her bunk with her mouth stuffed full of sheet so that she would make no noise.

"I like film music," said Sandro. "It's good." He made a roll-up and took it out to sit in the bow where the bowsprit would have been in an older boat. He hung his legs over the edge and leant through the rail to look at the phosphorescence when it came to wipe the water with a winged gauze that lit and sank, lit up, lifted, and sank.

In the stern stood Alec, feeling the boat swing slightly but giddily in the context of all those profligate stars. The lights on the island that had seemed mysterious before had become things to name and recognise. He was already collecting the place in order to feel in his heart he had been there. Yet he had left no trace there but some money, and it would leave no trace on him unless he somehow took its qualities and defined them. Already this definition would make the place artificial, a kind of double or false coin. Perhaps that was how places survived, by striking images of themselves just a little off the true. In the pursuit of others' false coinages of a place looted of its privacy, the form of travel arises that narrows the mind. It was his fear that this was how successful people managed to preserve their stock, by manufacturing false personae in whose lee to live in peace.

To paint such a place and convey it with truth, he thought, you would need to pitch the spectrum deepest at its green-blue-indigo-violet arches; to paint its people fairly their beauty should be shown like that of cats or horses. Otherwise a chill crept in, for the people seemed to carry a stillness that was sculptural; it was the land that buzzed with layers of movement, that seemed muscled.

The burring of the generator was a cosy noise, a sound like the passing of a goods train without end. The chunky noise seemed to recall the decent things of life on land away from this indifferent glamour of sea and sky.

"And don't," came Logan's voice, lowered and compressed, "invite your little friends again. You must learn to stop saying yes. Only people with nothing can safely say yes." The intensity had sliced all the Englishness from his tone. A frontiersman was speaking, a lone wolf, a decent man among lowlifes. There was a pained actorish quality to what Alec wished he were not hearing. Surely Logan was speaking lines.

Elspeth seemed to have her own script that at last, with a noise somewhat like the bark of a dog, led them both into silence. Alec had not dared do more than sink to his haunches in the stern and concentrate upon the island's lights so hard that, when later he came to sleep, the formation of the lights, roughly that of the Southern Cross, was burnt inside his eyelids.

Through the hatch of their cabin as he walked by it in the dark wishing he might have flown, he saw Logan's arm slung down over the side of his bunk, so that his own sleeping hand might hold his wife's.

Alec cleaned his teeth with salt water to save drinking water and went to bed with his mouth plump and skinless, burned with salt. He awoke with a hard throat. He thought that if he could cough he would bring up razor shells of salt.

The fo'c'sle was an arrowhead of old air. Alec could not get comfortable. In the night he heard a sound just beyond the human register that might have been an insect or an expiring star. He feared that it might be tinnitus. Ever since Muriel Bruce had been stricken by tinnitus, he had waited for the insistent co-resident in his head, another note to add to those of regret and conscience.

Muriel outlasted the Commander.

"It was as one might have wished," she said, over tea a week after her brother had been gathered. "If it had been me the first to go, he could never have set a tray."

The dog Dunvegan was long dead, but not gone. Alec's most enthusiastic taxidermist friend from the museum had compromised between his own affection for nineteenth-century anthropomorphism and the respect in which his owners held Dunvegan; the dog was as solid and hard-packed as he had been in life, the height of a nursing chair, and he stared out of glass eyes on to the decline of human powers, his black-lipped jaw set in the smile his owners swore he had in life. He was a ton-weight and had not been lifted since being placed at the foot of a curtain in the window's bow. His presence, ugly, heavy, not very clean, had been a continuing comfort.

When Muriel Bruce spoke of her brother after his death, she used the words "My dear brother". She put herself to this test, as she also maintained standards of dress, changing into a blouse with a fichu for tea, and for supper, that was rarely more than a cup of tea and a biscuit, into the shoes whose buttons had to be captured and secured with a silver hook on a pearl handle carved like a fish.

The tinnitus came to her soon after and to combat it she resumed the playing of the Scots harp, the clarsach, whose echo reproduces externally the inner sting of tinnitus's constant ring, with the blessing that it fades.

Songs written for the clarsach have been of a melancholy or a triumphalism that are generally held to pass away from us as we grow old, so it was a strange sight, Miss Bruce at her harp, extracting a Jacobite lament from it or the reproaching helpless song of love for a faithless man. If he heard the sound from the next room, Alec could believe it the celebrations of the house's ghosts, as he believed he heard their talk at night in the streets. He had seen a woman in Ann Street set her patch aright and pat her high wig before giving her arm to—he looked no further, lest it be a man in a suit.

The town was hospitable to those who wished to live in times generally gone. Edinburgh was ever behind the times, in some ways cruelly, in some tiresomely, but sometimes, too, beneficently. A man might live in a folly, eat gralloch and oats and do nothing but read and paint, if he could get money for his making.

The blind Commander died in May. By July, Alec wished to take Muriel out of the flat in Nelson Street for the first time. He had been shopping for her, and the neighbours watched to see that her milk bottles had been taken. It was a lie, the shopping list she gave him, but filling his basket at the slow, unexciting shops to which she gave her custom was part of the piety he owed for the rescue and constant education the old people had given him since the first morning at the Wreck.

Alec could not imagine the outing that might best lift Muriel's spirits, without causing her anguish when she reflected that her dear brother was not able to join in.

Alec was with Lorna by then, whose lighted window he had seen from his own, unlighted. Lorna was able to fix a car for the day, borrowed from her landlord, who was a careful man, discreet, a closer of shutters against the night, but who in this case understood the call for a car.

Alec met Lorna the usual way. He broke his window one night, forcing up the lower section so he could hang out and look into the distant window he had chosen for his beacon, and it came crashing down on him like a guillotine, shedding glass for good measure. Across his back were stripes made by the downward slice of seasoned wood.

He went to bed after a bath in Dettol and woke up stuck to the sheets with long straps of hardened blood. Tucking the sheet about him, he cycled to the Infirmary.

The late watch had brought in the driftwood beached by

drink and the windy fights it brings about. Alec sat reading a book that he had chosen for its dullness, hoping to numb himself; the wait, he knew, would be long.

"Curatorial Obligations in a Modern Context", read the drunk opposite him from the spine of Alec's book. Drink gave him words for everything, a benefit greatly enjoyed by Scots. In Glasgow the mode of polylalia is an unceasing mock-heroic deflation through magnification, the fantastic development of grand themes. In Edinburgh a mort of information is discovered in the mind's back room by the gallant torch beam of the drink.

"Will that be curatorial as regards," the talking drunk man seemed happy. He was better dressed than Alec though half his face was blown up like a pudding, "as regards some limited modern" (he said modren the Edinburgh way though his eyes were going like Yo-Yos) "context or do we have here as it might be the entirety of our context, *id est* things in general, the world as it is outside of ourselves, including all that therein is, fish, fowl, good red herring, lampposts, pipettes, stills, small beasts and vermin, millinery, honey bees, mustard, gas, mustard gas, tarpaulin, cigarettes all brands, and here we are not yet begun on the mineral kingdom or my wife's bedside table. What you will, what you will." He collected himself and resumed his list of all phenomena. Alec was attempting to assemble some drift to the list. "Evening pumps, the feet of a grouse mounted and set under glass, dogs, of course, and spindles, kidneystones, mirrors, sheepswool and if you must that of women, a kiln, worms, a rowing boat empty, onions again, I said them did I not, worms . . ."

"Come on, he'll be OK for a while. He's feeling good."

Alec, who had thought he heard something behind the words, turned in some impatience to the nurse. Her eyes were green or blue depending on how you caught them, pale in a pale face. The main part of her hair was the lively grey that runs in families, strikes young and emphasises youth, a grey without yellow and carrying its own light. Her eyebrows and lashes were black and in the sockets of her eyes lay olive-purple shadows.

This was still in the days of belts and starched hats. Alec concentrated on her belt while she bathed, pressed, unpicked his shrouded cuts. There were all but thirty of them. Two hours later she lifted the sheet away from him and set to the cleaning of the naked cuts.

"It's too late to stitch you."

Alec was coming round from the blush that had covered him when she took the sheet from him. He'd on his trousers, as well.

When he left, he asked her name.

"Sloops, columbaria, wrack, matter that can neither be created nor destroyed . . ." The list was growing, could never stop.

And her address. Worse liberties must have been taken in this ward. His pretext was that he must return the hospital overall she lent him for the cycle ride home. If she didn't want to give it, she could tell him to get lost and come to the hospital.

Lorna Agnew, she wrote, and the address.

As he made his way stiffly three days later to the place, he knew more certainly with each street that it was she who had been the cause of the accident that had brought him to her, she at whom he had been staring through his weak-sashed window all this time, she whose life, imagined so wholesomely in his own less wholesome evenings, he had lifted the glass to watch. He had been awaiting rescue from the trap of his perversity, his unnatural feelings for his stepmother. What could be more natural now than this impossible coincidence? The circumstances made of these untidy, uncomfortable events, a predisposition in Alec to be at once in love. The encounter in the hospital was soon a story, then a turn, then a game between them.

The misery that Alec had diverted and banked up in his shame, the grief for his mother that had appeared to him indecent while he tore his aunt's clothes in his dreams, came slowly from him over Lorna's table in the months that followed, and he wept eventually into sheets they took together to the launderette, a new place down by Canonmills where it was cheaper than the pictures.

It was Lorna's fixed notion that they must take Muriel Bruce out today for three things, sustenance spiritual, bodily and inessential.

They helped Muriel down the stairs at Nelson Street slowly. At the bottom the journey seemed to Alec to have taken so long that he knew something of the extraordinary achievement a sustained life is in age, leave alone further responsibilities. Alec got into the back of the green Austin, so that Muriel might have the view and be soothed by Lorna's driving, which she undertook without drawing attention to herself and with confidence.

He tugged down the arm in the middle of the seat and leant on it like a man about to tell a story. Muriel settled herself and put up her left hand to hold the leather loop that hung there solely for reassurance, with no pretence of life saving.

"Are we all here?" said Lorna.

Alec rolled his eyes, irritated at what he feared might hurt the old woman as she recalled her absent brother, having to express it and hoping also that Lorna had not felt it. She was driving, she had planned the day out, she was entitled to some clumsiness.

"Oh yes, my dear," said Muriel Bruce. "All of us indeed. My dear brother also." Alec was disappointed; was Muriel going to succumb to the afterlife? She had always been rational. With most manifestations of the other world she was brusque. Alec had not liked to confide his own notions about the streets' ectoplasmic strollers, nor the listening he did at old eaves; she would, he thought, have pricked his whimsy before he'd tied on the string.

It was a striped July day, the streets marked by shadows, the gardens in the squares a full midsummer green, tossed by the wind that set the sun chasing clouds so that you could not keep up with the changes of plot in the air. The drama of such summer weather is high in Georgian streets expressly built for silhouette, proportion and gravity. An exaggeration emerges that shows another side, something baroque, akin to the secretive, tall, but more humanly featured Old Town. Detail, blown up by the sun's angle and thrown black to the ground by the shadow, comes to dominate. When this happens, pastiche and caricature, the fast effect of a stage set, preponderate. The impression is high, melodramatic and festive, more than elegant. Add to this the salt that loads the air in an Edinburgh summer when it is not falling in rain.

The green Austin lent by Lorna's landlord smelt inside as Alec imagined the instructional tortoise might. They took the road out to Penicuik and to the cliffs at the Esk where lay hidden the small castle of Hawthornden and the less hospitable-looking castle of Roslin.

Lorna turned the car into a muddy entrance and parked before a building that seemed to have been cooked at different temperatures over much time.

"Have you been to the chapel before?" she asked Muriel.

"Twice. My Christening and my dear brother's."

"Does it spoil it for you to come now? Might you be sad?"

"I have no true idea of it, only the stories that go with it."

"It always rains here," said Lorna, "and then the sun shines and it rains again."

They went through the old door into a dense plantation of stone trees. They were observed, it seemed, by faces hidden everywhere as they are hidden in the movement and angles of branches in a summer wood. No single simple holiness struck Alec as it did in white kirks or cathedrals full of light and turned repeatedly to the cross. This building was a chapel but the term was a plain one and not comprehensive.

History salted down with story and fables had lain here and fermented until it had the light and dark, the packed murmurous involutions, of an old wood. Under the chapel the Catholic Kings of Scotland lay buried. On the flange of one of the columns, some ribbed as cardoons, others topped with acanthus, was carved a fruit that no man had recorded at that time five centuries ago. The Earl of Orkney of that old century was said to have, in effect, discovered America.

Muriel spoke of the chapel's past; its stories, rich beyond accuracy, were part of her life's own story.

"The angle a person takes to time, that may tell you about their life and its end. In the corner is the Apprentice Pillar, held to be the finest of all the different stone trees you see. The Master Mason left it for his apprentice to complete, came back and found it too good." It was ornate certainly and deeply corded with ornament. "In his jealous rage, the Master smote the apprentice, who died from that smiting." The old unused word sealed the story's freedom from reliability. "Up there you see the apprentice, there his wailing mother, small in stone. In the pillar it is said there are shards of the Grail. Such stories rush to each other and cling together. I do not find it the loveliest pillar, in fact. The whole place seems never to settle for one to be able to decide for certain."

Alec looked up at the ceiling of the chapel's body. He shed the earlier resistance he had held like a lost man holding a map. The drum of the stone was chiselled in clear sections, each studded with repeated emblems, stars, lilies, roses. The ceiling was less naturalistic than all the other turbulent, peopled, seething stone, but it had the formality and indifference of sky and weather, and, for those who take Him, God. The small scale of the chapel intensified its sway, the stern devotional ebullience of the carvings, green men, cabbage and plum and chameleon-shaped bosses, moved through work to art without insulting craft. Unconfined nature under the dropping stone stars of the chapel echoed a rectitude nothing to do with repression.

"You might say the place was pagan," said Muriel. "It is certainly forgiving. The marks of the Masons are everywhere." She pointed to signs shaped like fish hooks and the feet of birds. "In time they will say there are dragon's teeth in the graveyard.

Beside the font there are some tender words for a more recent descendant by marriage of the High Kings of Scotland, a Russian lady. I used to listen to my father speak of the unlighted tiny refuge in the crypt where lepers came to die on holy ground, and I held my limbs to me with a will. Under us now men have died who can bear to be looked at only by God, and then in the dark."

"I found you in the register," said Lorna, "both of you. I am sorry that he was the younger one, too."

"No, it was better. That way he had my life about his own at either edge of it. I was born before him and have lived beyond him."

The wind began to get up outside the chapel. The shifting of small panes in their leads and the peaty cold of the place made it like a cave now within a wood. It seemed surprising that the stone creatures held still inside their stone boles and knots. The impression was of verve, mischief and the ascertainable.

"Here it is," said Muriel. She stood back from the rail of one of the tiny chapels, each the size of a desk, and traced along a column a row of merry-making skeletons. "The bit they never let you see. More *danse banale* than *danse macabre* to me, though not so to you. The bones seem to me the least of it. Quite smart really. Let me sit alone for a bit."

Alec took Lorna down the stair into the crypt, and they stood together outside the cell of the lepers. He said to her the hard words he had seen cut in a lintel in the museum, the letters clean and whiskered with the cursive energy of the chisel: "*Abbas, Episcopus, Princeps. Pulvis, Umbra, Nihil.*" He sounded frightened and thrilled together.

She knew only the echoes of the words but was too shrewd for him. She knew the flavour of gloom and glory was too easily sucked.

"I love you also," she said, her pale eyes in their dark sockets feverish with health.

Sure enough, there was rain to meet them as they left the chapel and walked towards the car.

"Shall we find somewhere to dry ourselves, now?" asked Lorna, though she had it planned. Muriel was leaning back in her seat, eyes shut.

"Do you hear anything?" she asked them.

"No."

"The usual. Wipers, engine."

"Your answers distinguish you. Alec is idle."

"And I am dull."

"No, you are truthful. Do you wish to hear something? The noise in my head is gone. I left it behind at Rosslyn."

The tinnitus that had tired her with its whine, perforating the silence she wanted, had left her at last like an earwig taking its leave.

"Can you walk if we park in Charlotte Square? Or will I drop you?"

"Better the walk, today."

Once they had parked the car back at the peak of town, tucked in below the stepped pavement, the three of them set off towards Princes Street, past the linked rhythmic frontages of the grand square, with their princely but rational abundance of glass shining from raised lunettes like brows over some of the plain high windows. In the octagonal garden that filled the square within, trees tossed wide sections of green and showed grey beneath. From the far side of the square came the buzzing sound of stone being cleaned, the persistent trickle of strong solutions over flayed detail and harmed subtlety.

But the square was still an almost perfect sequence of confident order, free of self-importance, enlightened, accommodating.

The three of them made it to the Chocolate House. The Johnsonian name was misleading. The place was as up-to-the-minute as the grey-and-primrose Terylene button-down smocks of the waitresses, the only spot in town to serve hot mocktails and small savouries all day. The floors were pierced at intervals to admit the penetration of iron cocoa palms, built at blistering expense by a gang from Clydeside with experience in tropical themes. The wallpaper showed cocoa pods in cross-section.

Hot chocolate came in cups to be set in stainless-steel holders and with heatproof straws that did not guarantee a heatproof mouth. In the roof large carved pods were tied to the rigid fronds of the palms that appeared to brace the flimsy restaurant. On each floor of the Chocolate House a crucible of chocolate breathed out steam. Tinny tubes and electrical whisks modified the beverages accordingly. A hum of sugar-powered conversation filled the three floors.

Lorna found a table between a palm trunk and an old woman staring with vigilant dislike at a younger man. They shared an ice without touching long spoons. When something notable loomed, such as a cherry or a stratum of syrup, the woman held back and allowed the man to do his worst. Then she regarded him with an expression of satisfied distaste. Her scarf was the pelt of some animal with six legs and two adjacent heads. On her locally woven shopping basket was sewn in raffia the untruth "Sunny Italy".

The sugar came in jars with beaks that dispensed suitable quantities. At tables all about were ladies who could take the day broken into small pieces only. Muriel knew her good fortune was not to be one of these. She was never alone in the way a more apprehendably feminine woman of her time might have found herself. Her appearance had never distracted her from life into dissatisfaction. A mural of toiling harvesters of the cocoa pod struck her with its impracticality. So merry were the pod-gatherers at their labour that they looked not at the pods and the activities involved in their harvest and processing but out at the sippers of cocoa, merry smiles filling their faces with bare teeth.

The bitter smell, thought Muriel, the bitter smell is what I remember of chocolate when we took it in Mexico with Mother and Father.

"I'll have tea, if I may," she said to Lorna, who had nevertheless been right to bring her here. It was full of young people and even children, though the general tone was a little too fast for the main body of Edinburgh motherhood.

"Tea, then, please, for two, and a Freezing Hot here." She indicated Alec by letting her hand drop on to his. He started. The woman at the next table disapproved, checked to see whether the gaze of her son was with her own and then, seeing that it was, bestowed a long squeezing gaze of tender indulgence upon Lorna and Alec.

She was going to be denied every mother's rightful reward, a daughter-in-law. Even that ugly old besom—she looked at Muriel—had someone to punish. Grey-headed, the daughter-in-law was, she noticed, conning Lorna for other marks; the old woman must be a force to reckon with.

The Castle's hard hem was to be seen through the window. Drumming and the crack of boots came and bent away under a cloud of pipe music that lingered after it ceased to be audible, become part of the ear's fluctuations and balances as sea legs stay with you back on shore.

"A grown man and you can't finish an ice," said the mother at the next table. Her son would not eat the last cherry for some reason she made no sense of. He had seen her put it into her mouth and extract it whole once more, never noticing what she did, as a woman will pull out her chewing gum to kiss a man and put it in again; but this was the other way about.

Freezing Hot was an item from a part of the dessert menu entitled, "And now let Us tempt You"; the ice-cream was ginger flavour, the hot bit. It came with two wafers.

Alec observed the man and the woman at the next table. Only between a mother and her son could good manners have offered such offence. He saw the son take up and emphasise each unconscious gesture of the mother. The isolation of the two and their sentence one to the other was set and ingrown as some unkind graft of skin. Unless she died soon he would have to make his own way out, that son.

"I am not ready for it yet," said the mother, "but when my time comes I know you will see your way to doing the right thing."

He did not know what she was talking about. Nor did she. She sometimes spoke like this to pass the time, in the unsurprising formulae of domestic speech. From her son's response to whatever it was that she said, his state of mind might be gathered. For example, had he said, "Oh no, Mother, you'll live a long time yet," she would know he contemplated murder. If he were to reply, "Things can be perfectly comfortable for you for a long while yet," she would know he had in mind a retirement home where they would feed her on kitekat and ground glass.

She repeated a sentence she had heard at another table, to check whether her son was listening at all: "Miss Livingston-Learmont is of the old school and makes sure never to take tea indoors." Perhaps she would find out from her son the meaning of this mysterious pronouncement.

Her son said, "I'm sorry, I don't know her."

The mother resumed her staring match with the cherry in the depths of the sundae glass.

Lorna and Muriel each took a bit of Alec's ice. He loved seeing them spoon it up. The happiness shed by small treats had never bloomed quite freely for his mother, who would not please herself at all for fear of the wolf within. No appetite aroused was safe; she feared consumption of the mildest sort as though it were its namesake, a disease that burnt you up. In consequence Alec had, and knew he had, a greedy, appetitive, streak. He had a first twitch towards quantity that filled him with a mouthwatering impulse to give in. Sometimes softness seemed so easy that it made sense until he contemplated its sad habits. Luxury had been to his mother an abstract noun, a vice the colour of seamy finery. It began with arising from your bed when you wished and ended God knew where.

Very likely the Chocolate House.

The last place Lorna had taken Muriel Bruce that first afternoon of her return from her brother's death had been the establishment of a milliner, up on the lateral ridgeback boulevard of George Street, among shops selling ironmongery made with the care of jewellery, selling ladies' gowns and school uniforms, and all presenting themselves as though these transactions were as much of a social pleasure for the assistants as they were for the patrons of the establishments.

The hat they bought went into her last home with Muriel Bruce. Mr James the milliner took his time looking at the face that had improved with age, becoming undeceived and open where it had been apologetic. He told no lies.

"I do not need it to last, Mr James," said Muriel.

"I rarely consider lifespan when it comes to hats. It is so short." It was clear he meant the lifespan of hats. That of humans interested him less. It was an age of time. It was like asking a butterfly collector to watch the teeth of a crocodile grow in.

"Something cheerful and not over-useful." Muriel looked around the room. On pegs like giant pins perched hats you would not see in a street unless they should be flying along looking for a flock of parakeets in which to hide.

The eventual hat was not much, a wisp, in fact, just a kind of lettuce made of black net, dotted in places with beauty spots of plush, also black. The effect was Edwardian, elongated, quizzical. It took three weeks to make, during which time Mr James sought and found a hatpin of Whitby jet that was cut like a star. He threw it in with the hat, a festive mourning gift.

The stairs at Nelson Street began to be too much for even the few journeys Muriel was obliged to make. Lorna had given up her room in the flat behind the Parisian curlicues of iron, and was living with Alec.

The two of them set to finding a place for Muriel to live. The Infirmary gave them addresses. They visited each recommended home together, without Muriel, and came away in the first three cases glad they had not brought her.

She knew of the plan, mentioning it often as though inoculating herself.

"What sort of old lady is she?" asked the keepers of the first last home. "Cheerful, friendly, down-to-earth, incontinent?"

"Oh yes," lied Lorna desperately before the question's end. Then she was glad to have bothered her complacent questioner.

The second place was full of whimpers. There were no men, who make old people's homes smell but also give the old ladies something to live for beyond spite. On the walls were strung messages of Life Beautiful, penned in the prose of girlish serfdom and laminated. The bathroom contained an old woman being washed when they were shown around. When Alec withdrew to save her feelings, the woman sponging her said, "Don't worry, she doesn't know the difference." By then Lorna was out too. The confiscation of privacy seemed to kill the old ladies more quickly than widowhood and bitter winters.

The third home was in the country, by Gogar. It had been a real house; that was in its favour. The house was a central octagon with two short but graceful wings, faintly curved.

Within the octagon the space had been partitioned like a cake. The soundproofing consisted of softboard. The place was like a hellish carousel. From one room came the cry of an abandoned woman, without once stopping except to collect air to

109

start again, "Oh God, get me out of here, Oh let me die, please, God, Oh God, get me out of here, let me die."

"They stop it after a bit," said an orderly, fixing the lid on to a beaker. An old woman with a hairband was rushing around calling, "I love you, I love you," now in the voice of a child, now in a hot voice that chilled. In each of these places Alec was bursting to pee but could not. He was moved by the unfairness of the paraphernalia from second childhood producing none of the fondness the kit of a baby evokes. The fragility of the old women in their triangular rooms, the old men kept away from temptation in the wings, seemed to interest no one, to hold no use and to exact no honour. Age had one thing above all other states, its abundance of the past, but the past no longer had a place.

Muriel grew ill. She wanted to go to a place where she might lie in a bed and look out on water. In the end, Alec asked his father and Jean if she could come to their home to die. The move shook some life out of her, and the rest she surrendered quietly one evening. The hatbox with its weightless contents was under the bed. The stuffed Dunvegan had not made the journey. Alec had set up a sprinkler mechanism on the garden hose. It was a kind of view over water, to be carried to a window to see water fan-dancing among lupins and over shining grass.

"I see a bird come for me. At the window." Alec's heart stopped at the words. He looked down at Muriel. He wanted to remember this time in which he either saw the Holy Ghost or saw someone who saw it. When he turned he saw what the woman herself and her life should have led him to expect, a seagull, watching for food to snatch. It was a bird of appetite, not of the spirit.

"You were my chosen son," said Muriel.

He had not thought of it. The tastes of his own adulthood, its habits and adaptations, had been sheltered by the Bruces quite as surely as they grew from the enthusiasms and anathemata sown by his parents.

"I will see you later, with tea. We will read."

"I think not," said Muriel, very clearly.

But again he did not hear it until after he had to, wishing not to set an edge to life.

Four

The boat emerged from the gap through the reef, out into the darker water and away from the air about Moorea that smelt that morning of macaroons.

"To be certain we were covered for anything that could happen, we'd have to have spares of everything. It would mean sailing in convoy with a double, another *Ardent Spirit* down to the last pin and cleat." Logan was streaming the Walker log, a geared mechanical tally of miles hung over the side into the water, simpler than almost any device on the boat, just a long bit of string attached to some spinners that clocked up nautical miles.

His gestures were calm. He was entering the life that best suited him, where the thinking, if necessary, was quick, its effects external.

Leaving places fixed them in his mind. He would be happy never again to be tied up in the boulevard Pomare in Tahiti with the cars honking all night. The fishermen carrying fish yoked over their shoulders on a stick through the gills, a silver fan of fish over each shoulder, he had forgotten. The place had failed him in not being far enough from home. Like America Tahiti's capital was full of borrowings; like Scotland it was afire with sullen endurance, set with the tinder of unbridled wrath in drink.

Logan was not prepared to look at the living confusion travel and cash had brought the town and to be amused by the mix of habits and cultures growing there, too stirred together to extricate, as hard as unravelling a tapestry on to spools of different-coloured rewound wool. A place that offered flying-fish pizza in a neon-lettered bar named Chang's Gaff, a meal for which one paid in francs before taking a bus to a neatly labelled site of human sacrifice; this could not amuse him. In such confusion he saw not energy but degeneration. He wanted a place to be like itself, or what was the point of going to it? His own part in the modification he did not see. He arrived in the most silent way, on a breath, under sail, and gave more than he took, as he saw it.

He shared with money itself a powerful transforming knack; he could weigh heavy on the earth in hard coin or evaporate and move invisibly between lands. At sea he most respected himself for something free at last of money. His loneliness was strength at sea, his strange longsightedness in matters of personality not at all disabling. On land only strong flavours reached him, and fewer places tasted of themselves unmixed now than ever.

He would have said that it was time he did not have. Senti-

114

mentally, he might admit that there was no price he would not pay for more time. In truth he had enough but did not invest it.

"Life's too short," he said, meaning that increasingly a gap was coming between himself and life, the gap children feel and recognise as boredom. His introspection had been done in the adolescent years when he had been sick for certainty; he had not needed to look in again, for, like a grown boy, he was strong but still sheltered. His temperament was more burdened and intricate than his harsh understanding gave him the means to interpret.

Any offence he gave to men his open way dispelled; the offence he gave to women was received differently, often as intimacy. Since he found women becoming, like small countries, increasingly similar, he took advantage of the reputation he had for charm without needing consistently to show it. Certain women will take it upon the word of another that a man is desirable; it is a matter of publicity. With such a man as Logan, for these women, between whom he sometimes could not tell the difference, the retrospect was what they held on to. So they became women who spoke of him in a way that intrigued the next woman. It is a process that holds regimes in place.

"We'll start with watch-partners as in cabins and see how that takes," said Logan. "Two to six to ten to two to six. No breaking of the pattern, no matter how she's creaming, or we can go off course. If we get weather I'll spread the strength."

The wind freshened, its strength uniting evenly behind and into the mainsail. White sail became one half of the sky. Gabriel sat at the high point of the tipped aft cabin, peeling carrots into a bowl that filled her lap. Below, Elspeth was laying out the log book.

She came up to sharpen Logan's pencils over the side. Thinking of the company, not of the wind, she turned the pencils in the sharpener as she talked with Gabriel.

"Now it's almost beginning, our time at sea," she said. The pencil rotated sixty degrees of the sharpener's bird's-eye circle at a time.

Gabriel was too young to enjoy such loose conversation that relied upon drift and exchange and comparison. Elspeth did not seem to have much to show for her life. Gabriel imagined how she would wear such a life. She scraped the carrots with an artistic look on her face.

"There is a bit of a swell always deep in the Pacific," Logan said. "It's long so you don't always notice it. Spit it out if you need to chuck at all, Gabriel."

Then he smacked at his eye, remaining turned round from the wheel at the waist.

"Hornet, or something sharp in my eye." He started to pull at his lid with his right hand, steering the course with his left. Elspeth vaulted over Gabriel into the aft cabin to get his antidote. The carrots spilt and rolled down the deck. Some stayed in the white gutter under the gunwhale. Most went under the sea and then like matchwood were there again but soon left behind.

"That antidote has to be where I am," said Logan. "Not near by or somewhere you know it is safe." His voice was raised so that Elspeth could hear. Everyone else, as they do on a boat, heard and naturally listened. Tension on a boat is like the wind and touches everyone aboard.

The mainsail began to flap a little at its most distended point, then it beat and whipped where it was tightest to the mast. The reefing ropes that had been hanging from it at exact angles, as safe as a fringe, seemed to trace some panic. They acted as tell-tales.

A gulping long wave moved sidelong under the hull, just enough to take the wind momentarily away from the smooth mainsail. The flapping began to punch and distort the sail. The boat began to twist.

"Nick, get up here, come and winch her in," called Logan. He did not speak angrily of his boat, sounding calmer than before.

Nick grabbed the heavy winch-handle from the cabin pocket, one of four slots aft of the wheel, wed it to the winch and wound till he felt the tension sit tight. It was not quite right. The poised silence that should have come was forestalled by something. He looked up at the mainsail. Somehow part of its head was folded on to the spreader. He could have torn the big sail.

"Sandro, will you let her out easy and I'll lift her off?"

They were all there, waiting for the sail to be reunited with the wind. Nick climbed the mainmast with the intelligence of a lemur, looping his feet on to cleats and soft bolls of rope. When he flicked the heavy mainsail off the spreader, the tension among them was such that the release of the sail was like that of a living thing. Sandro retensed the rope that held the wind at its best point for their use in the long white pouch of sail.

Logan, who had forgotten to die during this manoeuvre, remembered his hornet sting. Elspeth was dithering about with the syringe, he could feel it at his back.

Putting up his hand to his eye, he pulled from beneath it several tiny rough splinters.

"I've got a splinter," he said, part of his brain calculating which foresail to put up.

"Shall I get you a needle?" said Gabriel. Really, she could be a useful girl.

"Not in fact. It's for my eye," he said.

Elspeth began to laugh in an uncontrolled way.

"All we need is a camel."

"Was it you who was sharpening pencils into the wind?" her husband asked her. "Do I have to tell you again that on a boat *everything you do affects everything everyone else does.*" The voice he used for the talkings-to he gave Elspeth was less loving than the voice in which he spoke to the boat. He was severe with Elspeth when it was warranted and on principle; others saw the tough but fair way he dealt with her and thought before crossing him themselves.

"The genoa," said Logan. "I'll hold her still if you dress her."

Nick and Sandro moved forward over the deck, thin, light young men who knew what to do without talk. They pulled the long fanfolded sail forward and clipped its head ready to haul it up and set it. Before raising it, they tied to the sail's foot a rope the length of the boat, with a simple knot the size of Sandro's head. Logan turned the rope around and with the thread of the hefty winch. At the same time he steered a course that held the sails unmoving as robes, then he called out and Nick ran aft to grind up the enormous sail and Logan turned the wheel till the wind punched and then lay once more within the cloth, that this time pulled the boat along with more speed. The tilt was so high you could sit on the windward side and look down into the sea as it was taken away by the air pushing over it. As long as it lasted, the rushing of water along the tipped boat slaked Logan's great thirst.

Elspeth sat at the highest point she could find where she was not in Logan's sight and looked down into the blue water that was continually never the same. There in the sails and blue she was happy as a person can be in rich emptiness.

Occasionally the lowest edge of the genoa touched the water and cut it, drawing white in that instant.

Gabriel was in the sail bin, covered with bergamot oil. The second lot of carrots she had peeled was on the gimballed stove in a pan clamped over the bobbing gas. The water in which they boiled was at an angle more probable in ice. When their warm winter kitchen smell grew strong, Gabriel stretched herself out of the sail bin and walked gingerly down the sloping deck to look through the galley hatch at these travelling carrots. How miraculous normal things could be, thought Gabriel, wondering if she ought to fall in love.

Alec looked up into the sails white on white on blue, full of an invisible resource held in place and exploited by intelligence. He knew why he had come. This was it, the rare time when peace and purpose coincided in beauty. Logan would not put it like that, but to see the man achieving this angle, this flight, was like watching a builder at work. First Logan had set a trap for the wind, then he held it and built it into racing towers.

The pitch of Alec's thought had been lifted high by simple physical processes. Although the boat seemed sometimes vulgar to him, sometimes also squalid, that was to do more with human needs. This flying over water shook out the human dust.

He settled with himself that at the worst of the voyage he

would remember that things could be like this. That there would be bad points he was certain: he had felt like a man trapped in a roomful of birds when the mainsail flapped against itself: he had noted his skipper's temper.

He watched Logan and admired him. In many ways he seemed a creature well adapted to life. His disposition did not allow for the things upon which Alec feared he had wasted his life, shades, vagaries and tentative hues. Alec also allowed himself to feel superior to Logan, though he did not put it to himself like that.

All that day they were awake simultaneously, although Elspeth took herself off during the afternoon to read below. She did this from self-protective habit, in case there came a day when she must hide herself. If she were as a rule not there at a certain time, it would not be noticed that she was not there.

During the afternoon, she tied herself into her lee-cloth so that she did not fall out of the bunk. She read more slowly than she liked to, because the reading was one of the lures she used to get herself through the days. If she had read at her normal speed there would have been no room for the books she would need.

"Tell me why you need to look at all these books," said Logan.

"Just as you play with boats," she rejoined. The foolishness of replying in kind to a man who had not intended the slight he had given was typical of her, a woman who had chosen a life whose chief saboteur was herself. It was unfair of her to have lit upon him for his certainties if she was going continually to jib at his want of fluidity.

They had each chosen the other for the soothing sense they had of being to some degree balanced by the other; she felt braver, simpler, he felt less access to his rage and loneliness.

The speculations and scepticisms that had been the theme of her earliest life were dust kittens to him. He believed in Church and State; she was reared to mistrust them. The sanctity of fact filled his life; among the facts was religious belief. It was not so mystical as faith, being more a repository for exalted feelings, heightened fears and a sense of self.

She wanted to believe, for reasons as selfish as his own. Her highest bliss, in want of children, was aesthetic. She wanted to ascribe what she found transcendent to something. Elspeth had an impulse to praise.

Gabriel had been the surprise, to Elspeth. It was fortunate that this was a boat. On land, Elspeth was sure, there would have been trouble. The stags would have begun to rub away their velvet. On a boat the proximity to danger can hold off intrigue.

The big seashell was in the hatch at the foot of her bunk, its mottling subdued by the soak in soda crystals. It smelt a little, still, and moaned when held to the ear. At some stage she would give it to Gabriel as a souvenir. She wondered if it could be blown like a conch.

Getting it out from among her seaboots and oilskins, she shook the shell for roaches and put it to her lips.

The noise was tired, the sad greeting of a bus driver to his wife, pressing on a perishing rubber bulb, when he expects nothing much for dinner. Hoarser than a lowing, the sound emerged. The small hole at the tip of the shell's spiral that had marred its handsomeness was now its main point.

She blew again.

Feet moved indirectly up the deck over her head in the cabin.

She blew.

"Oh, sorry, Logan just thought you might be unhappy."

It was Alec. What could it have cost her husband to speak this way? How strange he could not come for himself.

"Does he think I make a noise like this?"

She held up the horn and smiled at Alec over its antique flourish. The sheet she wore was held over her in the Attic fashion, falling down from her nipping elbows behind. The lee-cloth was hauled-to.

Happy, there was something to her, he thought, warily, but something better handled by such a man as Logan.

Ardent Spirit reached Huahine in the dark. On the radio the local coastguard was telling boats outside the reef to hang off till morning. Through the night they watched in changing pairs in case the coral should scrape, although the boat was not close. It was a steep sharp reef, the spray burning off it all night in smoke and in the morning composing a white wreath around the island, lying slow around the lagoon like dry ice on a stage.

They took the boat in when daylight had filled the sky. Within the reef a band of pale blue encircled them. The island was dense green, its summit-high pasture planted with a shrub like a victor's garland of parsley.

From the shore came peals of church bells.

Sandro flinched.

"Better than the Mormons," said Nick. The interiors of

these islands, less remote than the Marquesas, and not, like them, protected by convinced Catholicism, were settled with one-storey churches of Jesus Christ of the Latter Day Saints.

A bureaucracy from France and a religion from America at present lay over the islands.

Alec and Nick swam in together after breakfast. Alec, stockier, had not Nick's otter's cunning against the current.

At the summit of the island, Alec saw as he swam, pretending to be taking his time because he was looking about him, were horned peaks, some of them with trees growing sideways out of them.

"The problems islands have—are they much the same wherever the island is, would you say?" asked Nick when they reached the shore. Alec had watched him nightly forbear to join in conversations. Perhaps it was tact? Nick combined with intense practicality a theoretical tendency that he protected by holding it in his head against oxidisation from exposure to windier minds.

"Incest, uncontrollable usurpations, postage?" said Alec.

"The balance between need and ruination, too." They were passing between irrigation canals in which stood blue lilies on one tall leg, heronwise.

In a square-backed Renault van, a family went by, elbows out of windows. They were driving in the direction of "The Open-Air Museum With One Hundred-Year-Old Fish Trap", indicated on a hand-painted sign.

"A hundred years is old for a fish." Nick spoke.

On the point of putting him right, Alec caught the over-straightness of Nick's face.

"About islands. We feel better coming here maybe because it's the French who have done most of the recent harm. But that is picking nits. There's not the time to explain that it's not one who threw the stone but someone very like one."

"There is time, there's not the inclination." Nick's correction moved the dawdling words to a clip. "Differences are not spoken of and at once there are none, because the bullies have won, like those snails in Moorea, and we all recall how pleasant and rewarding and eccentric, if you can say that about something spiral, the old snails were. So someone gets together some shells of the old snails and makes a display, correct in every important detail, the old snails to the life, and people feel much better after that. Replication and surrogacy are the future. You are participating in some of the last nonvicarious experiences of this century. Everything will have its substitute, its empty double. And a generation of people is already born that cannot tell the difference between the water and the mirror. Even when it has drunk the mirror."

"Are you *so* pessimistic? Is that why you are at sea?" asked Alec.

"I'm not pessimistic. It's not that. I'm afraid we'll be evolved beyond what is good for us, back into simpler, greedy organisms. Just appetite and controlled imaginations."

They passed the PTT. A girl in green was smiling and making eyes into the receiver. Her imagination showed her the face of the person at the other end.

"I come to sea for that reason. I want to see the last places that are not blurred, if I can. This is a way to live without money. I earn a bit and it goes. I own so little that I do not have to own more on its account. The combination of living intensely with people and of there being times when people are nothing seems to agree with me. I'm curious but uninterested in knowing other people through time."

"All other people?"

"I've a wife and when we meet it is a nice surprise. She married me for nationality but we had to part so soon after that the interest I had in her, which had been small, grew, and now if we coincide I am sad to part. She's a South African, the sea is covered with them, but mostly they are older. Liberal whites who couldn't bear it. The boat she's on at the moment should be round here somewhere. She sends me her position on the globe when she can. I think of her with the same stars over her. There are letters in boxes all over from one of us to the other, lost letters, but they'll do for the next time round." Not the next marriage, the next circumnavigation.

"Her name is Evelyn." He had known the only question Alec could ask and answered the one he did not. "We talk about family but not until we find a boat of our own. And I wonder how it is to be raised on the sea. It might make them mountaineers or turn them into plankton."

"Plankton?" So Nick, like many theorists, had an irrational streak.

"It's what Evelyn calls the numberless infinities of souls."

"Are you faithful?" It was a drunk man's question, a question that went too far; Alec took the licence to ask it from Nick's tone of sober openness. He was a man who would answer anything he wished to and let nothing drop without meaning to.

"I am. The gossip at sea travels faster than on land. Some

125

conventions are apparently loosened and talk is the other thing to.do in the evening. Boats are known oceanwide and who is on them. And messing about unbalances a ship, turns it sour and leads to mistakes. Inshore from here there should be an inner lagoon. We can look out for lipsticked bonito. I've not got my book on me, but I'm fairly reliable on fish."

Above, the sun was reaching the top of the sky, blinding their raised eyes through a star of palm.

"There'll be rain later in the afternoon," said Nick, "but before that shall we go for a beer?"

They stuck out their thumbs and were picked up by a Citroën DS that came round the corner on juicy wheels. In the back seat was a goat with gold eyes.

A group of old men around a tin table rested their stomachs in wide blue braces and salopettes worn without shirts. The shade over them seemed like old rough lace. Looking up, Alec saw that the proprietor of the nearby Café Snack Bar Ritz had rested over the branches of a spreading tree a flat tranche of coral the size of a large table. Among the beer and mineral-water bottles the old men drank from was a metal tray of langoustines. Some of the men smoked, others sucked long claws or bent out tail-flesh from the shell with wide thumbs.

"They are doing nothing. It's the best thing, the thing we are best at, but everyone does it differently. More art should be about doing nothing," said the driver of the DS. The sense of drunken talk increased for Alec, loosening him. He thought of the man's remark: "More art should be about doing nothing." He did not dismiss it as he would have almost all his life, except for during the short glowing spaces when babyhood or happiness had cancelled thought. He felt a shell crack from him, a shell of opinion and self-consciousness, and recognised a strong desire to be back at work, painting, and conveying in paint what he had not tried before to paint, a goodness in life. It was easier to think of an art that concerned itself with expressing the doing of nothing in a place like this, than in Scotland where to do nothing was to be worthless, or to be very cold.

The pleasure of holding such a conversation in French, a language well suited to statement, enclosed them. Alec enjoyed the concentration of speaking in another language and the liberation from certain forms of embarrassment.

He reflected that in the new life with new people he had been living on the boat he had also been concentrating. He had made his speech another language as one does with strangers. The strain of that had been greater than the pleasant effort he made now, to speak French. On the boat he had been thinking of how the others wanted him to be. Now he was thinking of what to say best to express what he wanted to say.

His faintly superstitious wariness of the types to which Logan corresponded (man of action, man of influence) had set up an anxiety in him to be some type or other recognisable to Logan. In so doing he had laid traps for himself, having picked his role as Scottish boffin.

A sweet-smiling man of about forty unloaded watermelons from a barge moored by a grocer's shop. Elephantiasis made his legs as full and thick as the long, shiveringly striped fruit.

The Citroën stopped and relapsed towards the dust. Alec and Nick went in to the store for stamps.

The rain came and went, warm drops filling every lifted vessel, mouth and flower until, at a swipe, it was gone and the sky renewed.

When they reached the inner lagoon it was hot again. Nick swam, in the same shorts he wore all the time and washed in the sea by letting them down on a line with a pocket full of saline-adapted soap. Alec took off his jeans and walked into the pale water; to dive smack into the water would be too violent. That was for paying back cold water that hurt you when you entered it.

They swam with rather than over fish that were so precisely marked, spotted, barred, dotted they seemed retouched. When the lagoon seemed suddenly to shatter, the shadows of many fish becoming one on its white floor and spurting away like a comet, Nick punched Alec and pointed out to him a grim-faced patrolling shark. The dead eye and cuneiform moves of the animal stayed with Alec, although he seemed not to have felt afraid when in the water with it.

Nick was neutral on the topic. He did not make more of the incident than there had been—a lot of small fish alarmed by a bigger one that very possibly feared himself and Alec.

When in the night it was time for Alec and Nick to take the dogwatch, Nick woke Alec with hot tea. It was a cool night, dripping with falling stars.

"Your dream was bad," said Nick. "Everyone is afraid of sharks unless they are one themselves."

After first confidences between people moving towards friendship, a rest between exchanges of information somehow hastens, not impedes, the growing trust. Alec and Nick had now to talk, in order to stay awake on watch, and with no sails to check for chafe or horizon to scan for container ships or unmarked yachts. There had been no time for Nick's story to ferment, but the slight hangover of over-intimacy did not brush the two men.

"You go below and read if you like, or you could catch some sleep," said Nick. "There's nothing to do but listen for mermaids."

They watched the sky. In falling, the stars shed chalkdust and were gone down the sky in a blink. The discrepancy in time between the actual hour of the death of the star and the eye receiving the news did not fit inside the head.

"Travelling light is what those stars are. I mean doing, obviously. But also what they are made of."

"The speed of a boat under sail is a better speed for my constitution than the speed of light," said Alec.

"It is a good speed. You arrive at places at the right time, not before it like on a plane, so all of you arrives at once."

"What would you say was the right speed on land? Horse?"

"Foot. Solar-powered sedan chair. I suppose horse but I resist it. They have personalities."

"So does a boat."

"But she is female."

"A horse may be that."

"But never as feminine."

The shrouds of another boat tinkled. The buoy at the teeth of the reef issued its tocsin.

"I suppose you are married," said Nick. Such convention in this unusual man annoyed Alec. He gave the usual irritating answer: "Yes and no." It was a reply that never pleased unless in reply to two separate questions. It forked the tongue.

"The only hope I've got with that fridge is to drain it right down, extract the plate and the element from behind the safety mesh, readjust the thermostat so it does not freeze over like hell, check the safety ducts, replenish the freon or is it argon, krypton, neon, xenon or radon . . ."

"I'm sorry," said Alec, "I hadn't meant to be as rude as I was. I lived with a woman for a long time."

"What is she doing?"

"If she and I were still together, I would say the answer to that would be crying. Or drinking. She's a nurse. A Scot."

"Does that explain it?"

Having said even so much about Lorna, Alec was swamped with feelings of disloyalty. He was a weak man, a seizer not of the occasion but of the easy way.

"Nurses *see* so much, as they call it. And we had seen a lot ourselves. All usual stuff. But she died, almost, of not taking herself seriously."

"That's not the way these days."

"Lorna and I are older than that, just. We were the lot that took other people seriously in a rather priggish way and then got selfish."

"You have children?"

"Not ours. Hers. One."

"She was married before you?"

"No."

"And when the fridge is thoroughly dismantled, I suppose I should give it a good clean with some strong but not alpine disinfectant. Dettol is a fine standby, available in many of the islands of the South Pacific, though Izal has taken hold in Noumea . . ."

"No, she wasn't married before me."

"Can you feel that biffing? It's something biffing the boat, a big fat wrasse or something. This hull is like skin, you feel for her, held back by barnacles and rubbed by things that may be the size of her. But the barnacles, though less dramatic, can weigh hundredweights; each of them's like a little stone lentil. When a boat with a long keel like this one gets careened, she must lose a third of her weight."

"She and I lived together for many years. I deceived her in the usual ways and allowed myself the upper hand in most things. She found a way round this that I did not notice until it was too late. Meanwhile I had set up an excellent system that excused me however I strayed. I was so strict, you might say ascetic, at home that there was a snowy uprightness to it. Home after all is the example for the next generation, although there were none of those. Also, I suspected that Lorna was more adroit at having fun than I was. There were nights I had, all Scotsmen do, when I feared I was turning into a Scandinavian. I saw the bones in things only because I so feared the flesh taking me over.

"Lorna was beautiful, more so as she got older, and I would not let this be seen. She had wanted to show herself innocently, but I made a vice of it. I did not confine her to our home but I belittled the light sides of her life. A *nurse*, for God's sake, and I grudged her lightness.

"I found a way in which to make her unsure of her beauty if it was due to be taken out into the hungry eyes of others. I encouraged her, pampered her, helped her find soap for the bath after work, washed her like a cat, fixed on the ear-rings I least approved. And before we entered whatever room it was I looked at her from top to bottom, slowly, till I withered her. I could take her from full summer to a frost in those looks. She loved me more, in a way no fair man can live with since it holds a hard mirror to his face, the more I cut her down. At her work all the time this went on there was the giving out that had to be done. She did come home like a dead star, no light left. Sometimes I invented jamborees for the two of us so that I could spoil them, in so doing, so I liked to think, teaching her the folly of diversion.

"After I had frozen over the life we shared, I went for the axe. I began to see other women is the Scots term. The English say seeing to, very dative.

"Most of the letters I kept at my place of work. The surgical tidiness and order I had made the rule at home did not leave room for strange letters on coloured, often pink, paper. I was not happy, of course, but did not know how to stop it all. The sternness I had set around my home like ice was what gave my outside wooings electricity. The women were often greedy and materialistic, animal in every way but the one. Lorna continued to love me. Her hair . . ."

Alec stopped. Not even Lorna knew this story, after all.

"It had been grey since our earliest time. An old woman died, whom I had loved. She was my other mother. My other other mother." He spoke to himself. "Lorna carried me, as she carried the death by smoke inhalation of her—only—mother, old but not to blame, curtailed by the insurance fire of a warehouse-holder a street away. Her hair took that day to go white. I watched it. I suppose thaw is the opposite of what it did: the

132

white did not so much slip from it as slip into it. It got softer. Her beauty remained in the more serious form I have seen come to women who are monogamous. Women are renewed by new love—any promiscuous woman will tell you she is fighting time by being remade again and again in the eyes of men.

"Lorna was not like that. The shortness of life was not a thing she conceived of being fought off by numbers of men, when it would not answer to good medicine and the knife. She grew beautiful in a different way, not from new attention, but out of a nature that was firm and at last emerging. She became quieter and more sure of her thoughts. Sometimes I saw what I had had and asked of myself how I could continue to live by repression at home, repression clothed in the garb of principle, and do what I liked, which by now I did not like, away from home.

"Lorna began to have bruises, even a contusion on her hip, but patients could hit and kick, even bite. I was often ashamed to look at her in case she saw in my eyes the little white body of the last woman they had looked at.

"She became so poised that I suspected something. A portentous formality came into her speech. Sometimes she explained things to me that she knew I knew. She asked for the same information repeatedly. But the real sign was that, for the first time in over a dozen years, she seemed to have found a way of eluding the hurt I knew how to give her. She began to answer me back. The respect I had not earned was not being paid. She smiled a lot, and drank tea. In the night I found her drinking tea, the pot by her side.

"It was cold, of course. Full of vodka. Tea also, mixed with it, so profoundly did her years of obedience to me connect with her desperate need to get away from me.

"I actually wondered whether to exploit this new strength in Lorna, pretending that under her sudden grace there was not a wretched paddling with the feet below the water. Then the teapot went, and all shame and concealment after that were mismanaged. I had humiliated her and must suffer. We went nowhere together.

"I marked bottles with a pencil, a Chinagraph like yours. In small ways she was cunning. She bought her own pencil. This was our life. Although I did not give up the other girls, I was with her more than I had been for years. I was with her like a jailer. She was happy when she drank for about half a sentence, like a lifted eyelid. Then the eyelid closed again and the dark came down.

"She said that, when her hours allowed her, she was happy drinking alone. It was I who made the pain. We were leaking money. Spirits cost more than fuel. It had to be spirits. It is a national passion with Scots, to ride the world having taken ardent spirits."

"Coming on this particular boat was for that reason?" asked Nick.

"It is a beautiful name."

"Not rash?"

"Can they know its meaning? Logan and Elspeth?"

"At least one of them, I think, yes. And you have missed out the child."

"The child she used to save us. And to punish me."

"Did you not want it?"

Like fumes a green dawn was joining with the spindrift from the reef to make a forest of rising light around them. The stars were pale, receding, falling unnoticed now by this turned cheek of the world.

"I am fond of children. I love this one."

"Yes." He waited.

"She cannot remember who the father is. It took place outdoors. In the town. She does not know who saw. Do I not know that there are people who live like that, watched even as they lie on the pavement together, she asks me. Asked. Am I so clean I can wash off these thoughts, so noble I can ignore what is right there in my own house, so pure I cannot see dirt? She asked me these things with pleasure. It was as though she were repainting our walls, with filth on a wide brush.

"The two things were excesses, my asceticism like a frozen sea, her wild dance with the spirits. For the time she carried the baby there was nothing much, the occasional woozy afternoon. But Lorna has that speaking trait, the feast-or-famine gene that afflicts Celts, so she was mainly off the drink until after . . ."

"He, I suppose?" A comforting normality in Nick's voice seemed to lift the pain of the telling.

"Yes, he—how did you know?—until after he came."

"He is her present to you, a fresh start. It was natural it should be like that."

"Look at the sun. I am cold now it's warming up."

"Go and sleep. I hear the others. What is his name?"

"It's Sorley."

"You can tell me more later if you want. Or no more. This watch is busier at sea."

135

"Is it possible?" Alec did not want to meet anyone below so he did not go down the companionway. He went up into the bow, prised open the fo'c'sle hatch that was ajar, and lowered himself into the tiny cabin that fitted, as he collapsed into his bunk, close around his soft tissue like a shell.

Five

"It's nothing, it will go away," announced Gabriel, causing more worry when she did not name the pain she had introduced to them all by moving as though she had swallowed a batten. Her voice too had become stiff. When she spoke, the others deferred by at once falling silent. Even Logan seemed to do this.

Clearly she was ill, if not as ill as her fierce denials of any need for attention were set on suggesting. Being young she remained in the state when discomfort can be curtailed. She was new, and did not care to share her body with illness.

Her hair had sunk like a wet cat's, her skin looked hot.

"We can put in at Raiatea," said Logan. "There will be a *pharmacie*." He emphasised the French accent. "Look in the *Ship's Captain*, Elspeth."

Elspeth took down *The Ship's Captain's Medical Book*.
"What shall I look up, Gabriel?"

"I'm aching really, and hot and cold, I suppose. Giddy."

"She needs something more specific, Gabriel," said Sandro.
"Swellings or green vomit."

"I think I've got it." Not Elspeth, but Nick, spoke. "Look at
her hands."

Gabriel held them out in the nail-polish-drying piano-player
gesture. Her left hand was a softer thing to look at than her
right. The skin seemed to have been gently inflated so there
were no tendons visible.

Nick stroked the back of this hand with his middle right
finger.

"Hurt?"

"A bit; numb more than anything."

"It will hurt," said Nick.

"Oh fine."

"You're lucky. With some coral cuts you get no warning, just
the fever and not much hope. This will be fine. You've a septic
hand."

Gabriel did not like the ugly name given to her romantically
fevered state.

"I'd hoped to save the drugs till we got out to sea," said
Logan. It was an unnecessary remark. They had all known this
was his intention. He rather liked mentioning the dangerous
drugs in the safe: the fallen bowels, torn ears, uprooted scalps
the drugs presided over. He spoke of these wounds like a war
veteran.

"It's nothing like that bad," said Nick. If he did not stop

Logan now he would tell the poor girl how septicaemia swept through a boat he'd been on once and a brace of right hands had been thrown overboard after a double amputation conducted with just a gag and a brandy bottle. He could not trim his conversation.

Purgation and entertainment lay close in Logan's talk. He had less time for conversation, associating it with women. To signify this sort of talk he and his intimates had a gesture; the right hand was folded over and made to yak like a set of false teeth.

"If we get to Raiatea fastish, we can get it cleaned up. Otherwise I'd've suggested we boil it, but no need."

At "boil", Gabriel sat with her forehead pinched in her hand. A solicitousness close to flirtation, now she was diagnosed, came over everyone on the boat, not only the men. Knowing little, pretty, a little difficult, Gabriel combined traits that encouraged attention of the happy sort that pleases the attention-giver. Her innocence without her wide smile and fresh eyes might not have been enough; without that innocence, pleasing her would not have offered so much pleasure.

"I'll make you a canopy over the afterdeck and you can lie in the air and shade. Feeling crook can take it right out of you," said Logan.

The boat was on an easy reach, her angle cradling, not steep.

Elspeth went below and squeezed the green grapefruit. The juice of one fruit half-filled a jug. Seeing the jug made her think of ice, and although she knew that ice-making tired the refrigerator's burning lungs more than any other function, she put some ice in Gabriel's weighted glass.

139

"Good idea, ice for Gabriel." Logan spoke to his wife in a warm voice as she took the drink to the girl. "Get me a glass, Elspeth, and I'll help her with that jug. If this wind tightens up and sets we'll take her to the chemist in style under a spinnaker."

The sea slid over itself in scales, shining. Nick and Sandro set the poles for the spinnaker and attached the guys. A breath seemed taken by the air, and held. The thin vast foresail went up light as a bubble, rearing out at the front of the boat that no longer roared along but moved as though pulled by a swan, so full was the silence.

The sun through the spinnaker glowed, spilling a light pure as the light that glows through the thin white marble windows of some old churches, warm without colour.

Under the bow, as you would expect when a boat was set upon the healing of a maiden, dolphins played, bounding out of the sea in a unison people cannot achieve, three by three, water falling off their glossy backs to itself.

Once at the *pharmacie*, Elspeth had bought the anti-inflammatory creams. The white-overalled assistant told her, after looking at Gabriel's hand with resignation, "It will grow fatter and pain more."

As Elspeth had up till this remark been speaking French, she was confused by the collision of courtesies. Also she wondered why the *pharmacienne* did not speak to Gabriel.

"But your daughter will be well soon as long as she keeps it clean and lays on the unction."

Elspeth's own age, that had not much interested or worried her before, came to her.

"I was seventeen when I had you, not impossible."

"Sorry?" said Gabriel. She had been looking at skin creams

140

in jars like little silver clams, unscrewing them and breathing up the pap inside.

She must be homesick, it was natural. Elspeth thought that Gabriel might even have been thinking of her mother, smelling the complexion creams; she wondered how she might include Gabriel more, make her into part of the family. Perhaps to do so would make Elspeth herself feel as though it were a family. She would ask Logan to have an eye to Gabriel.

Out of the white-and-silver *pharmacie* they turned. It was strange, among the palms and leaf-thatched huts, to see the islanders, open-faced and black-haired as their ancestors, carrying in one hand a pineapple by its stalk, like a head, in the other a Prisunic bag. The walk of the women was still comfortable, alluring before motherhood and capacious thereafter. Their heads have been meddled with, not yet their feet, she thought.

A woman approached them. Before she drew near, the street changed its dozy buzz. A beauty sheds a light before herself so that the world is prepared. Bandbox and animal together, a topaz-coloured woman in white linen sauntered along holding by the hand a child with skin dark grey-brown-green and hair the white-green of blonde babies who live by salt water. On crocodile pumps, the siren walked in triumph, her hair five-sixths the length of her white dress.

From the grocer's shed, came the voices of Logan and the other men. The disloyal instincts Elspeth underwent when with her own kind in other places grew worse the louder the voices of the men. They could always be heard. This she resented, it was true, but would she not have been pleased to hear this commanding boom were it dark and she afraid?

Alec was there, his voice, being Edinburgh, making different

141

assumptions from Logan's. He was eating slices of salami off a penknife. The whole shop was full of a chewy darkness like spores.

Strung from every slat that braced the palm-fibre walls were dehydrated shrunken organs and vegetables. Watered, these might swell to yield a menagerie, a congregation of monkeys, a ten-acre market of soft fruit and hard tubers; there were fish so dry they would crumble, shrunk perfectly from a size greater than that of a man. The detail on them was fossil-neat, like all reductions impossible to see completely, so that you had to take much on trust.

"Raoul here says," Logan began, "we should get you some peel of the fruit of love for that hand. I know it sounds like queer gear but you can't lose."

If he did, Raoul did not show he understood, unlike the girl in the pharmacy. A man like Logan may insult but he reassures, too. A woman like Elspeth subtracted certainty from the simplest acts.

"It's orange peel," said Nick. "It can be very useful stuff. Don't eat it in large amounts, though."

"Hardly," said Gabriel. It looked like dried tongue-skin.

"We'd best be going."

"Bora Bora?" asked Raoul, a wide, heavy man in a sarong over a stomach round and hairless as a melon.

"Yes indeed, *certainement*," replied Logan.

The beauty of Bora Bora was mentioned everywhere in this part of the Pacific.

"I'll tell you something about Bora Bora. It won't be free," said Logan as they set off. He pulled the outboard throttle on the Zodiac for emphasis.

Alec, momentarily misinterpreting, wondered who had most lately conquered it, then heard the words at their proper value, converted into figures.

After his confessional night with Nick he was slow and tired. He seemed to have talked all through those first hours of the day. Had he also said anything?

"All the time I am lying to you," Lorna had said to him, "I am free."

These hard words lay under his skin and pained him. He looked at Gabriel's coral cuts. The hand was coming up now, filling with liquid like a goat's udder. The places where the coral had cut, hardly visible this morning, were the bluish red of meat on the turn. For anything to touch the hand would be painful. At night, Nick said, she would have to sleep with her hand in a cage of some sort.

He would try to fix one by the time she wanted to sleep.

"Shall I take over your watch?" asked Nick, after he had held Gabriel and swung her up between the guard-rail posts from the steps up from the Zodiac.

It's odd, thought Alec, how I am beginning to pine for certain things; they aren't the things I would have imagined.

I thought I would miss solitude more than I do; that may be the good fortune of sharing that tiny cabin with Nick.

I used to require space, a cubicle of my own at the museum and no one near me when I painted, even to begin to think. But now there is no space and I am thinking all the time. The proximity is so close on a boat, there is a drama to it. The unities are forced upon us.

Did the sea count as space although it was outside the boat? Surely it was more an outer space, its extent too great to be comprehended as a quiet room in a house can be, or a studio. If he had been alone upon it, he knew, he would go mad and conjure mirages before the end of the first week.

The solitariness, he supposed, must have been a fear of having people know enough of him to encircle him, to include his life somehow within their own, like babies in whose bodies are found an embryo of their weaker sibling. He had not wanted someone to know so much about him they could put him in a bag and draw it tight.

Being here on the boat he was aware at last that it is rare ever to reach that stage. Up close against one another, people continue to disappear behind distracting clouds or to hide behind some self who is only their protecting double.

The solitude he had made important to himself, driving people off in the process, was a luxury. It had been nothing like loneliness, a condition that seemed to worsen in crowds, and nothing at all like being alone. The solitude he made was a worldly thing, dependent on people being there in order to be walked away from. He was not gregarious, he knew that, but he was dependent.

That word was not so bad now that he thought about it. His best paintings had, he must not deceive himself, been made of places empty of people, while he lived up against others. The distraction and clutter forced him to clear and reorder his mind and its translation of the world into paint. The asceticism he had forced upon Lorna that had left her gasping like a fish in a drained loch and thirsty like a fish too, that asceticism had chilled him.

He missed newspapers. In his life on land, he had almost

ceased to look at them. He knew he was not one of these people who are attached to the papers in the almost physical way that makes them smooth out the page of yellowed paper that falls out of an old drawer or tweak apart the balls of paper that pad the china in a house move.

Equally he was certain that he was not, unlike Logan, who listened whenever he could to the radio news, a man who needed to know what the world had done in the last day. News was murderous gossip and men who could talk of nothing but news thought their preoccupation profound because of the solemnity of death and the horror of human pain; but in frivolous fashion, men who did not share this suffering were buying it to legitimise their old prejudices. The news of a day, properly contemplated, would make you wish not to see another day.

Newspapers knew this and weighted their material accordingly, this much civil war, this much marvellous meals with mince. It was for this shameless packaging that he craved a newspaper now. The awful faultiness and garrulity of newspapers seemed to him charming; before, it had seemed meretricious. He remembered the intimate dislike in which certain columnists were held, the slithy tricks of the superior broadsheets in holding on to readers, their Chaucerian technique of announcing, "It will never be our way to describe how a certain contemporary monarch has been seen dining alone with a tiger . . ."

The horrible self-deceit of newspapers came to him and he laughed. His spirits were high.

He passed through the saloon and Gabriel and Sandro's cabin. Gabriel lay on her bunk, talking into the tape recorder.

". . . did not seem to like the idea of being my mother. Anyhow, she couldn't be. She never knows what I'm thinking, not like you. There were some face creams like you have and I did get sad then. Hello, Alec. This is Alec, Mother." She pressed off the small machine and said, "Say hello, Alec." She pressed Record, with her right ring finger, idly.

"Hello." The tape was still going. He saw that the blanket was raised over her left hand, so he lifted it, as you open a door carefully to see an animal.

"Leave my blanket," she said in a friendly voice.

The hand was inside a basket woven of some vine.

"What was in there?"

"Grapefruit."

"It's pretty," he said. Untypical gallantry, prompted by the breathy listening purling of the tape recorder, made him go on, "though not as pretty as what's inside."

She looked so bored by his remark that he had to kiss her. The engine of the boat was at that moment engaged, so she turned off the tape.

"We're motoring to Bora Bora," she said. The sea was taut, flat, directionless, faintly sloppy astern. At the head of the bunk below Gabriel's own, Sandro's rosary swung from a small brass hook, making a scuttling noise.

The closeness of the cohabitation Gabriel and Sandro were sharing was, Alec realised, what hindered any romantic attachment between the two. No mystery was open to them. The illusions that wrap even the most direct and straightforward of love affairs had never had the distance in which to flourish and shed their veils. Yet it was probably also true that they knew nothing of each other at heart, having established personae inside which to live and a mutual co-operative propriety about their physical selves. Alec could imagine feigning incuriosity. He could imagine feeling indifferent to someone forbidden—since enduring his discomforting morbid thirst for his second mother he flinched from reawakening that pain.

To sleep, however, twenty inches apart from a young female body lying over one's own, to dress and undress at dark junctions of the night with that body, at the beginning or end of a watch, would seem like a long frustrating dance leading, predictably, not voluntarily, towards some resolution. Yet the two were like infants, living in that first pod of self-absorption.

In the days when they had shared a life without secrets, Lorna had fed his own curiosity. This was characteristic of her practical intelligence. She recognised his wildness and let it sniff and stare at other women, reaping it for herself.

The voyeurism he cultivated in himself was applied to everything he saw. He saw secrets not only in bodies. The heart of his painting was its penetration to what underlay what he saw. He stripped back the land, the flowers, the faces that he was to paint, without sadism, curiously. Voyeurism had an ugly reputation as though its hidden motive was to humiliate its object. Alec wanted only to watch and to see. To have caught another soul in an act of pure kindness would thrill him as much as a glimpse into the lushest Turkish bath, he believed.

The life on *Ardent Spirit* combined two rich genres to observe, the domestic interior and the human body in its classically heroic mode. He found the sight of Nick and Elspeth pouring dried beans into canisters in the saloon at evening intensified by the outside bulk of water, the infinity of sky. When the men were hauling in the reacher, or Gabriel straining at a winch, their purposeful eyes and focused strength composed a picture he would use as a source, pared free like lay figures of everything but action.

"There's one with a beautiful neck," Lorna would say, as they did the shopping in Stockbridge, or walked out by Salisbury Crags. "Look at that shining hair." She managed neither to sound like a procuress, as women can when love has become dull to them, nor to make him feel that he must at once turn to her and say, "But you have a beautiful neck, your hair is lovely." Praising the beauty of others did not seem to diminish her sense of her own light-eyed handsomeness.

He had begun to act upon his curiosity, damaging his home and almost never gratifying himself beyond the first touch of new skin. The oath not sworn to Lorna, but held to, that he would be loyal, if not faithful, became a snake that coiled about his whole life, squeezing the air from it.

"See that one for her straight back and hard profile," said Lorna. They were queuing with a jug at the Italian shop on the way down to Leith and the sea, to give lunch to his father. They would fill the jug with red wine and fill a basket with some of the foods the old man, very surprisingly, had taken to; long hard bread full of holes, cheeses like the soles of sandshoes, strange vegetables that lived in a tank of oil and were lifted out in tongs, dry yellow cake, and the wine, even. The shop had become part of the city's growing cosmopolitan life. On Saturday mornings, people were starting to visit it the way that Europeans shopped, in order to find what was good on that day, or to pass time. For Edinburgh, it was new; a certain bohemianism had grown up around the Saturday queue. Alec recognised other painters, a woman weaver of Italian blood, a sculptor. The affinity between Scots and Poles, Scots and Italians, may have to do with the old religion; it is also concerned with food.

That day the sun lay as it can in Edinburgh so slanting and insinuating that even the grey stone of the terraces and the old paving stones were warmed. Women wore dresses and sandals, without stockings. The housewives at their doors had on aprons over blouses as they wiped off the Brasso at their doorbells. The city whose life was lived for the most part indoors was trying its own streets. Seagulls tramped along among the shoppers. At the docks a foghorn once in a while blared. Strangers fell into conversation, made bold by the oddness of being in a queue for food, a queue that they had chosen to be in.

Old men, the grandfathers of the two families of the shop, served food and conversed at a pace combining commercial and theatrical timing. They passed among the crowd, offering on small plates a piece of Parmesan ("Cheese, it's cheese, tell them"), some sugared violets, a plate of purple olives and pink tuna. The old men were attended by their dazzling grandsons, who climbed ladders to reach the top shelves of the narrow, high shop, and their granddaughters, gold hoops in their ears, who used lazy-tongs to bring down hard sacks of ground coffee or sachets of pink-and-white almonds. The third generation spoke pure Scots though they were entirely Italian; they interspersed their Edinburgh speech with fast-squashed Italian, falling into operatic Italian-English to flatter, wheedle, or declare large totals. Their upbringing had been strict; the grandfathers were bringing up the boys to be as shrewd and charming as they were, to carry on the bringing of oil and heat and flattery to the cool city and its evasive, bridling, seducible citizens.

"Is she Italian herself, d'you think?" Lorna asked.

The girl Lorna had pointed out was tall and narrow, straight-backed and somehow prancing, with heavy hair and the drooping, half-sneering, half-swooning profile of a Greek head. Her forehead, pale yellow like all her skin, as Alec knew, was edged with down such as grows on the calyx of some flowers that can tolerate a life near the sea. She banged her basket against her legs, this girl, puffing her skirt out each time behind as the basket hit the front of her calves. Each time the material returned to her legs it clung more, until it was creeping in a fold back through between, sucked by the basket and blown by the wind that is always passing down Leith Walk on the way to the sea. In a town the size of Edinburgh a man will identify the beautiful women who are resident over the years as he takes the gauge of the crowds he walks among; from among these he will eliminate some as being impossible. To others he will aspire, and he will dream of them. Some he may arrange to meet. A few he may come to know. One or two he may learn more of privately. Having seen this girl in the queue, Alec would have decided to course the streets for her, had he not already been spending afternoons with her in the dark, with the shutters folded to the window and oranges in a bowl by the bed.

When it came to the tall dark girl being served, one of the grandfathers deliberately beat the other to it.

"And, *bella Signorina*, for you today?"

"Butter, half a pound, unsalted, please."

"It is my pleasure. Isabella, *presto*." He kept the grandsons away with other errands, the decanting of capers, the measuring out of crystallized citron, the chiselling of *torrone* off its sticky block.

The granddaughter near the butter-barrel took a knife, cut out a wedge of butter, set it on a paddle, paddled it into a pat, and then stamped it with a wooden mould that she drew from a zinc bucket of iced water. With her hands covered over by a muslin cloth, she lifted the thistle-badged butter on to waxed paper and folded it up with attention, not too tight.

"And *mortadella*, enough for two." The medieval woman had seen Alec and was tormenting him. He knew her husband liked the bland, oversized sausage. Or perhaps she really had not seen him and just wished for *mortadella*.

"He is truly fortunate," the Italian grandfather began, as civility demanded, "who shares this meat with you."

The people in the queue were enjoying the compliments themselves; it was a matter of national honour that such a beauty lived among them. Only a superb and heartless flatterer can achieve this effect of scattering his sweets.

"Yes, now, and bread, half a long loaf, if you would."

"I myself will eat the other half, dear," said the old man, forgetting and becoming less exotic as his sentence ended.

"Isabella, bring a little extra for the *Signorina*. You accept?" he asked. It was clear that Isabella knew where to get the little extra; a store of small tokens, chillis, muscatel raisins on the branch, small wedges of *panforte*, sticks of Edinburgh rock, even, had been accurately measured and wrapped for timely spontaneity.

"And I'd like a wine if I may. Bottle."

"What will you have today?" He said "today" often to his lady customers; they felt their presence marked. Newcomers believed themselves included. In these cold northern countries many women had become invisible by the time they reached the age of shopping for foods; he knew it from the vivacity that they learned to show him, their obedience, their willingness to learn. He was teaching the women of Edinburgh to shop, to eat, to cook to please their husbands and sons, in short he was teaching them how to be women, so he thought. He trained them.

"A wine we do not say. The wine, or a type of wine. A wine is like to say," he became truly continental, "a true love. Love it exists, a great thing, like the wine. The true love, not true love. Is not something you can find, just like that."

Lorna was shopping now, asking the other grandfather for her messages: "A loaf, a whole one, please, and three *tramezzini*."

"Certainly, dear. And?"

"Parma ham." An inconvenient thing to ask for on a Saturday morning, thought the grandfather, motioning one of the young men to hook down a dry mighty haunch and impale it ready to be sliced by the whizzing malicious machine in the corner.

"How much?" asked the grandfather who was dealing with Lorna. "Nine slices, please," she said, unromantic, truthful, practical and precise.

Comparing the two women in whose beds he had been in the past week, who were now shopping before his eyes, Alec reflected how you might make a town impossible for yourself if you continued in this way. No human could surely endure the accruing interest on debts of guilt and systems of lies?

The wine had been chosen for the dark girl, wrapped in tissue, probed snug into a long brown paper bag with secure string handles anchored by metal barrels like cuff links.

"See you next Saturday. Ta Ta. *Arrivederci*," sang the grand-father who had served her. Set up by his encounter, he would be able to wheedle the next twenty women with flattery whose sincerity would be meant for the sinewy neck and white flat teeth of the tall dark girl.

She turned and, not knowing Lorna, saw Alec.

"Alex," she said, "I should have thought it. Want a bit of *mortadella*?"

"I don't like it."

Lorna had not turned when the name Alex had been called. She did not use that name for him. She was in the corner of the shop, being shown a postcard, apparently, by the man who was serving her. She had a bag of biscuits under her arm. On the shiny paper was a putto of about eight, Caravaggiesque, eating a biscuit of the type in the bag with an expression on his face expressing all the deadly sins but the one most easy to identify with biscuits. The temperament of the many Italians who had settled in Scotland after being prisoners of war, often staying on to wed and to fill the Scots with ice cream, met and blended with the Scots nature as naturally as ice and sauce mixing in a bowl, the one just mutually chilled enough, the other just suffi-ciently intersweetened.

"Such a lot I don't know about you," said the girl, "but I mustn't tell the world."

At this, the queue fell quiet. Edinburgh is a city fond of hearsay.

Lorna continued to listen to the old man, who was indicating the shelves that bore tinned tomatoes, a panel of them three feet wide, twenty high.

Alec said, "I'll be off, Maria-Fiona, it was good to see you."
That could not but be true.

"Paint me!" Maria-Fiona cried out. "Paint me!" The verb was passionately enunciated, lasciviously imperative.

He left the shop, noticing as he did so the incidence of brogues and expensive ladies' pumps among the shoes of the customers of the shop. His own mother, not a slattern, had often enough gone over the road to fetch the messages in her bedroom slippers.

The little bags of silver balls and jellied citrus slices jangled as he left Valvona and Crolla. On the street some of the shoppers were looking after a dog that was not allowed inside, talking to it as though it too had decided to fetch some foreign foods into its life.

"Is it the salammy you're here for, then? Or would it be the baloney?"

Lorna emerged, smiling at the attempts to get across to the dog, which flopped its paws over each other and lowered its head on to them, looking at the changing queue tolerantly, though without interest. A gull ate chips from a bag outside the Deep Sea fish bar.

Alec was unpleasant to Lorna for a few minutes to punish her for behaving so naturally in the shop. Before meeting his father, though, by the boats at Leith Docks, he had adjusted his behaviour and with it his mood.

This small shift brought with it the customary spiritual relaxation as he allowed the chocks to be kicked away from under Maria-Fiona in his heart, and the woman herself to slide away down the slipway and away from him for good. The lightness he felt on each of these occasions, a lightness he could not confide, that Lorna would have hated for its coldness, was the most piercing pleasure he derived from his escapes from the rational home he had made for himself and herself.

Alec's father was in his coat today, despite the sun. The coat moved and exasperated Alec. He remembered the times they had spread out the coat to sit on for picnics, and a day when Alec himself had hidden within it under a tree while his father watched birds in the bitter wind out at Duddingston Loch, standing in his pullover and shirtsleeves among the old frozen gooseshit, counting the ducks and envisaging the extraordinary migration of the absent geese to the heat of North Africa. The coat was too small for Alec now, too big for his father, and Alec was ashamed of the aggression he felt towards his father for shrinking. It was as if it were irresponsible of him to be growing older.

"If you know what's good for you, *do not die*," he wanted to say. Inside its coat, his father's body was hiding from time, trying to be overlooked. Inside its shirt and wee knitted jerkin, the body was shrinking, everything pulling in so as to be closer to the heart.

They had the same conversations. Alec did not dare mention the sameness, that he loved, for fear his father did not realise it. His father did, and would have felt a change badly. These habits were like bridges to him between his memories of his own father and Alec's future, a span of bridges resting upon himself. Any change would have terribly aged him since to acknowledge resistance to change is to acknowledge one's own looming limit, the point in time beyond which it will be lonely to live, when every friend will be gone and one will be a slow-beating heart, alone.

"The crags, will it be?" asked his father.

155

"Indeed, if that suits." It would be colder up there, but they could take a rug. They had always taken a rug. It would not be an admission of susceptibility, therefore.

"Lorna's a small meal for us."

"Something hot, then?"

"No. A meal may be cold."

"The first I heard of it."

This was a way of bringing Mairi and Jean, dead now of the same cancer, that has a taste for sisters, into the talk. They did not visit the graves over the once a year, since what was the point? Each time they visited, the bereaved father and his son hoped but never confided their hope to surprise Mairi and Jean sitting and talking, short legs crossed, hair permed afresh, under the rowan trees on a labelled bench, their graves ordinarily, unfrighteningly open in front of them, like the doors of a little car, a runabout.

It was never so: the labels on the empty benches: "Given in everloving memory of . . ." were never obscured. The benches looked out on the cemetery, the writing on their backs, their temporariness and application to the living somehow more desolate than the names upon the graves of Alec's mother and his stepmother. He would read these names in stupefaction. The repetitive beauty of Scots names, their combination of modesty and ancient grandeur, their unchangingness (a publican could be called Robert Bruce, a plasterer William Wallace. In Alec's form in school had been an Annie Laurie), perhaps all this had allowed of a mistake. Other women of the same name lay now in Alec's mother's grave and in his stepmother's, another Mairi Dundas, another Jean Dundas. Such comfort was no comfort.

156

They made memorial to the mothers in chat so dry a listener might have heard and thought: These are men that take their women overmuch for granted. Alec's father did what he said, said what he did, and stuck thereto in a way that was falling to disuse.

"Mairi and Jean did good meals," his father said today on this picnic with Alec and Lorna, quickly adding, "Jean and Mairi." He was a fair man all through.

"It's so."

"A bit of fish was what I liked," his father said. It was so, he no longer had a true appetite. These foreign feasts were a way for Lorna to cajole him into pecking. He spoke of himself as a man with dead feelings.

"I went there," he might say of a place, although he was actually at the spot.

They left the bus in the Queen's Park, where it stopped for a while for the driver to eat his piece looking down the town. Alec's long love for the city was still with him, stronger because affronted; he had shared some of his battling furies about buildings blown up and burnt down by greed and by planners with his father, even, after the morning a certain delicate, witty building was flattened, taking away a pair of finials that he set in his father's garden, black stone lupins among the flowers' own blue-and-yellow soft spires.

His father could see his son was angry, but he wanted to believe that good things could not be destroyed to make way for bad, so he continued to hope that the squares demolished and streets torn away would be replaced by buildings full of light and warmth for the safe shelter of human life. He was relieved when the tenements and lands began to be levelled. Anything would be an improvement on these eyeless tall towers, he thought, not envisaging the deaf inhuman towers, all eyes, to come.

They climbed a way towards the summit, through low green grass and tougher grass like straw that caught in loops sometimes around their ankles. When this happened to his father, Lorna signed him to go on and she disentangled the older man. When it became a little steeper, they began to walk along the hill by the paths the sheep had made, dense green turf just a few inches wide, sprung within with roots of tough small flowers. Lorna took his father's arm.

When they had gone high enough for the view to have opened itself up, but not so high that the wind caught them, Alec spread down the rug. Lorna began to extract blue-paper packets of food-stuffs; Alec unclasped the lid of the wine jug and poured three mugs.

"I'm unused to this," said his father, tipping the wine to see what lay below its horizon.

"Yes," said Lorna, "I know. So am I. I haven't had any since last Saturday." It wasn't true, Alec thought, but it was what it was right to say, to josh his father along.

She was drinking then, but without dedication, only to enhance the great pleasingness of their days together.

She went on: "Could you grow used to it with a bite to eat?" She passed over two loose, dripping sandwiches, neither Italian nor Scottish, but understood by the Scots as Italian.

Taking off her shoes, she lay back and drummed her feet on the grass, stretching. Her interesting long body lay all before

Alec's father and Alec was in the same moments angry with her and proud of her. She was covered entirely with her wool dress but he saw inside the blue wool and imagined his father doing so too.

His father was looking not at Lorna's limbs at all but at her face and at the top of her head, where all those thousands of grey hairs began. He thought of death so quickly all it did was give flavour to his wine.

Two blonde young women, one dressed in shorts, both with the full rippling stride of Americans or Swedes, came up the hill, arriving section by great section over the horizon. Such of their conversation as could be heard was implausibly simple, as though they were neither of them English speakers, but had no other common language.

". . . very green. And tall to ascend."

"But there will be many things to look on."

In time, Lorna stopped herself from doing what she always did when good-looking women passed close to Alec. As a rule, she would have protected herself by saying what was good, never deprecating, and always having a care to pre-empt Alec's very particular tastes.

Just before she began to talk, in the way she had devised, like a man, lying there on the hill, before she began to say, "Did you see the way they moved before she did, like cygnets before the swan . . ." she remembered that this habit was a private one and that Alec's father might not like to encounter it.

Anxious, though, to let Alec know he was on her mind, that she had no hard feelings about whatever had made him sharp that morning, she said, "What do we see from here, Eck?"

Depending upon the way she snapped off his name, her mood towards him was clear. Eck was good. Alex she never said, choosing to leave some name for anyone spare to their lives to address him by.

"He'd enjoy that, telling us about the place you and I have lived in all our lives," said his father.

"I'll do it, Dad, if you let me peel you a bit of fruit." He worried about his father's health, his resistance to germs. He cajoled the old man as a parent does a baby.

With his penknife, Alec quartered the skin of an orange, then peeled it back, and carefully picked off the pith from the fruit, leaving a ball within four leaves. Slowly, in order not to rip the membrane, he divided the orange inside into the fourteen segments and six tiny inner umbilical pieces, gently keeping them all just attached to the base of the peel. He sat with his knees up, arms around them, looking out over the city. As he spoke, he dispensed pieces of orange to his father, who ate the odd one and passed the others to Lorna, who swallowed them guiltily, failing to extract the juice.

"The Castle, that's obvious enough, up on its rock, with to the left of it, do you see, down a bit, very low, the shallow dome of the McEwan Hall, the dark circular building, built in the Venetian style. It's all built for the teaching of medicine, yet it's in the style of Italian church architecture. Think of that confidence. There are courtyards and parts of the building that are deliberately modelled on Italian palaces too. There's a huge balustraded hall with galleries, and paintings decorating it inside, including one of the goddess of wisdom accepting the McEwan Hall." By mistake, he ate a piece of orange, saw what he had done and began surreptitiously to peel another one so that his father would have sufficient fruit that day.

"Then past the Castle, there's the Tolbooth Church. It was designed by Pugin who did the Houses of Parliament down in England, and by the great James Gillespie Graham, who did much of the early nineteenth-century city. It's a church for congregations, though its own seems to be shrinking, and it's the meeting hall of the General Assembly of the Kirk, too. It's closely related to another church planned by Pugin, in England again. They were both close to the ideal church of the True Principles of Christian Architecture. Imagine having that certainty. I couldn't tell you the true principles of agnostic potato peeling."

He passed his father, who was now lying on the rug, two pieces of orange, then said, "Want a Polo?"

"I wouldn't say no after all that fruit," said his father. Though the lecture had been like the fruit, better if you forgot it was good for you.

"I'm not lecturing you am I, Dad? Lorna?"

Lorna enjoyed being told things by Alec, always had, knew more than him often enough but let him talk, happy to hear him working out what he thought. She felt close to him like that, hearing the habits of his mind. It was like watching him paint, which he rarely let her do, but when he did it was like seeing a swimming bird from below, through the water, up to the sun, while she paddled down low, tugged by weeds.

"Then you've the University Old Quad Dome, the crown of St Giles's, known as the High Kirk, a very un-Presbyterian term for it, the Cathedral of the Kirk, if you like, but that's worse. Famous for being where Jenny Geddes slung her stool at John Knox. It's a dark church full of old flags and old battles. It began as a big kirk in the Middle Ages. It was made newly Gothic by the Georgians and tarted up within by the Victorians. It has a ladies' vestry," he wanted a gesture from Lorna, so said a thing that might amuse her, "and dagger-shaped windows whose form is called mouchette. Are you awake, Little Fly, yourself?"

"Yes," she said, from her sleep.

"It is full of the dim, thrilling showing off of the noblemen of Scotland. It's crowded with memorials to their courage in arms and that of their men who have considerably less memorial. Among its stones are indigenous Scots marbles from Ailsa Craig and from Iona. It's a crowded dark place, yet it contains a chapel of youth. Its distinction is very Scots, old history still being found each time they set to build anew."

"And the little tower?" asked Lorna. Her eyes were closed, and anyway she knew, but she loved him and she believed the city was involved in their love in a way she had not got to the end of.

"It was built to house the congregation of St Giles's when that became a cathedral. It's plain and light in design, owes a lot to the Dutch. The interior has been gutted."

He had made himself sad. He remembered what had gone in his shortish life. He wondered as he often did what had made a child love a city in this way, a child who had turned into an adult positively unconservative, yet so anxious, in this case, to conserve. For more than two hundred summers the New Town and for more summers than could be counted the Old Town had been growing at a human pace. Now they were being lit from below like great rockets of stone, these buildings, and launched into the future and annihilation. The town that had been drained of a loch two centuries before was being drained of its own nature now.

Six

Ancient Romans preserved loved infants' corpses in honey, thought Alec, and that is what I have done with my mother and my stepmother, preserved them in a sweet suspending medium through which it's hard to see what they were like. Yet people flee their parents, that is clear, just as they cling on to their children. So perhaps I am lucky that they fled me, these two mothers, and allowed me to soak them in sweetness?

Our illusions matched one another, Elspeth was thinking. That is why we married, and now we are paying for it. He will not recover from the death of his first wife because he does not want to. She was perfect like all pretty women who die suddenly. Even the atrocious ones are endowed in the flash of the car hitting the tree with the virtues that might have replaced their beauty had they lived. I'm not jealous of her, but I do not like living up to someone unreal. If it came to that, I would rather live up to someone unreal but helpful, God in Man or something. Trying to be like Hortense would mean doing my nails in the way she did, or worse. For certain those nails are more characteristic of her than the spiritual qualities she grows when Logan is more than usually disappointed in life.

He is served well by the shade of Hortense. She is a standard for me, and a grief for him. For both of us, she is punishment. Her death was part of her life in a fashion one may try to achieve over a long and well-lived life but never achieve; it was fast and ostentatious and symbolic. She was twenty-five. After such an age so obviously symbolic a death would be out of keeping. The death I know and fear will come while I do something as symbolic for me as driving in a fast car was for Hortense; labelling jam, or trying to find out which pair of black stockings is laddered by putting it on up my arms. One thing in his obsessive telling of the life and death of Hortense makes me love him, though. It is when he tells me he went to have his eyelashes dyed so that he could cry safely at the funeral and not look too bad afterwards with the piggy look fair men get after tears. Each of us is maimed, but in a specialised way that seems to make it more difficult, not easier, for us to help the other.

How close I am to being sick; it's the engine and these long rollers. The sick's lying in my neck like the urge to tell a white lie. Under sail, I hardly ever feel sick. Is it the thinking about Hortense? No, I think it really is not. In a way, she is something to have in common between us. As a wife dead, not divorced, she is more alive than a living predecessor.

Elspeth went above. Ahead of them was the double peak of Bora Bora, under a sky like thrown pigment. The sun was a ball that did not shine. She wondered if anyone on the boat was expecting a letter. Letters were the thread along the days of her life on land and she missed them at sea more than any other contact. She wondered how it would be to have a child and to be apart from them for some reason for long periods of time. She thought, and pitied anyone who had to know, that it must be like it was for her to be without letters, but worse by a factor that was the difference between an inanimate letter and an envelope full of human life.

On shore, a fire was smoking in round puffs, iron grey. Within them, yellow smoke streamed out from the land in a thin plume that trailed over the smashed colours of the sky. The thin smoke was separate, bitter-looking, although its source was apparently the same as that of the looser smoke. A gall bladder of something chemical must be burning within something less toxic.

"Electric?" said Logan. There were areas of knowledge he did lay claim to.

"Nick would know," said Elspeth.

"Go and get some clothes on," he said, not turning round to speak to her. "You can't take the exposure."

Once they had felt their way between heads of coral and chosen a place to stop deep in a creek, the anchor went ripping down through the boat and held. When it struck bottom, *Ardent Spirit* rocked and a small island within the lagoon, a *motu*, seemed to rock also, like a tall green yacht with a surf of white sand at its base.

The sea was paler, more fragile-seeming, around this island than around any other they had reached. The lightness of the blue under the dusty smudged sky was thin, unreal, reality being to the Europeans on board something more loaded, thicker. To Sandro the blue was known; he had grown up within reach of such lightness. To Logan, nothing you saw was surprising. He spent a third of his life in America. Moreover he suffered from the feeling of seeing everything for the second time. He was waiting for something to hold his attention, and in the meantime his attention atrophied.

At the side of the creek in which they had anchored were ranked several palm-thatched huts, built out on stilts over the water. Elspeth found herself looking at the two other boats in the creek to see if either of them belonged to the family who had visited her with the shell. One was registered in Noumea, the other in Panama.

"We'll meet them later, I guess," said Sandro. It was his way to move between the islands, make friends, have a jump-up, fall asleep where he had to, and resume life under the discipline of the boat with an ease he did not question. It did not seem wrong or strange to him to use these plates of coral sand fallen into the ocean simply to feed from. The effect was of Edenic innocence. He consumed all experience in the same flat way. Elspeth would think up ways to shock him and then forget it. He'd just say, "Oh, right." He could not be teased because he was so easy-going that he allowed for all forms of oddity in others, markedly in Poms.

Sandro could not take unkindness. He would not have taken it himself and became shifty if he saw it shown to other people.

His trick was to shame the person who was being unkind by pretending not to understand what was going on. That way he disentangled the secrecy of the way people talked, though he did not do it between a man and his wife.

"I know those guys out of Panama," said Sandro. "She's an ugly tub, isn't she? Roller reefing," his voice was dismissive as it would not have been of a person, "and a rear end like a fur seal."

Alec looked at the transom of the boat. It was wide and sloped outwards towards the water. She was painted the brick red of anti-foul paint all over her hull.

"They're repainting her, look," said Sandro. He was right. A man in underpants was sitting in a swing over the side applying paint slowly from a small pot. It looked as though the paint was thick and sticky, hard to get off the brush.

"It's terrible stuff, that paint, smells like polar bears' pits and sticks fast. Hang a man over the side against that paint and he could hitch a ride around the Horn."

To Logan, Cape Horn was the Star of the Sea. It combined the history of courage with the certainty of nature's indifference in a way that thrilled and touched him. In his office in the States he kept videos hidden where no one but he could find them.

A woman called Sigrid had made these tapes for Logan over years. They were made of assembled old film transferred on to video tape and showed old men linking passages of old film, often speaking in thick Norwegian or Icelandic accents. Some few were Poles and others spoke in the rock-faced accents of Cornwall or the Shetlands. Most of the men had faces cut deep with wrinkles; several had stubble that glittered, or frosty overhanging eyebrows. A disproportionate number of the old men looked straight out of the screen with piercing pale eyes. These old men were Cape Horners, men who had been round Cape Horn under sail. Many of them had done it as cabin boys or as deck monkeys, on the tall ships with their more than a hundred sails, all made of hefty sailcloth pulled on hempen ropes, thousands of times heavier, even when dry, than the Terylene and nylon Logan knew.

The films before which he used to sit in his office and weep, as a boy will weep at the death of King Arthur, showed these old men as boys, in flickering black-and-white, high up in the trees of ships, their hair whipped back from grinning faces, the camera wobbling up at them from below as they climbed up masts with iron footholds, or were swung out on a rope to fix a block and tackle caught on a spar over a webby, boiling ocean, shorn and smoking around the Horn.

These short strips of film were like bits of memory, somehow held. The events shown on them, the queenly boats, seemed too magnificent, to Logan, for something so overused as film. For this reason, like a connoisseur, he rarely watched his films of Cape Horn. Each old man would introduce himself before the piece of film concerning his ship: "I am Captain Erikson and I was before the mast on the old *Walpurgis* before she was lost . . . Here she is in 'twenty-three, I believe the cargo was jute. I was fourteen at the time." The boy would appear, in a child's tight jersey, smiling and heaving at the same time on a top gallant or whatever it was. The mind supplied the sound of the sea more accurately than a soundtrack. The sea at its most extreme, recollected in tranquillity, may be Wagnerian. At the time its own great noise fills all the air and it was this Logan would recall.

Indeed, the massive orchestration of Wagner like the sea answered Logan's northern hunger for the tragic. He had less aptitude for the personal than for the wide scale. He had a great urge to patriotism, yet what was his country, Scotland or America?—the one too small, the other too large, in his view. He escaped from them; his urge to romantic patriotism attached itself to the sea.

The old films of old men surpassed incomparably his one home movie of his first wife, wearing short gloves and holding in the one hand a small dog like a mophead and in the other, as so often, a glass, just slightly listing, the Martini in it at a slope. They had visited his mother earlier that day before he made the film of Hortense. Just as they arrived at his mother's house, Hortense said to him, "You are an ugly and unpleasant man. You have no soul." Then she smiled at him very winningly and picked a fleck off his jacket. They were the worst words he had ever heard in his life.

He was surprised sometimes when he heard himself praising Hortense to Elspeth. He knew she understood, it was just a form of piety that set in after death. He had not the time to be intimate, so he was sentimental.

Poor Elspeth, but she probably would do, thought Logan. She was a borderline case really, a bit dreamy, too, but Scots through and through, and he had thought that would matter to him at the end when he came to be an old man. He had forgotten how her failures of competence had seemed sweet to him or how her insistent belief in his good motives had for some years given him a sense of being a good man. Now he had pulled too far away from her. It was his work to trust no one and it had become part of his private way too.

He did not look forward to going ashore unless he would be able to get into the island itself and away from the houses surrounding the harbour. Bora Bora was part of the small world; it was one of those conduits through which many of the rich, members of that world, would pass. Logan, though, was a purist and held himself above this geographical gossip. He would have worked his way around the world on boats had he not been as lucky as he was. He did not embark upon voyages to see people, about whom he had little curiosity, and certainly not to see people he could have met by picking up the telephone. He was not shopping by another means in his travels, unlike many of the rich.

He was also fearful of cosmopolitanism in case he should be caught out. The complications of Europe seemed to him like a fearful exam; he thought he had to know things, would be obscurely tested by masked art historians, not realising open eyes were all he required. His upbringing had combined what was most conventional of what was British with what was most puritanical of what was American. He felt obscurely abandoned by the consolation of art. He was uneasy with the secular since it threw you upon the human, and he mistrusted humans. Periodically, he tore up the books Elspeth left by her side of the bed. It seemed a way to get through to her. He liked music more, the crashing magnificent composers who put him in mind of the sea.

He had no idea that one could at any stage in one's life start to learn.

"Come in with me to the bar?" he said to Elspeth. "It's run by a character. Since everyone else has their own plans, apparently." He sounded piqued, or baffled.

"Yes? A character?"

"A character."

"Oh. I won't, then. But you go."

"I might have a walk. There's a visitors' book and carafe wine at the bar, so I'll give it a miss. A bit frequented for me. It's said to be very pretty, the bar."

"It must be. It's here."

"So, Sandro, off to chase some skirt, a *vahine* or three?" said Logan, a bit uneasy with Sandro's unfailing extraversion.

"If that suits you."

"Course. Could you just make sure she's not dragging and check all the tanks. We should take on water here before we go."

Sandro asked Alec to help him lift and lower the Zodiac over the side. The rubber boat had absorbed the smell of smoke from the shore and seemed slightly greasy. They unclasped the outboard and lowered it on to the Zodiac's stern plate, Sandro squatting in the boat, Alec holding it to with his feet tucking its edge in under the curve of *Ardent Spirit's* white hull.

"I'd like to take Gabriel, she's had a bad go," said Sandro. "But she's pretty crook, I'll leave her be."

"How about Nick coming with you?"

"I will indeed," said Nick, "but I might not go all the way. I might swim off the Zodiac and look for fish." He tapped his shorts pocket. There was the waterproof book on fish of the South Pacific.

Sandro laughed. Nick looked confused.

Alec thought he might wait till the next day. He was tired, and he liked reading in the tropical night, watching the stars.

173

With the dusk music came from the bar, French night-club music, Jacques Brel, Barbara:

Ami, remplis mon verre, ami, remplis mon verre . . .

The sea was black and full of stars, the sky violet.

The music was excitingly, confusingly, appropriate.

Elspeth was humming, flat.

"What slush this stuff is," said her husband. "Nothing to do with the place. What can this man have known of such islands?" Logan went below to find himself a drink. He put on Beethoven's Seventh Symphony turning it up very loud; it came as a salvo, a beautiful thing used as a weapon.

It's peculiar, thought Elspeth, to use serious things in that frivolous way, a kind of snobbery so far from art. And how sad to recall that I used to be touched by his listening to pop and feel I was learning something from him.

She strained to hear Brel.

Je chante et je suis gai, j'ai mal d'être moi.
Ami, remplis mon verre, ami, remplis mon verre.

She heard Logan pouring another drink. He would later collapse. How like their life it was that when they had visited Hiva Oa they had not been to see the grave of Jacques Brel. How like herself it was that she had found it more pacific not to suggest doing so to her husband.

The Zodiac, Alec saw, stopped by the boat registered in Noumea. Sandro stood and held the Zodiac into her side and

Nick climbed up and over the guard-rail. He took off his specs. Usually he just pulled them down and they hung around his neck on the greasy bit of string.

A woman came out of the cabin, carrying a plate that she held out to Nick. He took one of the flat things from the plate in his left hand then threw open his arms. The woman held the plate out behind his back, flat, for a time, while she kissed him.

Sandro was able to make fast the Zodiac, pull himself up on a fender, hop over the rail and take one of whatever it was on the plate, before Nick separated himself, and then he stood and every few moments flicked hair back off the woman's forehead.

Alec heard Logan talking on the radio telephone. He was shouting, though the coast guard on Bora Bora must have a decent line.

He heard Logan finish talking and then yell, "Elspeth."

She came at once. A boat was ideal for this genie and lamp trick.

"Guess what that fire was."

"I can't. Long pork? Or do the tourists turn up their noses at actually eating people?"

"How tired they must be of those comments, these poor people."

"I'm afraid it's an added tourist attraction. Cannibalism. Though God knows it's easy to see how a cannibal might have *his* stomach turned by tourism."

"*Guess what that fire was.*"

The Beethoven was protesting its use as background music by sounding at once stretched and soupy.

"Tell me."

"The post office. Phones melted, letters burnt. No news from home. I'm fine, but you might not like it."

Her disappointment was out of proportion. She expected no letter, though she had hoped for a couple. She had hoped Gabriel would have a letter, perhaps with news of small brothers and sisters, and maybe news from Scotland for Alec. She had begun the familiar pattern of these voyages, the anticipation of small ordinary pleasures to compensate for the large extraordinary ones she was so bad at enjoying.

She went to see Gabriel, who was asleep on her bunk under a white-cotton cloth printed with hibiscus flowers in dark blue. Her hand lay under the basket like a doe rabbit.

She knocked at the door of the fo'c'sle.

"Yes?" answered Alec.

"It's Elspeth." Then she felt foolish. She could not go in to what was his room. That would have some meaning. On a boat the vital prerequisite of feeling human is a small lozenge of space that is your own.

"Come on up," said Alec. She could not hear very clearly.

Elspeth pushed the fo'c'sle door. It gave. There was no one in there, though a reading light was on and under it were arrayed six or seven shells the size of pincushions, seemingly made out of mother-of-pearl. Nick had made casts in salt of some snail shells from Moorea.

Alec's head hung down through the hatch.

"Yes?"

"I was just worried," she said. The tentative word, the sort of word Logan did not receive on his verbal transmitter, made her feel weak.

"Yes?"

"In case you were getting a letter. The post office has burnt down, with all the things awaiting collection in there."

"Oh no," said Alec. He sat up and that lost Elspeth his face. She went back out between the bulkheads and down to the bow to him.

"I am sorry. Were you expecting something?"

"Not really, but now this has happened I can't hope. Now I know I am in the Pacific with, forgive me, a lot of strangers."

"I know."

"People say that."

"I mean it," she said.

Then he remembered. "Say 'post office'."

"Postoffice," she said, as it was pronounced in her part of the world, one word, with the emphasis on the "O".

"Yes indeed," he said. "Oh yes indeed. Of course you are one too. I was put off by the carry-on, all so very English."

"One what?"

"A Scot."

"My name is Elspeth Urquhart."

"Yes, but you get them called Deacon Brodie and they have gone English."

"I couldn't do that," she said, "though I dread the day I need a passport to be admitted. I was born there yet I sound like this." She exaggerated her English accent.

"Come on now; admit you like the feeling of being different in either country," he said. It was an argument he had perfected over the years. His own father thought he spoke in an English voice and abhorred it.

"It would be more patronising to slip into different accents on purpose, but yes, it is odd. There is less place for Anglo-Scots, whatever the word is, than there was. Things are bad. There could be a split. People want it. They sing about it. There was the fish, there is the oil. The stupidity of the South has hurt, the tactlessness that has looked like pillage, the willingness to treat the place like a plaid, to throw on for its ancient rustic glamour and to throw over puddles to save them getting their feet dirty. I fear for the border, I really do."

He laughed at her.

"Here we are," he said, "on debatable lands."

She looked into his face and turned away.

"Which of you is it that drinks?" he asked. "*Ardent Spirit*, that name, I mean. She is named for the drink, is she not, this boat? It's a fine passion, the Scot and the bottle, no doubt. Escape and engagement. And cheaper than all this, by all appearances." He indicated the white, glittering boat. She saw it in a bottle suddenly.

"The ardent spirit who did drink, you're right, is not him, not me. His first wife, and she was French Canadian. In both senses, it applied to her. She was more alive and more full of spirit in every way than most."

"Were *you* expecting a letter?" he asked her.

"No, not like that. But I like letters."

"How?"

"In the sentimental way, obviously."

"Obviously," he said, looking at her wide face with the face of a palaeontologist, or the face he thought a palaeontologist should have, and had practised in the museum mirror while the hot-air machine dried his hands. That was, he looked at her with grave, impassioned concentration, affecting to pity her extreme age and plainness, while also acknowledging in his expression that further research might be rewarding.

Logan came to see what was going on. The first half of the cassette of the Seventh Symphony had abruptly stopped and Elspeth was laughing too much. He had started from a stupor that was more sleep and sea than drink.

"Elspeth," he shouted, a little hoarse, rather deserted. "Where are you? Come to me." It sounded like the voice of a blind man.

She said goodnight to Alec with a nod, and took off back to the stern of the boat, leaning inwards when she came to the stays, a white figure on the long deck. The sea rocked so regularly it might have been breathing.

Logan had said the anchorage was firm enough and the creek sufficiently secure for there to be no watch again that night. So they were asleep, Nick on the yacht from Noumea and Sandro ashore, when the squall came like a gun. Alec recognised what he had heard of: the storm rising without rumour or promise. It was an assault by water and air, sudden as a bucket of water thrown over dogs.

Logan, who was used to springing alert from his sleep, straight on to his legs like a cat, was on deck at once.

"The hatches," he yelled. Gabriel awoke from so deep a sleep that she did not know where she was.

Alec and Elspeth closed the hatches and the companionway cover and were up on deck. The rain came down hard. The boat was twisting and thrashing. Her anchor had dragged. She was veering closer all the time to the red yacht from Panama, newly patched with sticky red paint. In no time, the sea's nature had changed. The boats approached each other through the battered water, determined as great magnets. Worse than red anti-foul all over the hull would be the crushing impact of boat on boat, which could finish them both off. There was no one to be seen on the red boat.

Ardent Spirit screwed over the water towards the red boat.

"Alec, bring up the anchor, I'm going to hold her off with the engine, there's no hope of holding them apart with the hooks."

Alec began to set the anchor-chain mechanism to go and Elspeth ran into the fo'c'sle to guide the chain.

The sea was lifting and suddenly lapsing with a crash. Purple lightning in curtains rolled over the island. An electric heat burst with thunder that never quite stopped between its hard claps. The red boat was close. It seemed futile to attempt to steer against this sea that was rubbing the boats in its jaws.

The anchor was at last up and Logan able to go to full throttle. He forced the boat astern of the red yacht and kept her off like that. On shore Alec saw a man, it may have been Sandro, standing in front of the thatched huts. Then the lights on shore went out.

The thunder grew heavier. It never stopped, just grew louder. The blue yacht was thrashing in the waves, pitching at fretful speed up and down on her chain. Suddenly, a light went on in the red boat. Someone was moving about on her. Under the sound of thunder came a long moan of metal. Her engine started, and she began to move, into the creek, away from any rocks there might be on the coast.

The boat that had felt like a house now felt like balsa to Alec. He heard *Ardent Spirit* strain and fight the engine. She felt like a thing burning, writhing in the fire, no longer possessed of itself.

Then, like a bird falling shot from the sky, the squall dropped and was gone.

"Take her back to where we were," said Logan to Alec, who took the wheel. He could feel the heavy tug of weather helm in the disturbed water, the sulky disturbed low water fighting the boat's rational, designed, directedness. The angered water was less biddable than water after calm.

"I'll drop the hook," said Logan, from up by the anchor. "Elspeth, get below and check how she pays out. Thank God someone's had the sense to move that ugly red monster. We could have been matches and dog chow."

The sky was calm again, the new stars visible, unshaken. The moon appeared with no aura and no face. It was pale yellow.

Though the sea was still loose and running at a spate, its waves had sunk.

Elspeth heard the Zodiac: "Sandro, Nick, are you OK?"

"More to the point, are you?" Sandro held up a Tilley lamp that put his young dark face into deep shadows and made his olive skin glow yellow where the light lay on it. On the thwart of the Zodiac sat Nick, all wet.

"Nick, come and dry, what did you do?"

"Skin dries on its own. I'm great, thanks, Elspeth."

"What did you do?"

"He swam over to the red boat from his wi—"

"I just moved the red one a bit," interrupted Nick. Both matters he would rather leave, Elspeth saw.

"Well, thanks," said Logan. "Quick thinking."

"It could've been a bad scene," said Nick. He was embarrassed, as he often was, by the response of others to things he did that he could not have done.

"I've been thinking," said Logan. The squall had left clear air but on the boat it thickened. "The post office is down. It's a loss for those of you expecting letters. For me it's a grave inconvenience." The things were evidently not of equal weight. "I was wondering if you, Alec, would like to go back to Papeete and do a couple of things for me. I'll enlighten you about them later." When no one else is about, his words suggested.

It was curious, Alec thought, that he had not asked his wife to do whatever it was for him, if he was not anxious to go back to the town. This voyage, presumably intended as a flight from the implications and involvements of dry land, was taking its time in hauling free of them.

"Elspeth can go with you, if you want." If *she* wants, at all? thought Alec, impressed at the way some men have of declaring the outrageous quite normal and making it so. He was so tired he agreed, will-less. The squall had pulped him. It had had the same effect as the alternating kindness and unpredictable cruelty that break the will of trainee soldiers. Was he becoming Logan's man in some way?

Before he slept, he asked Nick, "That was your wife?"

"Indeed. And because of your trip to Papeete, I get to see her for more time. Thanks."

"Don't thank me, thank Logan," said Alec.

He was too tired to sleep, he thought, but was soon below the glassy thin dreams that presage some sort of test.

"It's the certificate to show that the bank has returned the bond I placed with the representatives of the French Government. It's a thing you have to do if you take a boat to an island the French own. They ask for these bonds. Kilo of flesh. When they asked me for it I had a hard time keeping cool. To pay for three feet of the rue Pomare and night after night of polluted air and klaxons seems rich, but there. You seem the type to hold his temper when they take you through the forms." Logan was speaking to Alec.

"Will they not need you there?"

"To *give* the cash, they did. Now they've given it back, any fool will do. I just need the duplicate certificate. The bond's been transferred. It's back in an account of mine. I just want to show them they can't go burning up things that I need for the proper conduct of my affairs." This odd selection of words struck Alec as showing what money had done to words. "I want to keep face."

"But with *my* face." Alec chanced this remark.

"I'll give you a covering letter. There's a word they allow you to choose, a kind of password, as a security precaution, and I'll enclose it. I'm also giving you telegrams to send to various interests of mine. Do not send them from a post office. Use the bank."

Alec used a bank as little as possible, and for such matters as paying a bill. He had no idea a bank could be used as a factotum.

"Here's the stuff," said Logan. Instead of producing it right away, which would surely have been more discreet, he moved the tantalus and swivelled two discs until he had displayed a combination of figures that seemed to satisfy him. He pushed the safe handle down thirty degrees from the straight, and pulled the slow chunky door forward. There was the grey little cupboard.

"If we'd gone on fire like that post office, that safe and what's inside it would have been all that remained," he said. It was a deep safe; before extracting what he wanted, he pulled out a case of brown leather.

"Stupid to have them in a case really," he said, "as if they're going to wait till you've opened it and only shoot after you've armed yourself."

He's showing off, thought Alec. All this performance is a show. Yet he's packing me off with his wife. What has he in mind? Logan pulled out a stiff package so repeatedly wrapped in transparent polythene that it was blue.

It was not obviously threatening. Alec couldn't see what it was. He was fairly sure he'd be told.

He felt a bump as a rowing boat came alongside and he heard the chatter that he had been vaguely conscious of since the dawn. "T-shirts, palm-fibre paintings, truly excellent barbecue pig-out prepared by family only in old ovens . . . T-shirts, all cheap." The boys doing the selling were well fed, listless. There were no girls.

"Ah, here she is," said Logan. He handed Alec a brown envelope, ungummed. "I've put a few francs in there too. As we know, Tahiti's not a cheap place to stay. And I've radioed to book you into the Roi Soleil on the Boulevard Pomare. It serves breakfast, lunch and dinner. Pass me that morphine, would you, and I'll shut up shop."

Logan was peaceful for the rest of the day. He seemed recharged by something. It struck Alec that he was not a fully confident man, that he was undergoing some ordeal he did not vouchsafe.

184

In the Fokker that flew Elspeth and Alec from Bora Bora's small airstrip back to Faa'a Airport on Tahiti, they sat next to a Chinese woman who had a trug containing some new kittens and a bouquet of orchids bound together in damp tissue and then in foil. The purple orchids trembled at one end of the basket on her knees; the tiny cats mewed without making a sound. The Zodiac had brought Elspeth and Alec in to shore, where they had caught a bus for the airport, rather uneasy in dry-land clothes and properly shod in a manner neither had seen before in the other. The novelty seemed to hint at an erotic beginning.

The Air Polynésie hostesses handed out boiled sweets and old issues of French *Cosmopolitan*. "*Quand Bébé Arrive*," read Alec in the magazine on Elspeth's lap, "*ce n'est pas la fin de l'amour . . .*" He thought, as he did when he wanted to record the life he was presently living, of Lorna and Sorley.

Raiatea and Huahine lay so close below the plane that the fronds on the palm trees might be counted. When the plane passed from them back over the water, its shadow refracted neatly.

At Faa'a, Elspeth put on a cardigan and some scent. She was not a coquettish woman. Nor was Lorna. Alec loved coquettishness in short glimpses and enjoyed it when it was accompanied by guilt. Its operations however were too exhausting for companionship. He supposed his ideal was a natural coquettishness, if it could exist beyond childhood.

They made a pair that did not match but did not look so mismatched as they stood in the taxi queue at the freezingly air-conditioned Faa'a Airport.

The Hôtel Roi Soleil displayed a board with slotted-in white removable letters on a ribbed black board. Today it read: "Air-Con, Quiet Rooms, Swimming Poll. Modrate prices minutes from all shoping. Tahiti's most popular night spot, featuring Tiare Apetahi's Orgestra every night. Full Selection of American, Chinese, Frenchstyle Specialties *Trois repas par jour*."

A desk clerk made them welcome, eating from a tub of snacks that she carried cradled to her to the lift. In the lift was one insistent fly and a brass-framed photograph of the hotel itself taken at a flattering angle and transformed to colour from black-and-white. This technique gave a lift of hyper-real, menacing, domesticity. The arcades of the hotel's façade looked seductively sleazy. Alec did not know whether Elspeth was to accompany him on his errands, and was more embarrassed by this than by their being sent together by her husband to a hotel.

"Did you see her teeth?" asked Elspeth.

"The word in Edinburgh used to be that you might as well pull all a woman's teeth when she wed and save on the dentist."

"It's like that here. Some of the most beautiful ones are perfected by false teeth."

He looked at Elspeth's strong big teeth.

"Were you a sweetie eater?"

"In the dark, hiding. Sugar probably does worse things after you've cleaned your teeth. I was a midnight muncher. Shoplifted Mojos and Tunnock's Snowballs I'd pocketed and that had burst so you had to suck them off the cellophane."

The lift arrived. The rooms were off the same dark corridor, lit by a circlet of bud fairylights around a mirror at one end.

The stench of Baygon and Looklens burnt Alec's eyes as he entered his room. It was a room like a brown drawer, pulled out

186

and left cruelly open to the street. He heard car horns and felt the collected heat of the sun as it hung in the dusty brown curtains. A melting dust lay over everything. The bedspread was brown candlewick.

"Do you have roaches?" asked Elspeth. "I have three to welcome me in the bathroom. Did you see them on the plane?"

"I know they are there and try not to make it any more specific than that. Is your room a different brown?"

"Much the same. I have a bunch of dried flowers. Festal. More durable than a garland."

The air-conditioning clattered, wheezed, and brought up the old air.

"It must be noisier for people who haven't been here before. I mean we knew what not to expect."

"That's a dispiriting approach to paradise."

"When do you have to go to the bank? Have you an appointment?"

"Why do you take this treatment?" he wanted to ask her about Logan, feeling the familiar aggression towards a person who already accepts abuse, the underside of the impulse to defend and protect.

"It's at about six, in the cooler time. Will you come?"

"I might shop instead. We'll need some soap."

He went to look. "I hadn't gone into the bathroom yet." Did she want to shop for a couple of bars of soap, or was she making it less embarrassing for him?

The grimy light of the Hôtel Roi Soleil would pinch out the brightest, youngest love, thought Alec. If he were being used he preferred that it should be somewhere remotely pleasant.

"It's odd," he said, "that you didn't visit the Gauguin Mu-

187

seum when you and Logan spent all that time here kitting out the boat. Let's go there tomorrow."

"I know you are a painter," she said. "I am an admirer."

This was unexpected, not comfortable. How long had she had this advantage over him? Only one thing could let her off.

"I didn't know at first that you were you. It's a name you could find anywhere in the world. Logan doesn't know."

"Shall we go to the museum?"

"Uh huh," she said, "I'm off just now for the soap."

The Banque d'Indo-Chine et de Suez was cool, clean, marbled, sweet-smelling, all the hotel was not. Handmaidens in pareos tight as cheongsams stood behind sprays of orchids, daintily working little adding machines. The sensuality that reading and reputation had led him to expect would suffuse the island had struck him only when he saw beautiful individuals. Here in the bank was the sterile temptation of modern sex, sex gone to money. There was nothing sweet about this atmosphere, the sweetness the first European accounts of Tahiti suggested, the sweetness of lagoons below the island's steep black rock.

Monsieur Riquet, the manager, seemed to be expecting Alec, and not to mind that he was not Logan. He was formal, pleased to extend the hospitality of his bank. The telegrams were swiftly sent. A flickering clock told the exact time by flipping pages of white marks on black that joined together to make figures. Alec recalled the Hôtel Roi Soleil, and tried to linger a little. But his appointment was over, Monsieur Riquet pointed out, politely not indicating the clock that tapped time away and surely Monsieur would be wishing to return to his hotel?

Free of his task, at least of its declared demands, he enjoyed the streets of Papeete as he had not on the previous stay when he had been a yachtie, one of a vagrant, unliked community. Now he was able to become his eyes alone.

A khaki-skinned woman with a mouth like a bud, the upper lip brown, the lower hard pink, swayed by. At each joint she was made so small she looked triple-jointed. Her skin glowed over small bones that seemed filled with air. Her robe of hair was an unnatural lavender red. She wore a handbag and shoes that had been made to perfect a *tailleur* and apart from them only a white pareo. Alec walked behind her watching the way she flicked a strand of hair back over her shoulder like a lost child flinging rice, to make sure she was followed.

When he lost her, it was for others, as extreme, as titillatingly unlike one another as could be imagined. Some, even, had fair hair, the garish exciting blonde that suggests much more against skin outwith its own register. It was a hair colour only taken on by a woman wanting to be looked at lewdly. The lewdness, as neon began to hum over Papeete, seemed graceful, even suitable; a personal subversion by the Tahitians of the trade in their beauty. No longer was there a single Tahitian type. Too much blood had been mixed. But the same spirit that condoned the raising of boys as women, *rae raes*, seemed to condone all sexes turning themselves into a thing more artificial, more stirring, even, than flesh, a form of art.

"I've booked at the Soupe Chinoise," said Elspeth, when he got back. She was in the lobby, watching the other guests, who looked pale and old in the dismal room. His legs were tired from following women, his eyes burned out by looking at them. He had done her husband's errand. Need he also watch her eat?

189

"If you're tired, I'll bring something back for you," she said. She knew he could not do that, of course, he thought as he showered (she had bought Fleurs des Alpes) and put on again the pale suit the bank had kept cool and the streets had broiled.

Portraits of Chiang Kai-shek and maps of Taiwan covered the walls. The waiters were old Chinese with thin grey moustaches and starched white bellhop jackets. All the food was middling warm and served in silver baths, very slowly, with some surprise, like a lucky dip. The tangs of seafood in the air, of wine and cigars, were more nourishing and delectable than the pieces of pale rockpool contents they chewed and could swallow only with more beer.

Elspeth said, "How shall we go to the museum?"

"When I went, I hitched. But maybe that's not for you. I checked with the bank manager. He said taxi or bus. I favour bike if you do. It's by Port Phaeton of all lovely names. There is a garden. There are no paintings, never a one. But I still want to go. Do you?"

"This is a bit you can eat," she said. "It's good."

"It's a leek," said Alec.

"I do want to, yes of course, though I fear it will be sad as homes of the artist often are. The pipe, the hat, the slippers, the cradle, the cup; things are heartless. But I have a taste for re-creations. I like the way they never work, the more authentic the worse. Perhaps there will be something like that tomorrow, a half-eaten meal, a *vahine* chopping plaster onions for the artist's evening meal, another grinding pigments by the *tapa* cloth?"

"I think it's quite empty, though there's a *tiki*, if you like those."

"If they are not frightening they are plain ugly, but I like the way one gets awe *and* affection for them, quite hard with an idol."

"What about Ganesh?"

"More awe than affection for me in spite of the trunk."

"Anubis?"

"All awe. The poise."

"Did you go ever to the Royal Scottish Museum?" They had been avoiding their shared country. Talking about Scotland so far from it would be like starting on a bender; they might end up where they did not wish to.

"I saw my first mummy there, first scarabs, first stuffed animal, experienced my first vertigo in the central hall."

He would ask it. "Where are you from?" He dreaded that her reply would make them caught in some way, related by coincidences that would need servicing for the rest of the voyage, explaining to the others.

"Oh, the Borders." So she was wary of it too.

"And you came up to Edinburgh sometimes?"

"As girls from the English counties go to London; for haircuts, dances, book shopping, the theatre. Miss Middleton for brushing up the waltz, Greensmith Downes for sensible dresses."

"We had different cities, then."

"Of all the cities I know it must be the one whose buildings go furthest towards fairness. Maybe Rome, too. It's the past, I suppose, the concentration of things. And it's the seven hills. If you walk among these things you don't forget them."

Far from their homes, they were each struck by the fullness

of their hearts. Each thought they saw the confusion a less intelligent person might have between homesickness for a country and a prospect out down and over the hills ahead into love. Congratulating themselves on their lucky escape they walked back to the hotel, never touching. They spoke about Edinburgh and about the abbey, sacked at the Reformation, by the village where Elspeth was born. It was arches and air now, on the bank of a river over which thin birch trees grew and shook their small leaves. The Borders had the hardest skies to paint. They changed, Alec knew, six times an hour, taking the greens with them. It was the country of black skies, white light, black sky, and the slowest arriving blue on earth that opened like eyes.

"Do you know what I most miss at sea?" said Elspeth. "The walking. And the looking at things that are made by men."

"I don't know yet what I most miss," he said.

The password Logan gave Alec for the bank had been "gull".

Seven

Alec and Elspeth were in the wooden airport boat that wallowed in the dark over a sticky sea; its driver was holding the tiller, his mate shining an Ever Ready torch over the bows as they steered like blind men making lace through the coral reef.

They were listening to three elderly women who sat together on a banquette discussing a film-star for whose children one of them seemed to be a governess. They were comparing travel arrangements in Oregon with those in French Polynesia. Slowly it became clear that the governess used these flat-bottomed wooden boats as often as she might have used buses. Her destination was beyond Bora Bora, on the remote island where her charges lived. She spoke in the dark, not whispering, where the roaches could be heard walking over one another, of the order she had put at the *tabac* in Bora Bora for a regular newspaper from home to be kept to await collection by her employer's boat; the yacht club were very good and kept Nesquik for her and Pillsbury ready-makes that she kept in an Eskimo till they got back to the island and set to bake up in the microwave. She missed nothing but company, she said, and that wasn't everything. Her two friends, who were nearing the end of a long, probably unfamiliar journey, agreed with her. Although they were three old women with white hair and flat rubber shoes, it was possible to feel their strength of personality, their curiosity and impatience with fuss. They reminded Alec of gorse, tough workaday stuff that holds the turf together, flinging out under sun a honeyed, dusty, homely smell.

It took him years before he realised that Lorna would speak to him through the remarks she chanced to make about plants and flowers. She did not want to talk about herself, feeling it burdensome, but if she went round the flat twisting off souring leaves or washing the plants with a cloth, she was hiding something under her nipping orderliness. If she remarked on a drooping clematis in next door's area, or observed the grappling spread of a hard-wearing cotoneaster close to a softer plant dear to her, he had to untwist her meaning, that even she didn't know, that had wound itself around the stem of what she said.

So what was he saying by his reaction that the old women reminded him of gorse? That Scotland had come once more to the fore of his sensuous memory, and, perhaps, that the place had laid down his first and deepest means of comparison. The Bruces, his first companions to introduce him to adults who were both worldly and forgiving, would have enjoyed these islands, would have been old enough to indulge and understand the reason for their vulgar exploitation of their own traditions, their only resource but beauty that could go in a flash.

"Of course, he's world famous, but here he's just another person," said the governess.

Provincial fame cuts the world into parishes, thought Elspeth. It can only be entirely entertaining for very self-important people, distinguished men of letters holding court over mint tea in a café of the *souk* for two hours before the heat of the day, playboy drug addicts hoping to score from passers-through although they have settled in shacks where only cormorants share the garden. Logan's life in contrast has been burdened by his sense of fiscal importance.

The greatest man I ever met was free of himself also, an old thin man in a dressing gown in a room with a bare bulb and a bed as narrow as a pallet, all the walls of the room covered frame to frame with drawings bought for shillings throughout a long life, dedicated with single-mindedness to the appreciation of lines, in chalk, in pastel, in conté. The blessing of such innate certainty relieves people of themselves, thought Elspeth. Perhaps saints were only people of freak aptitude.

Yet certain kinds of intelligence are one-dimensional, exhausting for the possessor often, and sometimes invisible to the world because their application is so rarefied. She thought, as she considered, of the crowning repugnant dish that her grandmother had served on high days, potted head. That was exactly what the unrounded intelligence ended up as, ugly, unpopular, spurned, lost to its body, and passed by other people from hand to hand, at a loss where to stick in the fork: potted head.

The sea was moving less. They had turned into the creek. She saw the lights on *Ardent Spirit* and prepared herself for the reunion with her husband and the look he would give her, like someone threading a needle. He is a man reduced by riches, she thought, and prepared to return to him all balm, to soothe him into feeling, with her, rested, ordinary. Ever since they had first been together, she had felt this optimism just before seeing him. Who, after all, she wondered, has a life that is whole? We are handed broken plates and must fit them together.

What is worst, thought Alec, is that my work has grown in its control, almost classical control, as my life has disintegrated. Does it follow that the classicism must be corrupt, just a cold mineral deposit made by the steam my life gives off? If I see disaster will my work free itself, while holding on to form? But you cannot choose disaster. Will horror heat me through?

The stars seemed to move among themselves, coming forward and receding in brightness.

The wooden ferry moored at the jetty opposite *Ardent Spirit*. Nick was waiting there for them, holding the painter of the rubber boat as it flopped up and down in the ferry's wake.

"I can see the lights of just the one boat besides *Spirit*. Who is she?" asked Alec.

"The tub out of Panama."

"The other's gone then?"

"This afternoon. Bound for Samoa. Maybe Papua New Guinea after that if they can get the papers."

"Might you join them?" asked Alec.

Elspeth looked surprised. She did not speak because she did not want Nick to take any conversational interest she showed for something more, making her her husband's spy.

"Could be. I won't force it. You can always get a lift round here if you're ready to work."

"Glad to hear you say so." Logan spoke from the deck above them, just as Nick brought the Zodiac alongside. It was extraordinary how much you could hear over water.

"How was it, Alec?" he asked. "I rang London and told them to get the bank in Papeete tuned up for you."

If he could ring London, why did he send me? thought Alec. Was not the point of having an unfair amount supposed to be that it simplified life? Yet Logan set up complications like a man putting nails in his own mattress.

Gabriel was on deck, leaning against the mainmast holding a book against her breasts like a napkin after a small but good meal. She wore her white nightdress. In the breeze its collar lifted, a turning page.

"Hi, guys," called Sandro.

"I grounded him because we sail tomorrow," said Logan. "He was out all night the night before."

So may Nick have been, thought Alec, the last night with his wife till they meet by accident again. The randomness of Nick's life briefly seemed more rational to him than the planned lives of those who never spend a night apart. Yet were Sandro's and Nick's absences random or had they been organised as his own had been? Logan had not struck him as a man with an interest in that sort of plotting; it was too untidy, too connected with the personal. He could not see in Logan a bent towards romance of this kind, machinating to secure a night with a pretty girl.

Alec wondered, uncomfortably, if there were some sort of pact between Elspeth and Logan, an arrangement whereby reciprocity cancelled blame. He wondered if he had fallen short and if she would now be in trouble because she had done nothing wrong and thus failed to absolve her husband.

The reef sucked at the edge of the night.

"How is your hand, Gabriel?" said Elspeth. "I hope you rested."

"It's gone," said Gabriel, and giggled.

"Your hand's still there, goose." Logan spoke in a voice Elspeth was surprised to remember that she knew. He was happy at a certain point with a woman, where he had found her weaknesses and remained unchallenged by her strengths.

Elspeth, leaning over the side to get her breath ready for a new stage in her life, held on to her handbag. For one moment she had almost let the earthly thing, containing all the papers that placed her precisely where she *was* placed on the globe, age, place of birth, credit rating, nationality, into the sea. Letting go was easy if you did it so fast.

Would she fight what seemed to have happened? Did she mind? As she cleaned her face in their cabin, she suspected herself of caring more for the short-term peace on the boat than for her own life in the longer view. She preferred not to think of her life over years, either with him or without him. She was, though she did not know it, awaiting a disaster.

Logan slept on deck that night, though he came below to see her. She was wrapping the shoes she had taken to Papeete in tissue and then in polythene, to preserve the leather from the salt that got everywhere.

"How was the hotel?" he asked. "I chose it for the name."

"You couldn't have chosen it for anything else."

"Tell me."

She told him, exaggerating a bit, describing the roach that lived in the towel, the flush that trickled into your hair, the bath that filled from the plug up, very slowly throughout the day, with the water from the air-conditioner's cooling system. She translated the slight things she found funny into broad slapstick for him. The result was that she did not introduce him to her way of seeing, but to some cruder intermediary world. This comforted him but left him unsatisfied too in a way he had not the time to track down.

"How was Alec?"

"He's a nice Edinburgh lad." Not mentioning the painting, she protected Alec.

"Should suit you."

"We talked about museums."

"That's good then. You'll've liked that."

"We visited a museum."

"What?" He sounded both angry and offended.

"Gauguin, you know. It's pleasant, but it's not a museum."

"You said it was."

"It's called one."

"Then I suppose it is one."

"Not in the way you mean."

"Oh. What do I mean by museum? In actual fact?"

She wondered whether to head off the exchange that was coming but couldn't see the difference it would make if she did, so continued: "A dark boring place full of old things you can't have," she said.

"You have made something out of me I am not. And if I am, that is your fault," he said.

Elspeth lay very calmly on her back until the tears had seeped back into her eyes. The difference between the reunion she had imagined and the uncomfortable encounter that had taken place mocked her. How she had failed. The only kind of married love that works is patient without end, she said to herself, yet I gratify myself by jabbing again and again at things I don't even much mind, and he makes himself feel better by having the last word.

Logan did not have his wife in mind as he lay looking up at the stars, arms under his head. Gabriel had flitted along the deck with a cup of tea with a slug of rum in it, and had had the sense to disappear without a word.

He sang to himself the words of the Skye boat song, allowing his rather sweet voice to blur and insert grace notes. He made a handsome picture, Gabriel thought as she watched him unseen, or if not unseen, unwatched. The picture of loneliness he made at the apex of labour he represented enslaved her, as she was ready to be enslaved.

> *Speed, bonny boat, like a bird on the wing,*
> *Onward the sailors cry.*
> *Speed, bonny boat, like a bird on the wing,*
> *Over the sea to Skye.*

Soothed, as he slid through the verses, giving strong emphasis to the theme of death and betrayal, by the vague thoughts of grandeur that came to him in this mood, he contemplated the stars and acknowledged to them, and only to them, his own unimportance.

His wife heard his voice, slack but still sweet like a pear on the turn, and rued her foolhardiness and haste. Nonetheless, she knew not to go to him.

Many's the lad fought on that day,
Well the claymore could wield.
When the night came, silently lay
Dead on Culloden's field.

He would be angry, thought Elspeth, that the bar on shore had put on a loud tape before he had come to the end of the refrain. He did not like the atmosphere he was emanating to be broken. The song from on shore was "Tiger Feet". She did not know the meaning of the title though she welcomed the song's repetitive beat. "Tiger Feet" sounded like a poem by William Blake. She began to play the game that put her to sleep faster than any other, the invention of first lines of books she wouldn't want to read. For the whole of this voyage, her favourite had been: "Mother had given up attending evensong these light evenings and substituted for her devotions some undivided digging." But she remained awake, finding herself many sentences later into the book, apparently a preferable reality to her own.

Logan was humming the song now, stopping to sip something. At one point he made the gasp of satisfaction that beer advertising had taught men to make after drinking.

Elspeth lost the safe thread of the soporific novel and remembered her own first visit to Culloden, where Butcher Cumberland slaughtered the Jacobites. It was the first place she had been to in her life whose air seemed heavy with grief. She was six at the time and did not know much about the battle though it shocked her how numerous was one side and how small the other. She thought battles must be fair. The thought of the big Englishmen on horses and the small Highlanders in their leg-rags and plaids was so obviously wrong that she did not see how the battle had been allowed. Why had someone not, seeing the unevenness in might, called it off? She experienced the ageing realisation that no one can stop things after a certain point. She also thought, and could not remember being told this on that day that she and her mother and father visited the battlefield of Culloden, that believing something a very great deal must kill either pain or fear.

They had driven north to Inverness from Kelso, over roads often not metalled and sometimes blocked by a fall of shale. Her mother drove, looking into the back in the mirror to see she was not getting sick. When she did get sick, which was about once an hour, her mother pulled in at a passing place on the single-track road, held her bent over at a wide angle so that she did not splash herself, wiped her mouth with a handkerchief, gave her the water-bottle for swigging, and handed her back the lemon to smell. Every long journey required a lemon. A man off the MTBs in the war had told her father lemons were excellent against seasickness. On that MTB her father had not had a lemon, of course, but even the thought had helped, he assured Elspeth. She loved lemons but the smell had become associated for life with vomiting.

After being sick, the sense of lightness and the airy head were almost worth it. As they drove further north, there were heather and bog cotton and bog myrtle growing in the roadside, and the puddles on the road were full of bright blue sky. She had seen no blue like this blue of the Highland sky, a thin colour without any weight in it and full of wind like a sail or a bell. The country was brown and gold on either side of the road and up ahead where the same road curved back and over at the summit of the lower range of peaks she could see; along huge stretches it was purple, then tawny, and through it off all the slopes cut clefts within which water ran.

Sometimes the sides of the mountains had fallen away and the blue or black or green stone shone in the sunshine or deepened the shadows that rushed over the land. A flash like quartz or mirror glass at intervals shot out, a deep pool of standing peat water catching the sun. Sheep lay on the road and got up on their knees and then their hoof-tips to teeter off. There was blue snow at the heads of the furthest mountains and the air seemed to grow wider all the time.

Rushes in the corner of a bend might indicate a loch to come, a thin forearm of water reaching inside a fold of land, blue-feathered and abruptly brown-feathered again as the light fell. The greater lochs they passed turned to black when you could see their mass, though the rims were brown and a coal blue shone out of them before they seemed like huge clouds themselves to remove all the colours, until Elspeth would suddenly see, against all that flickering deep black, something small and natty, a heron dipping and withdrawing its filled beak, or a clump of yellow flags, blowing with the white bog cotton. Trees save those planted like soldiers for a game of war, battle formations in evergreen, had given up, though around big houses tough windbreaks flowered a washed-out purple, the ineradica-

203

ble stain of ponticum. In the heart of such thickets a tall house with small eyes and silver towers might wink. Smaller houses clustered together around roadsigns, barrels of old rain at their sides, the daffodils of the second spring she had seen that year just turning to paper. In the borders they had been gone for three weeks, in the South for over six weeks.

The sky even as it darkened over Loch Ness was full of light, right up to when her mother put her to bed at the bed and breakfast in a village outside Inverness.

"I know what the little one will have," said the woman whose house it was, smiling in agreement with something they had begun to see. Into a jelly glass she decanted half a tin of strawberries, purple and loose in the red juice, then sugared them amply and poured on milk from a tin.

Elspeth sat up in bed late with this treat, watching the sky through a window recess two feet deep. When she took the cover off the bed, whitewash rubbed from the wall on to her arm. She rubbed her hands on the wall and transferred the bloom to her cheeks. In the propped dressing-table mirror she saw the good effect tinned strawberry juice and whitewash had upon her lips and skin. The grass and reeds and leaves and rocks outside shone with all the water they held. She watched them through the deep window with her new face. Then she lay down and shut her eyes. When her mother came to see her, she went away leaving her shoes behind so as to make less noise and came back with Elspeth's father.

"It's not what we'd hoped for, Callum," she said, "but she is beautiful."

"I don't suppose," said her father, who may have known fine

that she was not sleeping, "she cleaned her teeth." Elspeth heard him pick up the jelly glass and the spoon off the crochet runner by the bed.

"Bring your shoes, we'll go a walk," he said to her mother. "We've two hours of light." It was half-past nine at night, she'd seen it on his wristwatch as he bent to look at her and she peeped at him as she had learned to do from watching dogs at work in their sleep.

She woke later, when they came in after their walk, their cheeks that they laid to her own cold in different ways, her father's like a leather book and her mother's like a satin cushion that should not have been left out. When she looked out of the deep window she saw the sun's last whiteness lie so close to the land that all the water held in it seemed to rise and glisten to hold the sun from departing, while its skin of light showed every blade of vegetation sharp and doubled by reflection.

The morning came too soon for a family used to the darker-for-longer nights of a Borders spring, not stretched open by the Arctic Circle.

It was a wet sky. There was little to be seen beyond one's hand. Such days are not to be trusted. Within half an hour they may disrobe and let the eye pierce the thin air as far as Perthshire.

"Culloden this morning, I think. Vile weather's ideal for that."

"An open space, no cover, a child."

"Ideal. Do you want to honour such a place in comfort?"

The reverence Callum Kerr had towards his own Scottishness came out in his speech, which held on to Scots usages in an accent barely Scots except to the ear attuned to the Borders bite at words. He also wanted to keep the past alive; though his intelligence suspected that much of the tradition owed itself to nineteenth-century invention and a wish in the Scots to be other than the Irish, his heart swelled in a way he could not stop at the old songs and stories. This access to something he could not describe but that filled his heart when he heard, for instance, the word "Locheil" or the talking crackle of heather burning, he wanted to pass to his child. He supposed he wanted her to have those things he could not describe but knew he did possess, loyalty and a sense of place, as a father with faith might show the way to his child. They are things only taught over days and without speeches or set pieces or the child will smell a rat. It is this passing over of things neither generation can easily name that is lost to an absent parent, and lost to the orphan.

Culloden was the day's destination, then, because it was a place where a horrific thing had happened in the history of Scotland, and because he was a pacifist and hoped that there would never be a need again for his daughter to take that decision, but, if faced with it, to decide as he had, against war. He decided too late, after participating in war; not fear made him see it, but pity. He saw his friends' faces in the water, merry with terror, already like skulls, baring their teeth in burning water, drowning in and under fire.

Each time Callum Kerr had visited the field of the Battle of Culloden it had not been a place to put you in mind of glory, but somewhere so haunted that you might as well have seen the blood. Now he wanted to see if its effect upon him lay in his knowledge of the place or if his daughter, who, at six, knew nothing but how to please, would feel it too. His wife, he knew by now, would cleave to her scepticism; her principled atheism left her no room for atmospheres, though in this case she did allow for plenty of unacceptable facts.

Their Popular was two-tone, two shades of green like the contour lines on a hillock as shown on an Ordnance Survey map. It had not been what they selected at the showroom but it was undeniable what the attendant had said while he watched Callum write out his unprecedentedly large cheque: "A green car in the two shades will fit in wherever you go touring." It was a nice car, with a set smile to its face like some tolerant deaf person, and it took them about, no trouble. Like most men of his age, Callum drove in a way he had found out for himself; he was reliant on the brakes and turned round to talk to whoever was in the back with complete trust that his hands and feet would carry on regardless, never mind the whereabouts of his head.

"Lemon, rug, boots? Raincoats? Sunglasses? Jumpers, headscarf? Kodak, map, knife?"

Callum was poking his head in through the window at his wife and daughter to whom this list was addressed. They did not nod or interrupt until he had stopped entirely mentioning items. Elspeth wondered when these lists would begin to include things they could never need. The lists were the worried voice of domestic concern. Her mother did it back when they each set off to work, she with her music case and warm cardigan: "Hat, gloves, coat, pencils, paper, cough candy (if it was summer, Extra Strong Mints), ruler, petrol, keys, galoshes, graph paper, newspaper." With that list she could burden him with love, still mentioning only the necessities of his day at the map publishing house up in Edinburgh, to which he caught the train every day of the week.

"It's a pleasant journey, right enough. You can never tire of such multiplicative greens. And when you speed along the sea that's a holiday in itself. Imagine, what a great thing it must be to go to sea in time of peace. The journey gives me time, I always say, not takes it from me; anything I do on the journey has an extra aspect. I think: I'm doing two things at once. I'm riding on a train and I am drawing the riverbed of the Esk, which is gaining new wiggles from the juddering of the train. I am reading Herman Melville and I'm riding on a train."

The drive to Culloden was slow as they grew closer. A herd of small black cows belted with white walked without interest towards the next part of their day. They did not look to be dairy cattle. The straggler turned and showed the white edge of her eye to the Kerrs sometimes and once, as all cows must when watched intently, she let fall some cowpats without breaking step. The car was warm inside, the cows and the low mist also insulating. The combination of pastoral and comfort did not much suit Callum's idea of arriving at a place of blood. Elspeth was giggling at the cows' nonchalance.

Abruptly, the cows were gone, turned after their leader through a gate hard on the road, and hidden behind a dry stone wall now in some yard. All there was of them was a newsy mooing.

In the mist there seemed now to grin a little colour. There was a white centre to it somewhere ahead of them that sent out light. The grey seemed to cook out of the mist, like water out of an ironed sheet. It thinned. What had been solid became layers to be passed through and then swivelled to become layers to pass between, horizontal, lifting, light layers that with no hurry were gone, leaving a day shining like the inner face of an eggshell, exposed.

The yellow shorn glen on either side dried off tawny and began to stir under a wind. The mountains held a blue to their sides near the sun that ran down them where the clefts made shadows. Higher up, they were black and shone where snow was melting at a torrential rush that was from the green Ford Popular slow to invisibility.

Elspeth was not feeling sick. No one had asked if she felt sick, either.

"Are we nearly there?" she asked, which was the other way of getting attention.

"We are." Her father shut off the car with the key like a man shutting a cupboard. "Put on your overshoes, Elspeth."

These were thin boots with a flat button. It was like having each foot down the throat of a fat dead fish.

"Out you hop." Callum did not want to influence or load his child's impression of Culloden. He wanted to know if her skin crept as his first had when taken as a child to Glencoe where the Macdonalds were murdered as they slept, a fact he had not known when he began to shake with cold in that bleak glen in 1934. His sense of evil left behind to float free and reestablish itself was strong; he, at the age of six, had identified his feeling. He felt as though, just out of sight, there were wolves, grey among the rocks, brown among the bracken, furred but not warm, just covered to perfection.

What a dull old place anyway, thought Elspeth. Flat, brown,

dull. The sun was out now though the ground was wet. Her hair was taken up and shaken by the wind. There was slapping noise as some rooks got up from a stone some yards away, making it into the air with slow flaps. They were ugly, bald-cheeked birds with a smell like cats' breath.

The ground, she noticed, was not still. A minute shaking filled it. Something below was stirring or something very close by but silent was passing so close to them as to make the ground tremble. She had not imagined the solid earth might shake. She knew it rotated only as she knew her parents would die one day, as a rumour put about by people who had no proof to offer her.

The shaking under the earth seemed to be intensifying, forming itself around Elspeth. Could her mother and father feel it? Her father was writing in a notebook, her mother watching him with great interest while feeling in her bag for something. More of her mind is in her handbag looking for a cigarette than is with my father, thought Elspeth. She knew she was right. Her mother took out a cigarette and put it in the middle of her mouth, then turned with her back to the wind to coax a flame from her lighter. The dirty smell of lighter fuel spoiled the perfume of tobacco. Her mother put the cigarette between the first two fingers of her right hand and moved her mouth towards the hand, not the other way about. It made her look like an elegant lifesize doll. The smoke she seemed to drink, eat and then breathe out when she had taken all the goodness from it.

Neither parent, apparently, was receiving the persistent throbbing from under the earth. It was now beginning to steam up out of the ground, a beating without sound but reverberant, terribly reminding her of things she had heard of but did not want to understand. Most of all she feared that she was about to be shown something that would change her life. She did not want a changed life. She liked the one she had.

The shaking was not only in the air but in her own bones. Rumours of something she was unprepared to look in the eyes trembled through her legs, up through the basin of her pelvis, making her want to pee and cry at wanting to do so. She wondered if she was going to be sick, but it was not that. The trembling was distant and also inside her, not a fluttering but a deep redistribution of the rhythms of her organs. Something breaking out from below the earth or laying an unbearable burden on it was approaching, and it would arrive through her. She shook. Her face was alive with a concentration that was what Elspeth could in these moments accumulate of prayer, she who had been taught that prayer was not just useless but wrong. Feeling what she took to be the devil, she took up the only remedy she had heard of.

It had to be Elspeth who spoke first.

"Why didn't you tell me?" she said to her parents, believing them omniscient still, and knowing them good.

"Why did you bring me to this place? It is bad."

Callum Kerr shook himself for experimenting upon his child. He took her by the hand and walked towards the stone the crows had flown up from. Seeing what he had thought a stone was a dead sheep on its side, the head a bare trophy hanging skew off the sodden fleece, he turned her and they walked a different way. How had the Highlanders marched, men unused to flat fighting in company, preferring the hand-to-hand of skirmish, swordsmen not gunmen?

"There was a battle here."

"Is it that I feel?"

"It may be. Mother would say not."

"Doesn't she believe in evil?"

"She would say not. I fear I do. But I know there is good, more certainly."

"I'm tired."

"You should be. I have the rug. Will you sit on it?"

Callum spread the rug. It was made of mohair and bubbled under its soft long fibres with reassuring stitches that were raised like poodle fur. Elspeth lay down and slept for perhaps ten minutes, stroking a fold of rug again and again. The familiarity of the rug leaked in to her; when she awoke she was no longer trembling.

The sky was too clean, the earth too bare, to hold the complicated terror she had felt. She looked up.

The pouring song of the lark, hardly audible but quite clear, came down to them.

She and her father walked hand in hand over Culloden Moor, telling its inches and the weak parts yards wide where a man who fell would be drowned in black mud, and at half-past three in the afternoon, after eating the paste-and-tomato sandwiches provided by their landlady, they came upon what they could not have expected, the nest of the lark. They saw it from six feet away, noticeable though perfectly camouflaged, exactly because of the perfection of its needlework and fine freckling among the darned and mottled turf of Culloden. They left it alone.

———

That was the first time I consciously saw a white lie, and it was told by a bird, thought Elspeth, on the boat. The lark that was not singing but guarding the nest ran to and fro holding its wing at an odd angle as though it was broken, just to make the predator it thought we were take *it* and leave the eggs in peace. A white lie made for its nestlings.

Gabriel is not yet hatched, she thought, rocking in her berth inside the boat her father never saw and would have feared for its competence. He had been a man with superstitious, inhibiting misgivings about things that worked; he preferred the gentler challenge of things requiring a bit of going-over before they could be encouraged to splutter into life. He found something a little fascistic about things that worked first time.

The throwing away of a tool or machine because it did not work was decadence itself in his eyes. Something could always give its constituent parts to something else; nothing that was broken could not be saved with time and patience. The execution of the boat would have shocked him with its directness. Machines that worked lost a beauty for him.

"You sound almost like you are on his side," Logan would say, when she defended an underdog, even sometimes a villain, when she pleaded for reprieve for some person or thing that had fallen short of perfect function.

"I can't help it, I am like Dad." She had not realised it before.

"Yes, you are. And he is a failure." The faint shame about her father she had felt intermittently for years fell away for good on hearing those words. What Logan had said was true for a world that his judgement on her father freed her from for good.

The failure of her father struck her as pure and incorruptible, new and flexible and responsive. Success was a metallic thing with a brassy note, failure more modulated, harder to tune, but an instrument for the mutuality of man.

Each extremity of her conclusion was artificial and misleading. She had replaced success with failure as the right way to set about the world.

"You either ride the tiger, or get eaten," Logan said. "And your father would get eaten. In the real world."

"The Real World" was the place Logan knew and Elspeth did not. It was home to almost everyone who lived "Real Life", people who understood how the world worked and could explain it to you in sixty words or fewer.

"My father would get eaten, but the tiger would get tremendous indigestion," said Elspeth. "He might have to change his stripes."

"A leopard changes its spots, not a tiger its stripes. Your father is an idealist." Logan left the conversation at the point where it could sink no lower.

" 'Your father is an idealist,' " repeated Elspeth to herself, almost ready to sleep, testing Logan's sentence pronounced upon her father in her own game of sentences. It was not offputting enough to get anywhere much in her game of offputting first sentences, addicted novel readers having a taste for reading about failure, whose implications are so free and aerated beside the certainties of success.

Gabriel lay in her bunk, talking into the tape machine, cupping her hands around it as she had cupped her hands around her schoolwork as a girl. Neither secrecy was, or had been, needed.

Below her, in his bunk, Sandro planned the homecoming he would hit his parents with. He reckoned they could get a few days off if he warned them. Then he was going to take them down to Geyserland and put them up in a motel with sulphur baths. His mother moved stiffly around the kitchen; she insisted on using black pots made of iron that each weighed more than a pig. She cleaned the risotto pans with salt and lemon after the last eater had gone, and sluiced the kitchen down whatever the time. Her hands were impregnated with the smells of bleach and garlic. He would soak the work out of her. He planned the country drives he would take them on if he could borrow a pick-up. He knew a guy with a fruit farm; the farm was a failure, but as far as Sandro knew the guy still had his pick-up.

"It's the fault of you guys my yield's got to be pulped or sold cheap for syrup. Kiwi fruit was good gear till the Eyeties come into it. Christ knows what I'm to do with an acreage of hedgehog bollocks that I could've kept down to sheep."

In the end Sandro's friend Norm pulled out of kiwi fruit after getting a reasonable deal from a frozen luxury desserts manufacturer who operated by one of the wharves in Auckland and did not go bust till after the cheque to Norm had gone through. Insecurity added ill-temper to the normal Kiwi xeno-phobia, but Sandro did not mind it for himself; he relished hav-ing easy jokes among his friends.

The types they made out of every nationality other than their own were so crude they could only be jokes. The only place it struck him as bad was with the Maoris; there was a big wide street in Auckland where there was a shop that sold small things you might need, snap-shackles, hammers, buckram tape, and a couple of things for women like soap and disinfectant and nappies. It was a depressed shop, but in its way it flourished. There were two reasons for this: one was that many people forget the thing they most need, and have to buy it unplanned; the other was that people came to the shop, which was named The Necessary, to read its windows.

Every inch of window space in the shop was taped from within with long messages from the keeper of the shop and those who thought as she did. The messages were addressed to any Maori who might be passing by. "You think yous the same but yous not animal scum. Dare to come in show yourselfs not chicken. Fist time I met one of yous he had a bone in the nose no garments to speak of and was illitrtit now it's the dollar and where does it all go. DOWN THE THROATS of begging men that eats lizards and gets kids twelve a year." These notices were written in close, small lettering that moved in and out of capitals like the voice of a blind drunk.

Sandro had only ever seen non-Maoris reading these notices, which changed frequently and must be brought in by some shoppers. He wondered if Maori passers-by identified the shop for a place of hostility, if it was famously putrid like the tramp whom you stepped over the road not to smell, the one who ate soap and consequently thought he was washing each time he peed in his clothes. Sandro's mother gave this old guy—Soapy was his name not surprisingly—soap in bargain lots, shrink-wrapped; she hid cakes of cake in with it, for Soapy to eat and get the nutrition.

He would take his parents away from the town where people feared those different from themselves. He would show his mother and father the hot blue sulphur lakes of Rotorua and in the evening they would have trout he had tickled himself, cleaned and cooked in the blue, like in a restaurant where you did not do the cooking yourself.

He had grown so used to the talking of Gabriel and found her English voice so uptight that he could not understand it very well. Sleep began to cover him. He heard through the hull the swill inside the waves.

"I've met someone very nice here," said Gabriel into her tape recorder. "I think you would agree."

Where the hell did you meet people cooped up in a boat like this, Sandro barely wondered, though he tried to hook into his mind that in the morning he must take a fresh look at that Alec.

Eight

The retreating view of Bora Bora was at first fresh and overbright like a paste gem. *Ardent Spirit* put out to sea, at last, beyond the reef. Land left by boat appears to slip away at the same rate as time. Time comes alongside.

Every space within the boat was once more loaded for the voyage to Tonga. The last thing they had bought on Bora Bora was a tank of outboard fuel for the dinghy. Elspeth carried it home in a plastic demijohn. It sat fair on the slats in the bottom of the dinghy, plastic top secured by a springy loop on the base. The thread could not have been properly engaged, though, because when she passed the demijohn up to Alec, a little fuel trickled from the neck. On the deck, absorbed at once, it seeped,

shockingly wide, over the teak. It was sudden and disproportionate as a nosebleed.

Gabriel was watching. "Don't worry, Elspeth," she called,
"I'll clean the deck."

So Logan heard, and came, as he would not have had Alec
gone below without comment to find the holy stone.

"Lovely work, Gabriel. Careless or what, Elspeth?"

By the second day at sea, when they were settled into the
watch system, the sense of dedication to making a passage involved them all. Thoughts of the boat came before thoughts of
themselves. This was so even for Alec who had not lived at sea
before.

Sandro was the lightest and best at handling canvas, so he
was busy on the foredeck when he was not doing his turn at the
wheel. He slept quite often in the sail bin, a privilege earned by
being the one who mended the sails, folded them with Nick or
Alec's help and returned them to their light bags. Sandro had
made long trips in boats not merely without the refinements of
this one but with only two sails and no cover but tarpaulin. This
did not make him despise the elaborateness of this boat, but
made him aware of how much more could go wrong on *Ardent
Spirit*. The boat he loved most was a simple metal craft named
Joshua. He had never been in her, but looked at her in awe
whenever they shared a harbour. She had been around the Horn
the wrong way. Her skipper was her sole sailor, though sometimes he travelled with his wife, who was beautiful. *Joshua's*
surface was fitted at intervals with metal handholds, so that you
could sail her in all dimensions, at all angles. She was a hull and
sails, tough and refined.

Sandro remembered to look for signs of an attachment between Alec and Gabriel, but he would rather watch waves than courting couples, so he could not be sure there was not something he'd missed. Nothing was visible to the naked eye, but.

Once, as he was helming, and the stars were so many they seemed about to join up the dots, he wondered if Gabriel was interested in him. He let it go because he knew the only way to live in a cabin the size of a double coffin with a pretty girl was to cut all that out from day one. Anyhow, he liked Gabriel OK, but she was so English she was foreign to him. "Dear Mummy," she would say into her machine, talking into it so quietly and politely.

It made him think her home must be like a nice game of tennis, fluffy white balls of talk moving to and fro between people who knew how to reply and manoeuvre their feet at the same time. She *was* a pretty girl, helpful and a decent sea cook as far as they could tell in the reasonable weather there had been so far, but sometimes he thought her acts of unselfishness were not made to be accepted and forgotten as they should be on a boat or in a family. She was an orderly girl with white teeth who folded her clothes although she was keeping them stuffed in a sail bag, a nice girl whom he could not fault, did not want to; he watched her for signs of the openness he admired in New Zealand girls and found little of it. By openness he did not mean coarseness, but the adventurous refusal to be upset by new things that distinguished many of the girls he knew, and almost all the ones he'd met at sea. Gabriel was dangling herself in front of life when life was there up ahead of her waiting to be grabbed. He thought she had things the wrong way about. Instead of harnessing life, she was waiting to be harnessed.

He supposed he could blame it on her being a Pom, but he

was not mad about doing that. Still, if there was one race you could roundly abuse, it had to be the Poms. They were truly the root vegetables at the barbecue.

The ruminative pace continued, dayless, divided into blocks of four hours. Nick and Alec did the two till six, Gabriel and Sandro the six till ten, Logan and Elspeth the ten till two, and then again. In practice, everyone was available for an emergency by night or day. Gabriel and Nick did most of the cooking. Alec found that he liked washing clothes in a bucket by hand. For jeans they used salt water so the jeans were never completely dry, because of the hydroptic salt in them.

"The only time I get to read is when I'm at sea," Logan would say, before returning below to mark his charts, leaving the book in the wheelhouse. It would be a book of utter dryness, business memoirs of the unimpeachable kind, perhaps, or the analysis of certain stock performances. If someone had given him such a thing, it might be the memoirs of a politician without reputation and with less to come. All of these subjects fertile in good and evil and bursting with lesser skulduggery interested Logan when they were least human. The human content in fiction was what put him off. "It's all lies. Why should people want to read lies? I don't see it. Poetry, maybe. The point of it is to take your mind off life."

Alec looked up at this. They were on a broad reach, an angle to the wind when a sense of almost personal power and strength flows through the people borne by a boat. The water below them was deep as mountains, as cities.

Alec could not agree that the point of poetry was to take your mind off life, nor was it the point of any other art. When he looked at Logan, who stood at the wheel, blond hair whipping his head, eyes looking into the sun, he realised that Logan's words had not been the pure expression of his thought. They were what he said on this particular topic, poetry, when it came up. Thought had not entangled them. Logan was a man of whom it was said that he was deep, by people who had never been near water.

Elspeth read novels, Alec observed. Where was she keeping them and where had she found them?

He met her eye after her husband had defined the point of poetry. Her look was calm but preoccupied. She might have been answering back in her head, but it was not possible to tell. She sat at her customary highest point in the stern. She had told him she called her position there the coward's crouch, because she was furthest from the foredeck where the sails were handled, yet could show willing at once with additional winching or the making fast or stowing of ropes.

"Where do you get your books?" Alec asked Elspeth.

"I swap them with other people on boats. We write where the book travelled from and to and pass them on again. I had a Somerset Maugham that'd been one and a half times round the world. It was a good binding. Most paperbacks are getting crackly or have mould by the end of a circumnavigation. The West Indies finish off most books, too. The suntan oil and the drink combined. The things people fight over are funny."

"What do you mean?" asked Alec. He noticed that the skin of her shoulders, nose, collarbones had settled down now and lost its high colour. She was a dark pink brown, and the skin had toughened up. She was weathered, literally, he thought, and it is more becoming to be tanned.

"In the hot parts of the world they will give anything for

books about cold places or coldish things, the law or stories set in London. Antarctic and Arctic ordeals are very popular. In the cold parts, it's steamy tales of slavery, the Deep South, juleps, all that. It must be that people are interested in where they aren't. And diet books and Shakespeare are the most popular of all."

"What do you like best?"

"At sea? Or on land?"

"At sea," said Alec.

"That's lucky," she said. "I can't remember having been on land."

"What is it, your favourite?"

This was the most intimate conversation he had had since speaking to Nick about his son. It was in a way more intimate, since he was showing interest in another person.

"I like dry, sad comedies about the lives of women and children. I find picture books get lost among the sea, though reading about pictures at sea is wonderful. Your mind's eye is cleaner. Adventure stories, all that, as you would expect, Conrad, Stevenson. I read them on land and remember how I hated the sea and how I miss it. Nothing in all that bowsprit and binnacle lingo. It holds back the human life and reeks of the salt."

"You mean the lamp?" asked Alec.

"That's right," said Logan, "you just chat away."

Elspeth refocused her eyes to find out the source of his ill-temper.

"Take the wheel," he said to Elspeth, "if you feel you can afford the time."

It was halfway through his and her watch and she had forgotten. She put down her book, went into the open wheelhouse and took the wheel from her husband. It was heavy this day and pulling deeply. A slight twisting from under the boat added to the thick bias to port the wheel seemed to show. She let the wheel go momentarily to let it untwist itself so it felt looser in her hands, easier on itself.

Logan reached over in front of her and held the course, passing the wheel back to her when he had balanced it exactly with the wind. He had a musical sense of the water and the wind and the wheel.

When he gave her back the wheel the boat almost flew. She would never want to be free of him. He had entrusted her with himself aloof and she must take it for the trust it was.

"Gabriel," called Logan, "get up here and do yourself some good. Leave those pots." But it was Nick in the galley. Gabriel's brown small face emerged from the sail bin, then the rest of her, in a pair of yellow bloomers with a frill, and no more.

Alec looked at Logan who said, "Get yourself and me a drink. And anyone else who wants."

Sandro had worked on boats where the girls went bare all day, and if they were pretty he was fine.

Alec realised he was the one who was looking for something to say. All along, this expedition had never been spoken of as a holiday, though he supposed that was what it was. Gabriel's dainty brown near-naked form aroused a holiday feeling. He looked at Logan, a man testing himself for no reason Alec could guess, and decided to say nothing.

It was an odd holiday for Alec, after all. He had come on this boat to repossess his innocence. The pleased childlike reaction to the sight of Gabriel rising from the sail bin might have been a step towards that recovery.

"Sprite," he said to Gabriel, a request and a light compliment.

"I'll have the same, and Elspeth," said Logan. Because the wheel was live but not quarrelsome in her grip, Elspeth was pleased by his assumption of her wants as she would not have been if other things hadn't been going well. How hard for men to be married to women, she thought. How we talk to each other and the sound does not carry because of the tempests we ourselves set up.

"I'll take over from you in a while and we'll put up the biggest spinnaker," said Logan. "You'd like that, wouldn't you."

The boat righted herself as the reacher came down, wet all along the lower edge that had sometimes been in the water. The lowering sail came down with a sound like broken bells, a combined ringing and clacking of metal from the blocks and shrouds. Everyone was up top for the setting of the spinnaker, a piece of cloth that looked fine like silk but was made to take the attack of the wind and exploit it. As the poles were set, it began a liquid slapping in the bows, accompanied by a sharp loud rustle. It was like the arrival of a robed queen. The white and silver-grey sail was up to its fullest, high out over the bow of the boat. The silence surrounded only one distinct sound, the running of the water.

So still and soundless was the huge segment of material that they felt as though they were not moving, although they were going as fast as they had been before.

The boat cut over the ocean in state so free of interruption as almost to be abstract, achieved by simple practical means. Alec thought that this state was something like the state of the mind when thinking is going well, or work.

I said to him things that never could be true; it is what one does in love, thought Elspeth, and now I must go with them as the heavy boat goes behind its beautiful, unbelievable sail.

Nick had brought up the onions he was peeling, and sat amidships dropping papery skin overboard. They were a day out from Bora Bora, too far from land for a bird to come at once to take the peelings and not far enough south for the albatross.

Gabriel and Sandro were playing magnetic draughts. She was good at games and very interested in winning. Sandro was good at games but couldn't care less.

The silent exertion of the still but hauling spinnaker seemed to extract the force from each particle of air that pushed it from within, pressing on into and displacing at the same time the caves of air it pushed aside as it advanced. It was as hollow and full as a dome looked up into from below, as daunting in its man-made suspension that held apparently apart from trivial man. To look at its top was to strain. Its sway over the space within it and the residents of its haul was architectural. It used air as a sacred building will.

It was Sandro who was watching the spinnaker when it exploded.

He looked to Logan, whose anger was such a great part of him, and waited for the reaction to the searing that had been so sudden and violent yet almost silent. It was like seeing a cartoon without its caption, the huge white spinnaker with its silver star being thrashed through by another star, the blue sky.

"It's past mending," Logan murmured. "They all go quite soon. It's the fineness of the fibre."

When impersonal events might merit anger, he did not have it where his boat was concerned. He indulged her as he did not his wife.

Ardent Spirit settled but progressed before the wind.

Alec wondered whether to say what was in his mind.

"It could be getting tangled round the screw," said Sandro. "I'll take a look."

"Take all her sail down, now," said Logan. Nick, Alec, Sandro and Gabriel hauled down canvas, bundled and bound it, while Elspeth held the boat across her previous course a little, hoping that the sail had not wound itself around the shaft that responded to the wheel under the stern; certainly she felt no impediment. The tentacles of even so fine a sail would clog the steering horribly, spinning on to it fast, inextricably and with all its field-sized inertia.

Sandro jumped into the sea, did not dive, which Alec thought strange. He knew that a man overboard from a boat under racing sail was all but a man lost, but the boat was moving loosely and all her sail was down. As for sharks and all that lay under the sea, the only way to meet them was with unbelief, or, to put it more positively, faith in something else. Alec thought Sandro might still be at the immortal stage of his life.

Preceded by a plume of bubbles, Sandro's head came up close to the boat. He swam to the stern and dived under the boat.

Nick meanwhile had let down the steps.

Sandro called up from the water: "She's clean."

228

"Where's the kite got to?" shouted Logan.

"Melted in threads. Sunk." Sandro used the words that came to him first after his deep dive into a blue that did not hear voices and through which time seemed to stretch and boom like a drumskin. His ears were drilling towards one another through his head.

I am cold, he thought, and came out of the water laughing in shock.

"Give us a hand folding the mainsail. That'll dry you out," said Logan.

At night the sails were checked every fifteen minutes by whoever was on watch. If there had to be a sail-change they all got up to help. The sails were blue by night sometimes, sometimes grey. Alec was surprised at how the palette of the Pacific night was full of white, like the nights of the North. The speed they made was mysterious in the dark; they felt to Alec like a company confidential and outlawed as well. The Pacific seemed undiscovered, a great country that could not reveal itself because it had no consistency but its own nature to display, that took no account of human life.

When night came, although it might be clear and full of stars, to Alec it was obscure, because he could not think of words or images that would later remind him of this time. He was not surprised by that, but he wanted to remember and feared that once back within the parentheses of his life he would forget this vast fearful place because he would have no picture in his head to remember it by. Increasingly, he pored over the charts on the table like a mystic over texts. They looked nothing like the place, conveyed nothing of its height nor depth nor any other thing, but they made manifest the little that was known about the Pacific.

At night the boat became a thing so buoyant it might have been weightless. Alec stayed up to see the sun sink and was on watch for its arrival each morning. To see for as far as one can to the edges of sight only sea at dawn is to start the day resolved to make it good since it has arrived so perfect. Each day was like a resolution itself, taking from him the burden of himself as he tended the boat. He was serving a late maritime novitiate on *Ardent Spirit*.

At last after these reordered, watch-shaped days he began to trust those around him, because he had to, it is true, but the trust he had that they would conspire to stay alive, which was what he also wanted, made him realise that any thoughts he had had of despair in his life were frivolous; he wanted to stay alive.

He began vividly to dream of Lorna, and to write to her. Nick was writing to his wife, he said. He wrapped the notebook in an inflatable pocket when he had finished.

"In case it could float. Like in a bottle."

"Are you planning some misadventure?"

"It's not up to me. I'm just careful. It's like having no green on board."

Sure enough, there was no green on board.

"Why not?"

"I could make up plenty of reasons. I guess it's because if you have a few simple superstitions and obey them even if you don't understand them, you may ward off whatever it is so that it passes on to the guy who has green on board or says '*Macbeth*' or whatever it is."

Towards the next destination, Tonga, tropic birds began to fly astern, dipping from their hover into the wake and arising with serifs of water finishing their long wings and tails.

The air began to be colder at night, without the bloom that tropical heat settles over everything.

Alec began a chain of sneezes one night as he watched the vang on the mizzen boom for slippage. Each sneeze banged in his heart. I suppose I am unfit, he thought. I've used my arms and shoulders but we walk nowhere in the day. By the end of this long passage that he could not measure in land days, they were out of almost everything to eat except baked beans and sausages that looked like fingers with bad papercuts.

Yet he did not pine for land. The meditative passing of the time, with tasks allotted, and the unbroken steadiness of the wind that never sank and had not changed or risen suddenly on this passage, had an effect upon the six of them that was a little like brainwashing. Because they were living to a system that was working, they trusted the system, not thinking that this time was more emptied of self than it had been before, but aware of the benefits of some alleviation they could not place.

Logan, whose pessimism was dear to him in its impersonation of profundity and its implication of arcane knowledge, did not lay aside the pessimism, but allowed himself to fill with other feelings too. He anticipated some sort of new beginning in his life. How it would come about he was not sure, but he planned towards it and often found himself dreaming of a life after it. The event itself he avoided in his mind, however it would take place. Meanwhile, he remembered how fond he had once been of Elspeth.

With the next one loaded and in place, a man need never grow old but take his youth from his wives. It was Gabriel's passivity he held to be witness to her suitability. His distaste for steps not instigated by himself was thorough.

Logan preferred to be at sea, there was no doubt of that, but so unclouded a long passage grew uneventful for him and he began to invent difficulties against which to chafe. In his character lay something fine and well made, sunk beneath his power and turbulence and over time turning into a wreck, that stirred sometimes and gave out putrefaction sometimes and sometimes a glitter that was his charm.

It was at once apparent when they dropped anchor in the harbour at Nuku'alofa that this was a place not administered by France.

After registering their arrival, Logan said he was going ashore. Did anyone want to come with him?

Elspeth wanted to scour the boat within; it was her celebration of a return to land after even a short passage. Alec was growing used to this. He wondered if she performed the same expiation upon the houses they lived in. Nick said that he would post Alec's letter to Lorna, pages of talk on to the paper of a ringbound notebook, if Alec wanted to stay and help Elspeth clean.

Nick's grasp of the ambivalence Alec had not wanted to look into at sea was not crude. He saw, did not comment, understood human fluidity.

Three Tongan boys in shorts had come aboard with hardwood tortoises to sell. The famous tortoise of Captain Cook had died only a few years before in the Royal Palace. Perhaps these were its effigy? The boys did not know. The biggest boy said, "Please give us all your baked beans and similar before the harbourmaster comes to guzzle them. My mother favours."

Elspeth lifted out the saloon seats and took out the few remaining tins. A roach clung to the paper label of one of the tins. She flicked it off. No one wanted to kill the creatures directly by squashing them. The crack and release of oyster-sized innards was unpleasant. A fear of multiplication through death in insects seemed to stop them, too, a kind of medieval theory of spontaneous generation. The roach Elspeth had flicked away walked off with sectioned purposefulness.

She found some marmalade and two tins of Swiss Fondue and a jar of *confiture aux myrtilles*, and handed them over.

"Don't have them together, perhaps."

"Is it likely?" asked the youngest boy. He had hair rough in texture like the other boys' and the same height and solidity and bulk of face, but his hair was a kind of rough gold.

"We'll be off if there's nothing else you want," said the oldest boy. They had arrived just after the departure of the Zodiac with Logan, Sandro, Nick and Gabriel. Elspeth heard in the boy's speech the assumption that he would be taken from, as his people, immemoriably, had been. All his life he could take and never tip the compounded heaping of the scales.

Elspeth went forward to her cabin and came back with her head tied up under a scarf. She had put on a dress that flapped like a scarecrow's coat.

"Cup of tea?" asked Alec.

"After, not before," she said.

Beginning in the fo'c'sle they dug out mess from every

233

cranny. Alec pumped the bilges and serviced the three heads on board. The first smells of sewage and Parazone they dismissed with the delicious sweetness of beeswax polish and Dettol.

Elspeth kneeled on the floor of the saloon, that they had lifted and cleaned under, replacing in their compartments beneath it a foot pump and sealed packs of bandages, two bottles of champagne and fifteen bottles of Johnny Walker Black Label.

"It's the official bribe nearly everywhere," she said. "Do you want some?"

"Have you to bribe me?" he asked.

She went back to beeswax-feeding the floor. Her scarf and the floppy dress, the household smells mixed with the harbour smells, concocted a scene less romantic than their normal expected context had been for the past watch-broken days.

What was beautiful was the plainness of the scene, and the earthbound vigour of the woman scrubbing. He thought, and went to find paper and a pencil.

He drew Elspeth as she did the housework on the boat in the harbour.

"You want flowers," he said.

"I want more disinfectant more."

"I mean for the picture. You want some bleak daisies or wiry chrysanths. I have not seen a sight so northern, so far from the Tropics, for a while. It does me good."

"I'll carry on, if that's all right."

"You scrub, I'll draw; that's how it is with artists and women," he said, but she was not looking at his face, so he had to make an ironic cough to show his meaning, and that was clumsy.

"Where did you get your passion for a tidy boat?" he asked her. "Does it extend to houses?"

"I started tidying places I lived as soon as I began living away from home. Our house was not filthy but its disorder was held to show the purity of my parents' ideals; and they were pure. But I didn't see why that meant we'd to allow the cats to lick the cheese at table or why we had to have cobwebs hanging down to our faces. I wanted to live in a place with light bulbs that were not like strange rare fish that might or might not go phosphorescent if you fed them with some weak electricity from the failing wires. I wanted to see the pattern in the carpet, not to be dominated by it, but to see it. I longed for clean clothes and floors that could be trusted not to buzz with worm. And I wanted to stop my parents taking pity on everything. They included not only people in their pity. They had broken things around them too."

"What kinds of things?"

"Things that might have been Jacobean high chairs and might have been parts of a wheelbarrow, hundreds of tartan boxes with transfers on of castles, stags, steamships and brigs, tables covered with powder horns and patent ironing boards for the fixing of ecclesiastical muslin and stuffed fish in lifelike positions, as if fish ever got into lifelike positions, and old nurses' capes lined with red they thought I might want to dress up in and military buttons tied on a leather bootlace."

"The first house I went to like that, cluttered with old things, changed my life, I think."

"Well, I hung about at school hoping to get asked home by the wee girl who said you could eat your dinner off their floor. I would pointedly tidy my room and say my prayers before bed to offend their liberal free-thinking ways."

"How conventional you were."

"Now I think violent anarchic thoughts, but I have to have a tidy house."

"What was the biggest thing they took pity on?"

"There were people who lived with us for months at a time, but they moved about at least and sometimes shook off the dust they collected. Most of the time I was trying to come between my parents and houses. They pursued old houses that were in danger of demolition."

"Do you know what demolition is called now?"

"No."

"Change of use, advice and salvage. Moreover the demolition experts are furious because there's nothing much left to demolish, which is circular."

"You remember what I said in the Chinese restaurant in Tahiti? We would come up to Edinburgh for the reasons I said to you in the restaurant, it's true, but the main reason was to pay our respects to buildings. How I disliked it."

"Buildings were the great escape for me. I had never found anything so thrilling."

"Can it be usual to have this relationship with buildings, either way?"

"It's not usual maybe for the person to be so aware of the attachment. But the moral link with houses and streets seems to me, always has seemed, a deep one. It's irreplaceable in children."

She scrubbed hard at the table, kneeling up.

"Well, you are a man after my poor pa's heart. Let's see the picture."

It was a dark drawing and not kind. Elspeth looked out of it with begging eyes.

"Do I look so anxious all the time? You can't tell it's a boat, that's a pity."

"Usually you look about that anxious. At the moment you are looking more. The mysterious thing is that it's stopped being a boat just for now. Tell me about the houses you trailed round. I will have been the boy with an old woman or a brindle dog and his owner that you just did not see as you drooped about counting to a hundred and wishing for an ice-cream with your dad."

He was writing himself into her story. If she took this from him, he would know how it was with her. Then, he might make some move.

"Maybe. We would go in to houses full of twigs. They'd been empty so long, in the city right enough, that the jackdaws nesting in the chimney had sent down sufficient twigs to fill a room. Some landlords just lit the twigs after a good dook of paraffin. Some picked a few slates off the roof to help the rain in. Plenty knocked down whole squares, absolutely within the law."

"You are angry about it now. It's caught up with you."

"Now it is almost too late. Even places like this, that were once remote, are being developed. Life is being speeded up beyond the human. You're right, I didn't care when I was dragged as I saw it around all these condemned streets and houses, and now I care enough to want to go back and live in them, even."

"It's the obvious question. Do you dream of them?"

"One of the reasons I long for sleep is to be back with the houses that have been destroyed. If that could be death, walking a resurrected city, I would not fear it. I can remember the writing in some attics, pencilled lists of names of men come to do the guttering or store apples, and girls' names written on night-nursery windows with a diamond. I remember big houses where the owner lived in one room with a chamber pot. I wish I had listened."

"If it were not the houses it would be another thing. Only a very brusque character can refrain from going over the past again."

"It saves time if one can be free of it."

"Only if you are going to do new things every new moment of your life. I think it is good to remember the past if one is not posing it in fanciful new ways just to make one's own case."

"I will not talk about Logan," she said, shocking herself.

He decided not to have heard.

"Let me take the carpet on deck with you. We can hang it over the boom and beat it."

"You are domesticated too."

"I tried to elude it, but it has come for me."

"Here we are," said Logan. "What an extraordinary sight you make, Elspeth. We have signed in with an official called Hepple-white or Sheraton and I've made times for the collection of fuel, gas and water. I suggest we go ashore. I've met a remarkable character who's offered us a traditional feast."

Demolition leads to those traditions, thought Alec.

"It is at a site," said Gabriel.

Elspeth and Alec waited for more.

Logan passed on to the other matter that had engaged him that afternoon: "I went to place some calls and make a couple of enquiries about a few things. It's a pleasant town. The Palace is made of shingle, or we'd call it that in America, whitewashed. People as substantial as you'd expect, and wearing these woven girdles of palm matting. It's a sign of respect for the royal family. The strangest thing is that on a Sunday, they tell me, the airport is closed so that one of the nobles can play with his remote-control planes. Apparently it's the same every Sunday. I approve of that, the big planes held up by the toy ones."

"It could also be that Tongans are very devout," said Nick. "They observe the sabbath and go to church two or three times."

It was Nick who volunteered to stay behind on the boat while the others went to the feast, which was to be cooked in an underground oven and would feature suckling pig.

The Zodiac was deep in the water as they set off for the harbour steps. When they got there the weed and slime made the steps treacherous and the dirty harbour water slapped up and down them. The party was met by a wide man who guided them to his Chevy pick-up. His skin was covered on cheeks and neck with small nodules of skin like the grains of dirt you rub off when you wash with a loofah. He was frantically hyperbolic, waving his dimpled arms in their blue shirtsleeves, pulling up and adjusting his long palm-mat girdle. He was smoking without stopping. They all got into the car.

Later they picked up four more people, Americans, at a place the host called the international dateline, though it wasn't clear to Alec if it was the thing itself or a hotel named for it. He

239

experienced no shift in time such as he longed to feel. The remarkable brilliance of Pacific islanders in the matters of navigation and time impressed him and depressed him, for he could not see how the islanders' new lives would use such a gift. Celestial navigation, that bent the impervious stars to human use and absorbed the brain in exercise that freed it from any but the clearest thought, was becoming redundant. Soon it would be revived only as a stunt, a card trick using tides and planets.

"Welcome to this evening's typical Tongan feast. Be seated on the carved chairs and tables. My dear wife has earlier prepared the *umu*, the oven underground, where it is so large you can fit in one man." No one knew whether to laugh, except Logan, who did.

The host looked gratified. Cannibalism was good for tourists. "I will come round to collect expenses of luxurious meal to come. Meanwhile I introduce my daughters."

Two noble-headed girls with poised bearing came forward with wooden trays on which toothpicks impaled pieces of pineapple and more oddly various cheese snacks that could have been lifted with the fingers. It appeared that the appetisers had been gingered up to look primitive, with a stick through the nose.

Coconut shells of *kava* were passed round. In the flickering light of a pitch torch its colour was invisible, its hot smell and burning taste nothing to its effect as the flames shuffled the faces of the four Tongans and their nine guests. A battery-operated cassette player was turned on. A girl's voice came out of it, telling the story of the life of Brigham Young.

One of the Tongan girls seemed choked by the smoke burping gently from the *umu*.

240

The host did some stately dancing, breaking off to sip *kava*, then later lemonade. The smoke continued to creep among those assembled.

At last the host clapped his hands. The guests stopped conversing among themselves about the mildness of the night, the atmosphere of the site (which was not to be seen), and what sort of insect-repellent is best.

"A few words," said the host, holding out a number of perfect sleeping crisp orange pigs on a stick and starting to carve them in straight lines like loaves without respect for their anatomy. "This feast I hold each Saturday and I am proud to. The voice you heard on the cassette player was the voice of my youngest daughter, who perished earlier today at the age of seven after much affliction." All the time he spoke he had a smile of great exaltation on his face, and when he finished speaking he clapped. There was nothing for it but to clap too. The handsome daughters hit the tears off their cheeks as if they were mosquitoes. It was impossible to know whether the family was continuing in this way through necessity or custom. The inhibition that lies upon strangers lay thicker than it had before.

"No doubt," said Logan, "you were a splendid father to her. I am sure that your wife, who has shown such skill and charm this evening, was a wonderful mother." Empty words were needed, and Logan had them. He put his arm tenderly around Gabriel, in a paternal way, so strong had his fellow feeling at once become for this wretched bereaved man.

Fortified by the touch of the female child, he went on: "We were uplifted to hear her sweet voice telling the story of the founder of your fine faith." God, he has his wits about him, thought Alec, it's crude rubbish but it is potent and it is what's

241

needed. The man has a freedom from timidity that makes leaders of coups. He was moved by Logan's finely spoken, sonorous, trite words as they came. The sisters of the dead child gave up holding off the tears they wept as they handed round the sliced piglets, as they dispensed bottled sauerkraut on the end of long forks, as they collected beer cans and *kava* shells from the turf where they had laid the finely figured *tapa* cloth to be admired in the light of the pitch by which little could be seen but the depths of sad dark eyes and the sleeping orange slick chopped-off faces of the suckling pigs.

"It was more than our money's worth, at any rate," said Logan as they passed over the water of the harbour to the boat, where Nick was sitting up in the fo'c'sle listening to the water and the sky.

Nine

In the high trees over the road hung umbrellas stuffed with red fur. These stirred occasionally, and put out a tentative hand, like an old lady feeling in her reticule for an indigestion mint. Here were the flying foxes of Tonga by day, huge russet furred bats comatose but reassuringly alive in counterpoint to the low-lying churches of Jesus Christ of the Latter Day Saints, tidy bungalows so numerous it was on this island as though prayer might have to be succumbed to at any time and had to take place in one of these facilities rather than in the open air, at will. The number of such facilities suggested that the prayer-bladders of the people of the Kingdom of Tonga were weak.

Having settled into the life around the harbour after six days at anchor just outside it, Alec and Gabriel, Logan and Elspeth had bicycled to another shore of the main island of the archipelago, away from Nuku'alofa. On their bicycles they overtook cars, which ambled along beneath their hefty drivers. The often moulting girdles of woven palm around the waists of the Tongans did not have the effect of making them look clumsy; being constrained to walk at a dignified pace suited their bulk. They were held back from trivial jerky movements by the matting.

"Perhaps we Scots would be easier to rule if the kilt was rigid," said Alec, to Logan. Logan smiled at him without focusing. If he heard a metaphor or a joke in a sentence, he could not always be bothered to fillet out its meaning. He did not think a man should speak in a whimsical way.

"It's like making the population walk about each with a book on their head," said Elspeth.

"Monarchy supported by deportment." Alec caught her meaning.

They were passing a cluster of long huts that were open on three sides and roofed in palm fibre. On the floor of the huts women sat beating palm into *tapa* cloths. Out of the dusty capital, there were Methodist Churches, Free Wesleyan Churches and the churches of Jesus Christ of the Latter Day Saints, more churches than there were family houses it seemed. Children in groups, usually conventionally dressed in grey shorts, white shirts, check dresses full in the skirt, came up to look as the four passed. The children were big, with adult legs and already the stately adult walk, though their matting belts were not as wide as the adults'.

In the heat of the day, as the shadows of the fruit bats filled trees black at their boles, they saw a sign that said, "Tongan specials and blow holes". There was a compound like the chil-

244

dren's zoo for farm animals found in large zoos. Smartly painted white palings were stuck into dryish earth around a collection of huts painted in saltworn versions of cheerful colours.

This melancholy shanty prettiness was emphasised by the presence of two white kids tethered to a post. One cleared its throat; the other contradicted it with narrowed yellow eyes. There was a hook-and-eye gate into the compound. Logan opened it and looked around. He saw no one awaiting him and was at a loss till he thought out the next move.

"Anyone here?" called Elspeth. She would have been happy for there not to have been, but a man came towards them from one of the larger huts.

"Australian, American, German? We do vegetarian specials from each country. We know what you like."

"British, in fact," said Logan.

Elspeth went off abruptly to scratch the kids, if they would let her. The geographical certainties in her husband's voice made her squeamish. "Other peoples like to know where they stand," he said to her.

"Do other people?" she asked, annoying him without trying to.

"We do a good mashed potato with chips and rice."

"It's more the blow holes we've come for, though food would be a bonus." The other annoying thing was that Logan did always get through to people he spoke to in this way. "I was thinking of seafood. That *is* the sea down there?" It was about twenty yards away, beyond what looked like a ha-ha at the edge of the coarse grass. Alec saw a splash of foam once, and once a jet of spray. Someone must be playing by the water.

Lower down the dusty slope of the compound, tables with

clipped-on oilcloths stood under an awning that was decked with pearl bulbs like pickled onions on strings. A serving station with another awning was to the side. Slapping and puffing sounds, loud as from walrus, came from the direction of the water, which could be seen now to have a constant edge of mist broken over it.

"Select from booth the seafood. Under Australian vegetarian." Heaps of newly boiled prawns and langoustines steamed on enamel trays. American vegetarian, bundles of franks, curled in the heat alongside.

"There are no cats. You'd expect cats, with this smell," said Gabriel.

"They're German vegetarian," said Logan.

Gabriel recoiled excitedly.

Elspeth had rejoined them by now where they sat at a table with beer and Saltines.

"Snacks travel by faster airlines than people," she said.

"Have you heard of a concession?" said Logan.

"I've heard of concession."

"There you are. Gabriel, forepaw for you, or tail?"

Gabriel looked as shocked as she had the first time. She was good company; you saw a fine picture of yourself in her.

Alec thought of the note he had seen on one of the Charts of the Pacific: "Caution is necessary when navigating among the low, reefy islands of the Pacific Ocean. The several details have been collected from the voyages of various navigators, extending over a long series of years; the relative positions of the many dangers may therefore not in all cases be exactly given; while it is possible there may be others still undiscovered."

How could they come to know a place at all by arriving at roughly the speed of handwriting and staying for enough time to leave with three tall tales and a seashell? He had met an old Englishman at one of the many milk bars on Tonga, who said, "I've not been home for fifty-six years and I've travelled all among these islands of Tonga, but I have more idea of England, which is a foreign country to me, than I do of here. I know the facts: small kingdom; intermarried nobles; remarkable girth of inhabitants; uncountable archipelago; regrettable fondness for starch and soft drinks; bisected by international dateline; touch of cannibalism surely atoned for by enthusiasm of converts to the American Way. But all that adds up to something quite different from the genial place that lies about me. All I can do is like it. And keep on noticing what it is actually like." He snapped his nose into a spotted handkerchief and wiped at it to keep up the shine. He wore a blazer and had feet of leather, bare hard feet and ankles that shone like boots. "At eleven I generally have my banana milk," he lifted the heavy beige glass, "and then walk down to see what's going forward at the Palace. Put these on for that." He pulled out some chappals from a shoebag labelled "shoes" and sewn with a nametape. "Otherwise it's barefoot. I go barefoot, barefoot. Feet like omelettes. It's perfect agony in shoes." Alec had been no good to this man who liked a few words with each visitor to Tonga, rather more words if they knew the South of England, and perhaps a few more if they followed the fate of the pine marten, whose scarcity, he said, had driven him from the place.

"The last man who remembers seeing one of those before him on a branch of Douglas Fir. That's me. It was a nicer relation of the mink, I seem to think. I'll have another, but half only, thanks, that's all I imbibe till sunset."

Also in that milkbar Alec and Elspeth together had met a dandy of over seventy who should have been in Capri, not in Tonga. His monocle and connoisseurial complexion, the thin cane set with a band of chipped nacre at the top, his unrealistic gait and astounded eyebrows were all signals it was doubtful many of the people to whom he spoke were attuned to. He bore out the theory that scientific discoveries or philosophical movements are transmitted through space by some telepathic means, often occurring almost simultaneously in different places. He had created for himself an idiom that was just expiring in Europe, but he had done it alone and having started out as the son of a medical missionary in the Cook Islands. The trait he seemed to have failed to evolve was predatoriness, so it was not likely that he would perpetuate his species by the grimy waters of Nuku'alofa. When Alec watched him watching the tough, good-looking yachties, he saw a taper unlit, a passion less vehement than the other man showed for the pine marten.

"We've done this lot justice," Logan looked at the plates of claws and whiskers, "even if it wasn't cat."

"The prawns were perfectly OK, Logan," said Elspeth. "I'm off. Come on, Gabriel."

Alec looked at Logan to see how he reacted to this. He did not. Women had things to speak of that frankly did not interest him.

"I thought we might take a rougher road home, you and I, Alec, later," he said. Alec was reminded of the safe and the wrapped morphine. There might be no menace to the man, but his methods relied on one not knowing this for certain.

Alec heard Elspeth yell and he ran to find her down the drop from grass on to rocks. What had Gabriel said to her? He knew how the words of the innocent can hurt, the innocent and stupid much more.

Elspeth and Gabriel stood together on a table of rock that was the start only of great grey-blue steps and landings of rock arranged with a rounded stacked precision like old silver plates made ready in a burial chamber. Vaults in the rock below them boomed and from below also came the walrus-slapping of hard waves breasting the giving rock. The water was forced up through holes it had worn like a drill through the rock by persistence and repetition, each abrasion painless, the effect of a million of them a perfect bore-hole through solid rock, through which water shot in jets straight up like poplars. The jets did not have the Italian water engineer's timing that the great renaissance gardens use to shock and thrill, but they showed the power and beauty of water, the invasive neutrality that makes it desirable to us, and fearful. These forcing jets standing for a moment forty feet in the air then falling back over stones shaped by themselves were only extreme examples of water finding its own level.

The jets rose and fell in no order. So artificial or so divinely inspired did their display seem that it was not possible to believe they fell without reason. Alec stood on the furthest stepping stone he could reach so as to see as many jets as possible at once, to crack their system. When two shot from the rocks close together, they gave each other rainbows.

The rock throbbed from below. When the waves receded, the stones minutely settled. On the wave's returning throw, the tall pipes of water, white all through with the force of the shov-

249

ing green water from below, stood for that moment in the air, and subsided. Their logic was the logic of the waves, forced through rock.

Elspeth's teeth were chattering and she was grinning as if embalmed. Dazzled by what she saw, she was rooted by the thrumming through the rock that she associated with terror and the depths of human pain. Inside and under the rock, packed tighter by each advancing wave, and then thrown to charnel by the swilling recessional of the water, she saw bodies of souls lying in the earth on this island, only one island in an archipelago, that archipelago only one in an ocean full of islands.

"I love this throbbing," said Gabriel. "It's like the start of something coming closer."

I might even welcome disaster, thought Elspeth, looking at Gabriel and finding it hard to fix upon her, so small and benign did she seem among the piled rocks with the rooves of coloured beach huts behind; perhaps disaster breeds certainty. I am not sure I believe in certainty, but perhaps I should try it.

"This is a sight worth sailing all these miles for," said Logan.

Alec looked at him. A man that unironic would be valuable in war.

"It's like fountains," said Gabriel. She was so free, thought Alec, of having to find the word or the line, exactly to represent something. She saw, and responded. Her words were almost always a weakening of her response. In his painting he tried to show the response with no interval of transition, and it was impossible. Why not give up and be innocent like Gabriel, who likened this inhuman force of water to things men made to adorn parks, those humane places.

She is an intact personality, intact, thought Elspeth. How can I compare? He wants a new thing to break. I thought we could be like many people who are happy, both broken, but he does not care for that. I sent my heart to him like a falcon but it came back with air in its talons and now it is starving.

"Just like a fountain," said Logan. "How stupid we are not to have seen that."

The bicycle ride for Elspeth and Gabriel was as it had been earlier in the day. They rode side by side, unless a vehicle approached, in which case it was Gabriel who hung back, and Elspeth who, as a mother would, took the lead.

In fact I feel maternal towards Gabriel. It is not only her age but the risk she is running that make me want to protect her. It cannot be unknown in a wife to feel protective to the woman who is trying out her husband. She may even be afraid of me. Why do I not fight against what is happening? Do I want it to happen? Or do I feel that I cannot stop it and might as well fight some neutral natural force as enter battle with Logan?

What Logan and I can never lose is having been married. It is like cigars in curtains, you can't air it out; when a new cigar is lit, the old ones are resurrected in the room, their scent shaking out of the cloth to join the newly burning leaves.

"Did *you* meet Logan on a boat?" asked Gabriel, anxious to talk about what she thought about, and being as subtle as she could. She did not say "too". Only with a girl as young as this could such a circumstance be so drastic, so perilous to a marriage. A man taking up a girl so innocent had to protect her.

"I met him on a bit of land so small it might have been a boat. We met on an island. In Scotland."

"Oh, Scotland." People speak of places they love in a way that suggests that here is a subject for resting on. Gabriel did not speak like that.

"It is the great thing we share." I am a fool, thought Elspeth, I have told her the truth.

The road curved past three trees full of flying foxes. They made noises like children getting ready to flit, rustlings as of wrappers and subdued squeaks. The trees leaned together to form a triangle beneath which had been placed a sturdy bench, made for the support of solid bodies. A massive couple sat on it. They were young, their hands were linked, but their bulk denied their youth, bestowing on them qualities more permanent than slippery beauty and enchantment; they seemed welded, married, made moral by their bulk, not light of love, in a world where there was no longer the time to give yourself for life to another person.

If she says anything inept about Scotland I shall find the energy to dislike her, perhaps, thought Elspeth.

"It must be very nice." It was safe enough.

"I love it."

"How did you meet—on this island?"

"I was moving sheep so that he could land in an aeroplane. I was up there making drawings of remains."

"Human?"

"Stones. Buildings."

This was not a story that so far offered much to Gabriel.

"Why were you doing that?"

"It was my job. What is yours?"

"Cooking on a boat. At the moment." She spoke without malice.

I am put in my place, thought Elspeth.

"And the sheep?" Gabriel went on.

"You have to move sheep off a field so a little plane can land. Also cows off a beach. They land on beaches too. Planes, not cows."

"What does a cow do at the beach?"

"On the beach a cow stands and cools her legs against flies in sandy pools. Sometimes they sit down and look odd with the waves and the seagulls. It is part of the place."

"And the *sheep*?"

"They are used as markers on the runway while the plane is descending. They tie them down to four pegs, red sheep to the left, green sheep on the right."

"I know I'm ignorant."

"You are right. It isn't true. The sheep are everywhere and the plane lands anywhere. When you see it coming you shoo the sheep and pen them if you can. Anyhow, that's how I met him. It was an island with one long meadow they used as a landing strip, and a beach used more often unless the tide was in and it was an emergency."

"So it was an emergency."

"No. Logan just does what he wants. He wanted to see the Scottish islands from the air. He was flying low, flew lower, saw me and made a few circles, asked the coastguard for permission to land, and did."

The emergency had been love at first sight, for which he was ripe after Hortense's death. Such melodrama was the pitch at which he lived or he did not believe in himself. He feared to take life plain. Reared to mistrust all artificial savour, Elspeth had fallen at once for the intensity, and later had come to hope they had wound down a little, to a palatable decent compromise. She had paid for the delusions she had swallowed in the early days and anticipated some lightness in casting them off.

"What did you do then? After the sheep?"

"He parked the aeroplane and shouted at me."

She was giving truthful answers because she had not thought about the encounter for so long that it had failed to get wrapped up in ways of turning it into romance. They had walked through a graveyard with turf like brocade. It was a Catholic island. The graveyard was full of angels, some of them reading books. Flowers lay on a rich compost heap within a stone wall, thrown away and renewed by the families of the dead. In these graveyards by the sea there are few names, repeated over and over, Euphemia, Colum, Ella, Angus, and fewer last names yet. The dead lie in families. Many of those who are mentioned in the stones are very old, kept at work into their eighties, eating modestly, living a hard life. The dead babies are many, and the drowned men. These are fishermen and the unnamed. Men without names have been washed up on the shores of the Western Isles after battles at sea since there was fighting. It was the place for us to fall in love, thought Elspeth. It filled our hearts with our respective indulgences, love of death and love of place. And there were flowers. He loves death as I love flowers.

The two cycled on. I should ask her about herself, it is the kind thing to do. And it would be kind to him. I can't let him go to someone who will not look after him, thought Elspeth.

"Are you fond of children?" she asked. It would not matter either way. If she really wanted him she would take his strictures.

"Yes." It was an agreement made as though there could be

no other answer. It was the answer Logan would want as a sign of good nature in the girl. He would take it no further. He would never give children life.

A pick-up went by, four children sitting in the back with a disdainful pig, the curl of whose nose showed him the most spoilt member of the family. One of the children had her arm around the pig, another scratched its back. The pig smiled like a drunk woman.

Alec and Logan took a longer way back to town. They started to count churches, then became dispirited by a guilt they did not discuss. Alec felt ashamed. Logan defected within himself from his American to his Scots blood. He felt the American missionaries had been the worst, taking tithes from the people to build the churches that seemed to mark the half-miles.

Half his childhood he spent in a big black house with small rooms, once outside the city of Glasgow but now within it. In the rooms there hung dark paintings of men in frock coats and women with the faces of misers. The paintings had been bought with the house by his Glasgow grandfather who had made the American fortune; he bought it without looking at it, on the number of its rooms and the reputed splendour of its great stair. To accommodate the staircase, the rooms of the house had had to breathe in. They never let out that breath in Logan's experience. The staircase had a balustrade of steel that shone like guns in the dark and the banister was ebony, inlaid with the knucklebones, his father told him, of fallen Englishmen. There could not have been so many ivory-handed men even in a country so decadent as England.

The drum of the great hall of the black house was eighty feet high, a blaze of knives and longswords, dirks, daggers and cutlass. Some of the blades were set like the rays of metal suns, some inwards like the irises of staring eyes. There was a panel of interwoven swords the height of the room and six feet wide, each sword being the length of a big man's arm. Pikes were crossed over each barrelled door out of the hall. Once a year for a fortnight four men came from Sheffield to sharpen the swords whose present aim was decoration and whose edges were mortal. At the same time the balustrade of the stairway was cleaned by three women with guncotton. This was the most companionable time in the year at the House of the Mearns, when the weapons came down to be sharpened and polished and made useless again in starry arrangements on the walls.

The garden of the house was dark too and wet, relieved by purple bells of fuchsia that made faint pomp in long hedges that led down to the tower where he could sit and watch the Clyde. He waited for launchings as other boys wait for birthdays. His father gave him binoculars early on, to watch the making of the ships in the yards on the Clyde. He saw the last great liner built at John Brown's Yard, a ship growing between cranes she came to dwarf, her wide swelling sides completed in a curve and turn that moved him more than anything had up till then in his life. The ship was the size of a town of men, but beautiful as an animal, as something inhuman. Logan already had a distaste for other humans. It came from his isolation in the House of the Mearns and his horror of crowds. His mistrust of himself led him to see the human race as himself, multiplied. Trained to be disgusted by weakness in himself, to be deathly proud, he saw in towns rat-runs. It was an illiberal upbringing for a child.

Through his binoculars in the Largs stone crow's nest built to give the house a fine view of the river, Logan saw the builders of the great ships carried on gantries, walking up gangplanks, letting down the ropes of the ships. The men here had a virtue to them, he could see that. They were of one mind, like a swarm. A taste for autocracy was established in him, for the mass moved as one by one; co-operation was not a word he heard and he could not be expected to imagine it for himself in a household such as his own.

His mother was quiet. Her power was in her puritanical temperament and in the wide fortune in wheatfields and mills she brought to her marriage.

In New York the apartment reproduced the heaviness of the House of the Mearns, on a more extended scale and without the knives. His mother wore a uniform; a grey dress with white cuffs in the day, black at night. Her face was strong, down-drawn, white. She took no perverse pleasure in the disciplines she lived by; they were right and she did not question them. This certainty helped her to compensate for shyness. A plain heiress will be shy. The pretty one fears her money is part of what is wanted. A plain one knows that she is not involved in her fate at all, she is merely the buoy marking the spot where the treasure is sunk.

Logan loved his mother but saw her little. No one said it, but his parents lived separately as much as they could. She came over from America in ships and he would imagine her always in a ship, filling it somehow on her own, with her own strict, fair decorum. He said his prayers at night to a God who was a ship with the face of his mother.

The warmest times for him were the launching of the ships,

when they fell free down the grooved slips into the river, trembled, splashed up two curves of light, and were afloat.

Logan swore that he would never bring life into the world as soon as he knew that it was possible to do so. He took up this position because of the pain his own growing had caused him and because he believed that the world was, being in the hands of men, bound to end in horror. The proliferation of humans made this more likely. He took comfort in his belief in doomsday. It also excused his failings, the difficulties he had at school, the temper that lived in him like a chained wolf, when he compared them with the baseness of human kind in general. He used such words as "base" and "scum".

But he became a man with a heart that was half-tender. Because he had known few people as a child he had not learned to be easy with them. He soon learned that his awkwardness, the sense that he did not belong, was attractive to women. They rested their own fantasies in his emptiness, and it suited him. He developed the attractiveness of the man who behaves badly on more than one continent. He was spoken of, said to have a broken heart, an illness all women believe they can heal.

He began the business of marrying because of the sensation of new life it offers, though he made it clear to each wife there should be no actual conception.

Alec did not know whether to talk. Logan was not used to initiatives from other people. Perhaps it might have relaxed him to be spoken to. Alec could not think that they had much to talk about except things too serious to mention, that people trying to live in the confined quarters of a boat did not mention. Although he was continually intrigued and surprised by life at sea and its particular discomforts and rewards, Alec had realised by now that he was a landsman. He missed the detail of life on land more each day. He wanted, as a man wants to eat again after illness, to work, to paint.

Their common ground was their homeland, a prickly place to grasp. Alec imagined the life of a rich man in Scotland. He could picture no real life lived thus. Blurry nineteenth-century oils, considerably greater than life-size, showing dovelike chieftainesses welcoming huge kilted lairds with knees like faces, came into his mind. Every available surface would be overwhelmed with tartan, the walls loaded with the heads of surprised stags, their antlers pointing to a groined ceiling dark with smoke from the fire before which long hounds twitched.

He was far from imagining the truth. The idea of a character, once formed, is dangerously quick to accoutre every aspect of the character's imagined life. To see what others are actually like is not the gift of the most imaginative, necessarily.

To invent was more interesting, too, though Alec would not have said he was inventing a life for Logan.

Logan did not think much about such things. When he did, he made assumptions based upon a certain amount of knowledge and no observation. Swift to grasp fear, subordination or weakness in others, he was not interested by the laminations and contradictions of human character. They did not strike him. He was like a bad king in this way, a person who must have a jester in order to know who is telling jokes. Logan made his mind up fast about people, did not like many of them, and was slow but sudden to confiscate affection.

"Were you near the docks where you grew up?" Logan spoke politely. He found talk around topics wasteful. There was something in Alec that was not effeminacy, he thought, but the man watched you while you spoke, and that was like a woman.

"Most days," Alec replied, and decided to be less mean with his words. "I went with my mother and father. They worked in Leith."

"To my mind that's the best part of the city. But then I'm Glaswegian." The accent was more English in that sentence than Alec had ever heard it, but Logan did not say things he did not mean.

"Did you use to come over then, from Glasgow?"

"In order to be with my mother when she gave the Christmas message to the Distressed Seamen in their hostel. She endowed it. She would not have a heated bedroom in our house herself. In the evenings she knitted socks for the seamen that were so thick you couldn't get them on. God knows what they did with them. The seamen were excellent blokes. My mother was one of these women who do not realise how people hate to have good done them. And she was temperance. After the speech, and the talking, and the tea and the buns that got taken out and dusted year after year, she would take me to Leith."

Here is his tenderness, thought Alec. It is to himself as a boy.

"What would you do?"

"Watch fishing boats. I more than anything wanted to get into one of them and run away to sea. I wanted to catch herring out of Leith. It was the thing I wanted above all. The sea, the company, it looked great to me. I sat in rope coils and looked at the old boats slapping up and down in the water. I stole glass floats from the docks and kept them in my room. There were seventeen by the time I was sent down to my English school."

Logan was enjoying himself. He calculated that he need never see Alec, in his view a rather unrewarding character, again, after he had paid him when the voyage came to its end in New Zealand. Besides, confidences on land did not prejudice the balance of the boat. Some people grew confidential at sea, lured into indiscretion by the unreality. To Logan the sea was the more solid thing.

Would he be envious of me if I were to tell him? thought Alec. Or would it spoil his fantasy to tell him about the gutting floor and the backs done in by pulling nets, and my great-grand-father lifted overboard by a wave?

"I know it was a hard life, and anyhow now it's all but gone, but that is the way of life I first coveted," said Logan, "like some boys want to be pirates or to drive trains. I wanted to be a seafisherman. The nearest I came was this." He made a face that indicated his burdensome freedom and shoals of silver.

Should I knock your head off, thought Alec, for the sake of my father, or should I simply watch you as one watches a rare animal and trust to your extinction? He did not feel a malevo-lence that was anything more than theoretical, now that he knew the man. He did not like Logan, he thought, but even to know a few things about someone was to fall away from wishing him and his like dead. He supposed it was corrupt, but he preferred corruption to the cleanliness of social purging.

Corruption of this sort, Alec thought, the mixing of people and the sheen and variety of these mixtures, has been the great thing of this voyage for me. I see that the sailing is, when not boring or frightening, beautiful, but it is the people and places I have learnt from. There is no human purity. It is a lie. The combinations of peoples are without end.

Logan assumed Alec's early life must have been pretty grim. It fitted in with the finickiness of the man now when you thought about it, he considered, pleased with his perception. He would tell Gabriel. The man obviously grew up in squalor and grime. That would explain his habits, his precision, the way he boned a fish perfectly before beginning to chivvy any flesh on to his fork.

In this way, Logan subdued Alec to himself and made him pitiable and comprehensible. If we were actually to comprehend other people we would not be able to use them for our own ends.

This is not an exchange of confidences, thought Alec. It is Logan honouring me. How shall I find myself paying for the honour?

They cycled up to and past the royal parish church and the palace beside it through the violet hour; in the air around each of them bats pinched at the breeze while in the mind of each man settled carefully coloured false pictures of the other's early life.

Sandro was waiting for them at the harbour.

"It was a good day," he both asked and stated.

"Good enough," said Logan, locking the bikes to the reception post at the quayside, though he knew they would not be stolen.

"Great with us too. We're all set. She's ready to go." Sandro nodded all along the sentence as he spoke. He had the energy to waste.

It was men like Sandro and Nick who best survived the life at sea and the cramped, overlooked life in the harbour, thought Alec. They carried no slack. He had been looking for goodness; he had found, certainly, good natures.

"Gabriel's made real fancy tucker," said Sandro. "It's a question of pancakes and corned beef hash."

"Great gear," said Logan, all American, no trace of the irritable superior with whom Alec had passed that afternoon.

The boy on the coiled rope watching fishing boats had not been an invention; he was still there.

Ten

The longest stretch of ocean lay before them, between Tonga and New Zealand. Logan set the course due south. Alec and Nick once again took the two-to-six watches, Logan and Elspeth the six to ten, Sandro and Gabriel the ten till two. Each of them had checked every set of oilskin trousers and jacket, shaken the roaches out of the seaboots over the side, and checked the clips on hard lengths of nylon webbing that were tucked deep in the oilskins, to be made fast to the deck in case of foul weather. The webbing was rolled around its biting clip and the packed discs of ribbon and metal tucked in an oilskin jacket pocket, a small measure against what the sea could do. The oilskins themselves made a busy sound like water running on an old wooden clinker-built dinghy in shallow water, a hissing noise, very light.

Anything insecure or superfluous in the boat was put away, given away or stored. Gabriel wrapped up the shells Logan had picked up for her on the sand in Moorea; among them was an empty crab, light as a moth and peasize-perfect. To Gabriel each shell was an hour and a place. To him they would have been little things he had picked up. She was taking the pills he had told her to take every four hours whether it was rough or not. They accommodated the sense of balance to the water's swell, he said. It had been tried on astronauts, who became very sick as they danced around weightless in air.

Every hour during each watch, the log was filled in, with weather conditions, point of sailing, mileage since the last reading taken from the Walker log, course, wind speed and wind direction.

Previously they had behaved in some ways as though it were a holiday they were engaged upon. Now, two hundred miles south-southwest of Tonga, Logan had assumed a sober authority. This was the part he preferred. He began to concentrate absolutely upon the boat in an unbreakable carapace of single-mindedness. Before he had concentrated but allowed himself freedoms. Now the boat and the sea were the boundaries of the world available to them. If anything went wrong there would be no more world.

With apparently little to fear, as far as Alec could gather from the unchanging light-hearted calm of Sandro, and Nick's sure competence, it was as though Logan were calling upon the Furies by his solemnity. Sometimes Alec thought he was acting. There was something frivolous in such overt solemnity, like a priest wearing too many robes. The immaculate concentration

Logan built upon his boat had a maniac, solipsistic edge. He was the boat, and it was he. He flinched if she fouled on a gybe or if something trivial failed.

He was like a man who knows the pain he has will certainly get worse. This intensifying was perfectly sincere, its suggestions alarming.

Did Logan know there awaited a maelstrom ahead? Did he enclose himself in this black mantle as a way of warding off disaster? Or was this barometric sinking of his glass just one of the habits he had fallen into as he tried to wear out the seas with crossing them?

Elspeth took to making thermos flasks full of soup and cocoa, standing with Gabriel, one or other of them in the galley, the angle of sailing fairly acute but settled. Elspeth was enjoying the female company as an escape from her husband who seemed to her sometimes to be conjuring something from the sea that he did not want and could not understand. He had been preoccupied and angry on long ocean passages before, but the anger had at least been animated, the preoccupation susceptible to interruption.

"Pass me an onion," she said to Gabriel, "please. The new string of them's under Sandro's bunk. As you probably realise too well."

Gabriel lifted the thin mattress of the bunk and pulled up the ring-pull of the hatch cover. She heard and ignored the scuttling of roaches.

Gabriel took the onion, twisting it off the crackly rope, and passed it round from where she crouched, trying to keep all her weight low, round to Elspeth in the galley.

The galley was like a crossword. If you could cook and carry (without spilling) and clean up a meal you had completed the puzzle. The long swells of the ocean seemed to tug the stomach down and along and turn it over as one swell passed the boat on to another one. Often whoever cooked the meal was sick. Sandro and Nick were sick like cats, neatly and fast, with the minimum distraction from what they were doing. Gabriel was dopey on some sickness drug she insisted on. Elspeth was sick only when they were close-hauled, heeled over to port. She was then sick till she was empty, in which state she found reading an almost psychedelic pleasure, until her stomach raised itself once more to her brain. The concentration that having been repeatedly emptied gave her was like exaltation. If empty-headedness was stupidity, empty-bodiedness made the fumes of the words rise at once to her mind and inebriate it.

If I can peel and chop this onion exactly as I would in a flat, unmoving kitchen, Logan will calm down, things will get better. Elspeth propitiated the domestic gods of the sea, who did not exist. She wedged her bottom under the galley drawer-clips and pushed her feet and calves over against the oven. Then she bent over in a half-crouch to hold herself against the sea's flexing and pored over the onion like someone operating with little hope of life and the next of kin watching.

The first incision at the top of the onion went well. As she had been taught, not in kitchen things only, she was avoiding the roots to keep away tears. Forcing her body to become weighty in the lowslung way of a baby, she peeled off the brown thin skin and put it in the bag, held with a clip at base and top, where they slung rubbish that could go into the sea. I will chop it the perfectionist's way, she thought, pressing the onion down on the board she had slotted within its battens, and making five cuts across the rings. She turned the onion through ninety degrees and cut again. She had a grid for noughts and crosses. Making ready a small pan, that she held cradled in her right elbow on the small kitchen surface as she cut, she sliced through the onion from the top, achieving a pearly heap of cubes of onion, each about a quarter of an inch square. That was one onion done towards soup for six people. The most satisfying thing about cooking in a galley *was* the puzzle aspect of it.

Logan never got sick to the stomach. He had a headache he was unaware of that hollowed out his head. He considered the pain inside there to be the power of his will, the tension of sustained emotion. It was a pain that he held to give him energy.

Soon the air had turned colder, the sea breathed out ice. The laughable bright cotton clothes were folded away and jeans and jerseys came out. Nothing was ever perfectly dry. The sun was withdrawing itself. The chill came from the wind, that was co-operative and not moody, though it repaid watching.

Logan looked out at the wind, reading it. The sea was unreadable. The only consistency its waves showed was in their deep blueness and an almost imperceptible mounting in their height as watch succeeded watch. The water was now bigger than the sky. Logan found this surrounding gratifying; it reassured him that they were progressing south at a roaring pace and that the sea was as tremendous as he knew it was. He worshipped it, but in his heart he was looking in a mirror that showed him his ennobled self, made a hero.

On the 21st of June it was the shortest day of the southern

hemisphere's year. The sky and sea held the sun when it appeared between them in jealous balance. The sea let it go with trails of red.

At noon the six met in the cockpit for soup. It was all they could face cooking. It was difficult to keep hold of the soup at such an angle. To move about with hot soup hauled against such waves was to learn once more to crawl. A lumbering infancy descended on them all, though they each maintained some dexterity in areas where they were already competent. Alec veered between feeling competent and feeling cowed, reduced to a state of nature.

The superfluities of the boat began to horrify Alec. He became convinced the sea was trying to repossess them all, to shake off the boat's graces and reduce it back to its elements. His own life seemed to him not replete with the subtleties and dilemmas that had obsessed him and sterilised his work, that had enticed him to come in on this voyage, but a declaration from first to last of false quantity, wrong emphasis and over-indulgence in complication. Life was showing its simplicity, as he had required of it; but still he fled. He did like the simplicity he now saw. He began to hope for the life he had abused and questioned, to wish for it back in every respect he had once shrunk from.

He began steadily to think of his parents and of his ancestors, even. He approached prayer, that is to say he began bargaining with indifferent forces. He did not know what possessed him.

"Here he is! Albert Ross!" called Sandro, who was holding the helm and had looked back for a moment hearing the mizzen flap.

The bird was twice as wide from wing-tip to wing-tip as *Ardent Spirit*'s transom, and so white it shone with snow's blinding silence. The heavy suspended bird did not appear to move under its own physical power, but was borne on the wind, making a mockery by its composure and haunting poise of the canvas the boat bore, lame and lashed short now as the wind rose. The sails had been moved aft from the sail bin and the bows, lashed to the deck or stowed in the fo'c'sle, the storm jib and mainsail twice reefed. The bows of the boat were often now covered by folding waves, falling like glass buildings in noise and shattering white.

The bill of the bird was the colour of spring, cruel yellow, a new colour that comes fresh and consigns old things to death. The bird's eye was fixed on the eye of whoever looked at it. To look at it was to look into it. It was black and told nothing.

"The barometer's down," called Logan. There was relief in his voice as he told the bad news.

Things will be worse, knew Elspeth.

Nick too knew this was so, though he did something about it. He moved forward to the mainmast, attached himself to the deck by his clip, hauled down the mainsail. Logan took down the mizzen, reluctance mixing with excitement in his face.

The personal matters that had filled part of his mind for the earlier part of the passage now seemed remote to him. He recorded the drop in the barometer in the log for that hour like a man who listens to his genius.

Here he was at home.

"It's down again," called Gabriel, an hour later, pulling down the companionway hatch to call down to Logan who was plotting at his charts. Rain had begun to dive out of the sky at all angles and along the waves and off them as spray. Logan smiled at Gabriel. He had a beautiful smile. She received it as the blessing of this ordeal she was undergoing for love.

Full of an energy that grew as though on course, Logan called, "It's about a degree an hour." Nick, amidships, watching the visibility shorten like walls dropped one within the last, saw that this must be so.

The sea began to climb. It was against the sky by the time night came, a night too obscure for stars. The Southern Cross was eaten by the sea and rain.

The albatross hung astern.

When Elspeth went above to join Logan on their watch, she was dizzy and careless. She greeted fear like this. Clipping herself into the cockpit, she thought she was seeing double, but there it was, another albatross, slightly behind the second. The bird in front was the size of a constellation in the blacked-out sky. Sometimes they were taken from sight by a wave that threw itself up like a mountain and then slid away with a sucking rush that threw the boat down a slope ending only with another climbing mountain of water under the bow.

Waves came over the boat, one after another, leaving no time to recover between the buffetings. The tightness of the grip the boat had upon her adornments, the things that did not matter and may have impeded her, cupboards full of glasses in nests like jewellery, the snapped-in tantalus, the mirrors set over bunks, was like the grip a woman keeps on pretty things as she fights decline. Now the important thing about the boat was her seaworthiness and that only. In spite of the damp within and her repeated covering by waves, she took it with discretion, emerging each time to be smashed again.

Elspeth did not look at the size of the waves. She took each one as if it were single, trying to forget in the three seconds before the next wave came that they were at sea at all. She was steering the course Logan had told her.

He was not able to take sights, so he had to rely on dead reckoning. His state of bliss was level now as he looked around him and his boat at the black water heaped high against them. He was fighting the storm as though it were meant for him.

"The compass light has gone", said Elspeth. The dome of light to which the helmsman steered a course had just gone out, snuffed.

"That's bad," said Logan.

"Damp in the connection," said Nick. He pulled a snap-on waterproof torch from his oilskin and trained it on the compass, squatting to fiddle with the wires exactly as he had throughout the voyage.

Is he taking it lightly because he is brave or because it is not as bad as it seems? Alec wondered.

Nick concentrated on the wires in the thin gibbering beam of the torch, while Logan raged at the sea, and admired it, and asked it to admire him.

For eighty hours the weather squeezed at the sea and cracked the sky. The noise was thick and pained the breathing. A tight panic-inducing howl of wind attacked with random unceasing roar of waters; the boat moaned and creaked. There was at length nothing to do but wait and attempt to keep the naked boat on some sort of course. Under no canvas she raced over the sea faster than they had gone behind the fleetest combinations of sails.

Within, the whole boat was alive with loosed electric shocks from the sodden wiring (What boat rightly has reading lights, thought Alec, we are paying for the overmuch) and with cockroaches that seemed to prefer human company now it was constantly sodden, smelly, reeking of wool. When they were able to eat, they opened tins.

The smell below was of beans and meat and bile and sewage.

"She's in her element," Logan said at one point. He was near to tears. The performance *Ardent Spirit* was putting up was herculean, he thought. What beauty there was in seeing her not down in spite of it all. Gabriel brought him tea. It was an act of love, and Elspeth acknowledged it. To make tea when you are sure you may die or would anyway rather die, with a rocking kettle in a near-horizontal cabin in which you are accompanied by a naked gas flame and a canister of gas, and being juggled by the sea from without, is more than a gesture. Gabriel poured the tea half-way up the weighted mug and took it, lurching, with the sticky rubber mat for securing it, to Logan.

He looked at her from the great distance of his isolation; she was pretty, he remembered that. He looked at her down a long corridor from high within his head, like a man who is dying seeing the world recede and knowing heaven is better.

Gabriel was consumed with the difficulty of doing anything on this sodden boat, far from home. It was like getting old suddenly. She had seen old women take seven minutes to undo a shoelace, watched an old man select pence from his pocket as though he had to read the coins with his thumb-tips, and now she felt like these old people. There was a solution to this continual dragging wretchedness, she thought, not naming death because she was a cheerful girl who had been taught that certain things you do not meddle with. She wanted, as a young person may, to be dead as a solution to not feeling wholly well.

Three waves came at the height of the storm, lifting the boat then hurling it down another and another and another mountain. The ship's decanters in the tantalus broke free of their dovetailed wooden rail and blattered around the stripped saloon like weights, eight pounds each of base-loaded lead crystal. The noise was like an explosion within the exploding wave. Everyone below shrank away, trying to scramble forward to avoid being cannoned or splintered. The glass seemed molten in its threat. When the decanters at last rattled to the lowest corner of the saloon, their necks had smashed. They lay rocking on their sides, the glass crazed with the violence of its crashing from wall to floor to ceiling off the sides of the saloon. The neck of one decanter had torn the dimpled seat of the captain's chair. Glass shards had marked the wood of the saloon like wolves' nails.

When Alec thought he could be no iller or more afraid, he saw a clear vision. It was a child, thin as its bones, moving like an old man, with eyes too open; or he would see old people, lying where they had been put, legs and arms at angles no flesh could bear. He was filled with his own unworthiness, and also a will to live that was so strong it felt as though he grew as he named it to himself.

The things he feared he tried to name to himself also. They were: horror of extinction; fear of the bond Logan seemed to have made with the sea; an end to seeing things and knowing love. The faces he saw in the shrieking foam when he held the helm by grey day or grey night were those of Sorley and Lorna.

Yet all the time the sea was beautiful and he made the lover's mistake of reading its indifferent face.

In Elspeth the will to live gave her the energy to fight she had lacked when things were favourable. My husband is slipping away from me, she thought, and I have made almost no move to keep him. He is not only the man he is now, he is the man he was when we met. And he is the child he holds on to as the best part of himself. I must try to fight for him, if he can still see me.

Purblind, bedevilled and bewitched by his affinity with the sea, Logan was plunged into himself. He could see nothing but the dark. He felt the weight of the sea on the boat and the weight of the boat on himself. He made no weak pact with the sea, nor a bargain for peace. He disliked the suppliant position and did not assume it, being quite certain by now that he was pitted against an adversary whose will was a match for his own. He spent hours in the bow, looking out over the sea as it did nothing but increase in height and violence. Logan shouted at it, not in defiance, it seemed, but pleasure. He surveyed the huge waters and reduced sky as though they bore a harvest for him. At night there was only a chimney-view of a few stars, withdrawn above sheared clouds that seemed to be made by the sea. Logan's face grew white. He left his beard to grow. They were all dirty.

"He is mad," Nick wrote in his spiralbound notebook. "It would be better if we made it before he cracks. I do not know what set him off. The sea, probably." Nick knew the sea had no will, no self, that to give it personality was to underestimate its power.

The capacity of the sea to do harm, that had been an intermittent topic of Logan's, became in those three days of the storm's height all he spoke of. He recalled deaths at sea and spoke of them dotingly.

Each piece of machinery that failed on his boat caused him annoyance on a superficial level but made him glad because he saw the power of the great thing, the sea.

"We're better without it," he said to Nick, when the first fridge broke. The second one broke and he threw food they could well come to need out into the lifting water. He was lightening some burden for himself. Observing him, the five other people were oppressed by fear of the human unknown, more alarming even than the sea that was their only context and could kill them as lightly as smudging over sandworms.

"I am longing to be at home with you, Mum, and forget everything about this voyage," said Gabriel into her machine, and began to cry for herself and her home in a field that was green and flat and never moved. She thought of every wrong thing her parents had done and saw that it may have been right. With each watch that passed she grew older in months not in hours.

Logan in the height of his possession by the storm was alluring to her, a hero, but she scented something frightening to which she did not want to consign herself yet, if ever. He seemed to give off electric shocks. He was full of fire and salt.

The theatricality that is so deep in Logan is dug into him by an oppression that has lain over him all his life, thought Elspeth. It is I who am the more balanced one, after all, and my choice is to leave him and save myself or to stay with him and work at it with the dedication of a woman panning for river gold and spin-

277

ning it. She did not see that he was burning himself up like a man in a fever, that he was the one, not she, who hoped to find clarity in disaster.

Now all she wished for was the chance to die in many years' time and in bed. When it was not her watch, she tied herself into her lee-cloth and prayed, no matter if God did not exist, no more did the fair and just society her parents had taught her would certainly come about. It is not religion that will help us now, she thought. It is, if anything, faith.

She chose to pray and she chose to read *A Winter's Tale*. When she did not sleep she did one or the other. She felt around for words that might be comfortable in which to pray, and when she found her prayers too stiff or too familiar, she read the play aloud and offered it as a prayer. It was the enduring best of human making.

The chaos that had been the greatest personal fear for Alec came and tormented him whenever he could snatch sleep. He dreamed of the destruction of paintings and manufactured things, the end to pointlessness and decoration, of human rationality and ebullience blown out by the wind and consumed by the waves. His fear had ceased to be personal. He now feared the end of the world, that he had always theoretically feared and now, with Logan as its conductor, he did fear.

Where does he keep the combination of the safe? thought Alec, suddenly, in his sleep. He did not know where the thought had come from.

It was late in the third day of the storm's height. The boat was heavy with water. She seemed to be moving more slowly, though the wind had not dropped. For half an hour they had all wondered at the silence; it had not been silence, but a different note in the wind, more soothing, steadier, the call of a siren. For that hour the wind had held near hurricane force.

Later the wind rose again, returning to the screaming pan-icky bullying of the boat it had kept up for days. It's a great tinnitus outside us all, thought Alec. He thought of Muriel Bruce, the Commander, his mother, his father and his second mother, of Lorna, of Sorley.

He had left Lorna in order to navigate by some star he dimly saw. If he returned, what would he take back to her? A few tales she would regard as tall and a lame story about not falling in love with a woman in spite of a homesickness that was killing him. Homesickness, he thought, must often be a motive for adultery.

"Tell me something to make me happy," he said to Nick, who had come into the fo'c'sle on his hands and knees to get a towel to keep the sea from tipping in down his neck.

"Sorley is your son," he said.

Sandro was on the wheel. The sea was white. Some of the waves groaned and creaked and had the stately profile of icebergs. Can't be ice; growlers don't come this far north, Sandro thought. He had a literal mind that served him and the others aboard well.

"You go in and get us hot tea. You look dead," said Logan.

Sandro turned and in that instant one of the tall grey waves cracked down over the boat like dynamited stone. The vang on the main boom burst off it. The boom swung free, loose, heavy, its freed weight weaving like the head of a dead horse. Another wave came and kicked *Ardent Spirit* in the other direction from the first.

"Look out," called Logan, and Sandro, holding the companionway grips like a child trying to get a view, got the boom to the side of his head hard as stone on the skull. The noise was single and tidy, a sharp report amid the warring shriek of wind and baying and sighing of sea. The boat seemed sunk between streets of tall grey water that were falling in on them. There was no order. The waters threw themselves up higher, becoming towers, castles, cathedrals, rocks, and then sank away with a low sound of explosion without settlement. The air was gritty with cold and salt. The wind wailed its warning that had not stopped for days. All the grey water massed like a town with no windows or stillness, a place not fit for fragile human lives.

Gabriel had unclipped herself and gone below before Logan told her to.

"Nick, Alec, come now, Sandro's hurt."

They found Logan at the wheel, Sandro lying on the wheel-house deck, his eyesockets weeping blood.

"Don't move him until you have done what I say. Check his pulse. His breathing. Is he breathing? Good. Here comes another of these brutes."

Logan, instead of attacking the wave, pressed across it a little, unravelling its sharp peak and deflecting its force. He lost the wave's danger but used its progress. He was calm. He spoke quietly.

"Find the combination for the safe, Alec. It's below. I keep it in my desk behind the rolling panel. I'm pretty sure."

"I know the number," said Alec. He suddenly realised that he did. The circumstances of his being with Logan by the safe had been so extreme, his nerves had been so primed, that he remembered the number. It was as it had been when he went to buy fish at the docks with his father; he could recall long numbers when he was excited, remembering them flat and unrationalised, like numbers off a rubber stamp. It was the pattern they made that he held.

Logan was gentle as he spoke to Nick, who was testing Sandro's reflexes carefully on the slamming deck, the thrashing boom held awkward but firm by a temporary rig he'd fixed from the bust vang and five yards of nylon rope from the cockpit pocket.

Alec lifted out the broken tantalus from its socket in the silky panels, pulled forward the concealing door, and spun till he got in the numbers he wanted: 0315561374.

The barrels settled back at one pull. Elspeth was standing there. "How odd Logan is. That's my father's last telephone number."

Do we do nothing for no reason? thought Alec.

"What is it with Sandro?" she asked.

"It could be a fractured skull, I suppose."

"Help me down here with him. He is a light boy."

Elspeth's old enough to be his mother, for God's sake, thought Alec. That is what she wants, a child. That is what I cannot give her though I will always regret, if we live, not having been homesick enough to hold her in that bleak hotel when she tried to seduce me with good soap.

They went up on deck. Sandro lay like a young man in abandoned sleep under the shade of a tree. The mast rattled in the wind. There was no end to the wind and the rain.

"You'll have to move him. I don't like it, but you will have to," said Logan. "Elspeth, go over his head with your eyes, don't feel for it, but go over again with a torch to see if there's a mark or contusion."

The raving exalted hero figure who had been all risk and mania ten minutes before had gone. In itself this was the passing of a storm. Logan seemed to have found the courage to be quiet.

They got Sandro to his bunk. The radio had ceased to function, saturated by the sea to uselessness, or impotent against the desert cities of waves. They had no clear idea where they were. Yet Alec felt relieved completely of the thoughts of death that had been with him.

"Does he mean us to give him morphine?" he asked Elspeth.

"No, there are other less extreme painkillers in there. It's like Logan not to tell you. He likes extremes."

Yet he is a kind of hero of calm when an actual horror occurs. That is his balance, thought Alec. He is unfit for normal life but he is fine in battle. He finds battles to fight. He is a type the race does not like but needs when blood is let. He is the inland man, not I. I never want to be alone as that man is happy to be. He abhors people, but is kind. He will make trouble in peace. But he is brave, and courage is as important as faith.

Elspeth was going through Sandro's hair with the torch. She found no breaks in the skin, but a rising egg on the top of the skull where the boom struck him.

"You look as though you're hunting headlice," said Alec. The boat lurched and righted itself a little. They heard a shout from aloft.

"How do you know about that? Headlice?" Elspeth asked, lifting Sandro's eyelid. She was calm in the aftermath, although around them and above and beneath them there was no calm from the air. Sandro began to stir and mumble, punching the air.

"I have a wee son."

That moment there seemed to begin for both of them a life beyond the cramped wet fear they had shared in the past days. It was not a life that they would share, but they would each remember that it began by the bunk of the reviving boy, under the ocean, but moving towards land that, all at once, could be believed in.

Another yell came from up aloft. Elspeth wiped Sandro's eyes with distilled water.

When he fully opened his eyes, both whites were red.

"My mother," he said.

"No, it's Elspeth. Logan's wife."

"I mean, what will she say? She's coming to meet me."

"Where?"

"I don't know, but she'll be there."

"She won't mind that your eyes are red if that's all."

"My mother's Italian. She notices what I look like."

Seeing he was not broken, Elspeth kissed Sandro for being less injured than he should have been, and for frightening her husband so that he had had to find true courage.

Nick was in the saloon. His calm was natural, as it had been all along.

"How do you work that out about Sorley?" asked Alec.

"She made him for you. Take him. Or are you still so attached to letting life go? It's Lorna you were hunting down, like it's Scotland you found at the back end of the Pacific," said Nick. It took the clear sight of an outsider to show him his own future.

Logan slammed down the companionway hatch and yelled,

"Is anyone interested? By my reckoning, it's thirty miles till we hit land." He stood with the albatrosses behind him at the wheel of his boat, disappointed once again in having found what he was aiming for.

Like a head of seeds, blown, the tight-packed boat would scatter the six back out over the world.

Alec looked at Sandro, a combination of two Souths, Italy and New Zealand. He held his arms out to Elspeth, "I'm to the North," he said.

She came into his arms and there felt to him already like the past.

She returned to Logan, up among the hard weather, at the wheel of his boat.

"Stay with me for a time," he said, "if you would like to."

Acknowledgements

I am grateful to William Kirk for permission to reproduce his lettering for the memorial tablet to Colin McWilliam in the Greyfriars Kirkyard, Edinburgh, and to the Trustees of Hawthornden Castle, where parts of the book were written.

A Note on the Author

Candia McWilliam was born in Edinburgh in 1955.
She is the author of *A Case of Knives* (1988) and
A Little Stranger (1989).

DATE DUE

APR 1 1 1995		
APR. 29 1995		
MAY 1 6 1995		
JUN. 29 1995		
AUG. 0 5 1995		
OCT. 0 3 1995		
NOV 3 0 1995		
Dec. 11-95 DEC 6 1995		
FEB. 2 7 1996		
SEP. 2 1 1996		
NOV 0 7 2000		